EVERY THING IS POISON

ALSO BY
Joy McCullough

NOVELS

Blood Water Paint

We Are the Ashes, We Are the Fire

Great or Nothing
(with Caroline Tung Richmond, Tess Sharpe, and Jessica Spotswood)

Enter the Body

PLAYS

Stage of Fools

Enter the Body

La Tofana's Poison Emporium

Smoke & Dust

Blood Water Paint

NOVELS FOR YOUNGER READERS

A Field Guide to Getting Lost

Across the Pond

Basil & Dahlia: A Tragical Tale of Sinister Sweetness

Not Starring Zadie Louise

Code Red

The Team Awkward series
(coauthored with Veeda Bybee)

PICTURE BOOKS

Champ and Major: First Dogs

Harriet's Ruffled Feathers: The Woman Who Saved Millions of Birds

The Story of a Book

EVERY THING IS POISON

JOY McCULLOUGH

DUTTON BOOKS

Dutton Books
An imprint of Penguin Random House LLC
1745 Broadway, New York, NY 10019
penguinrandomhouse.com

Design by Anna Booth
Text set in Requiem Text

THE LIBRARY OF CONGRESS HAS CATALOGED THE HARDCOVER EDITION AS FOLLOWS:
Names: McCullough, Joy, author.
Title: Everything is poison / Joy McCullough.
Description: New York, New York: Dutton Books, 2025. | Audience: Ages 14 and up. | Audience: Grades 10-12. | Summary: Sixteen-year-old Carmela Tofana finally gains access to her mother's apothecary in early 17th-century Rome, where she discovers that alongside healing remedies are dangerous potions that can change women's lives.
Identifiers: LCCN 2024028883 (print) | LCCN 2024028884 (ebook) | ISBN 9780593855874 (hardcover) | ISBN 9780593855898 (ebook)
Subjects: CYAC: Poisons—Fiction. | Healers—Fiction. | Mothers and daughters—Fiction. | Rome (Italy)—History—17th century—Fiction. | Italy—History—Fiction. 17th century. | LCGFT: Historical fiction. | Novels.
Classification: LCC PZ7.1.M43412 Ev 2025 (print) | LCC PZ7.1.M43412 (ebook) | DDC [Fic]—dc23
LC record available at https://lccn.loc.gov/2024028883
LC ebook record available at https://lccn.loc.gov/2024028884

First published by Dutton Books, 2025
First paperback edition published 2026

Manufactured in the United States of America
LSCC

ISBN 9780593855881
1st Printing

The authorized representative in the EU for product safety and compliance is Penguin Random House Ireland, Morrison Chambers, 32 Nassau Street, Dublin D02 YH68, Ireland, https://eu-contact.penguin.ie.

For Susan and Jim,
who gave me a safe place to turn

All things are poison
and nothing is without poison.

—Paracelsus
FATHER OF TOXICOLOGY

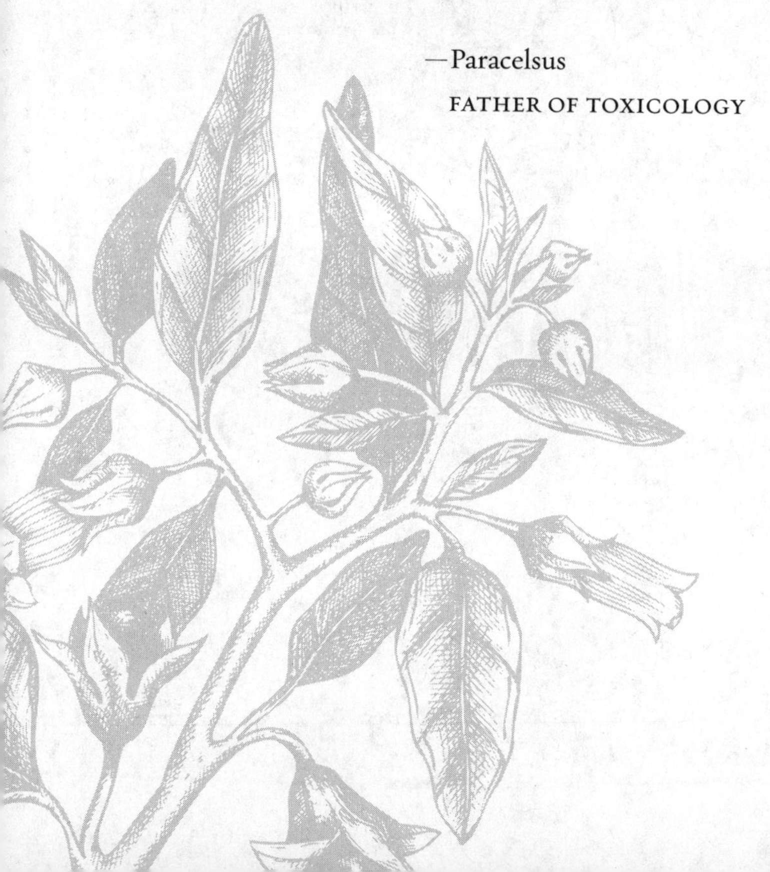

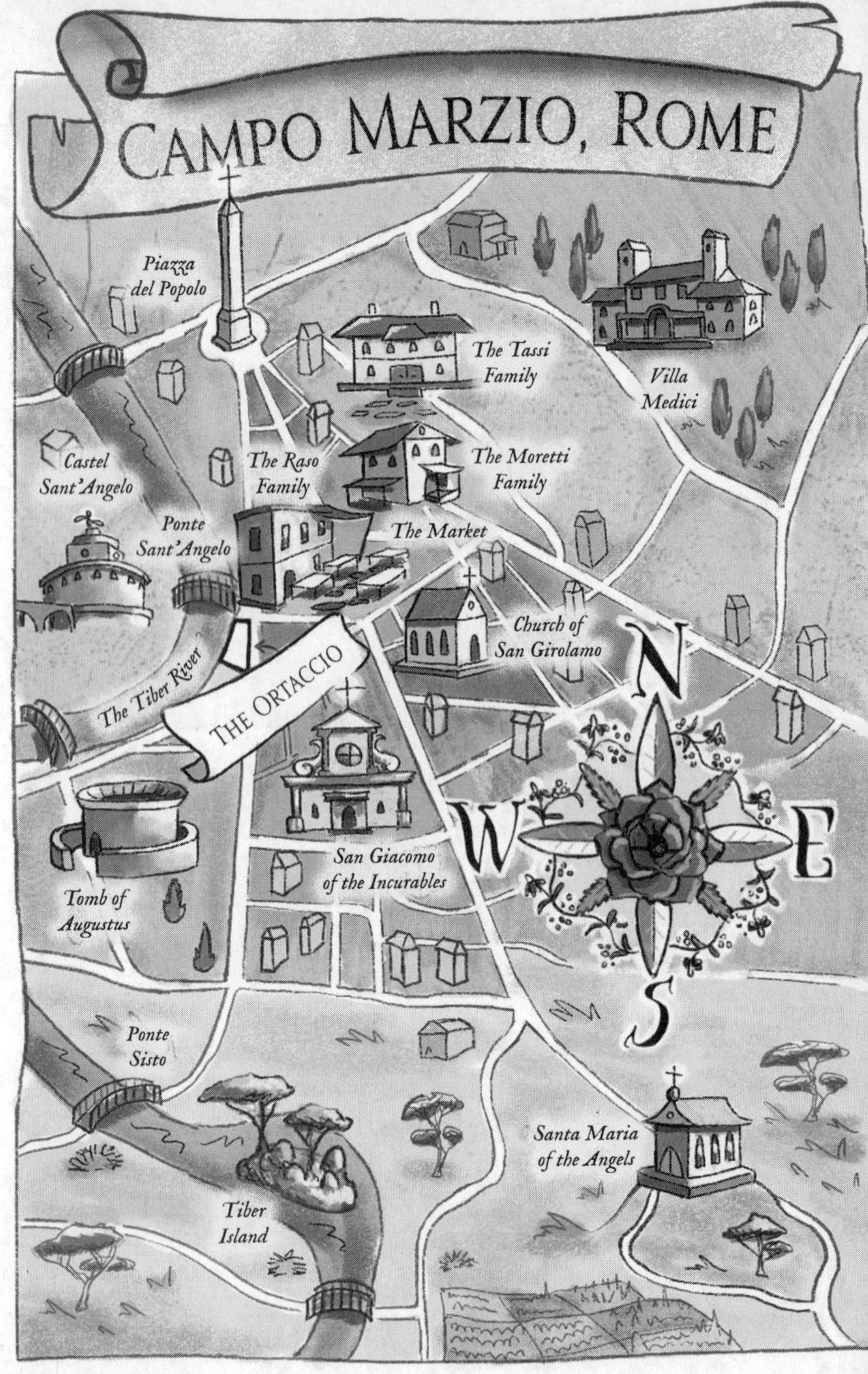

CAMPO MARZIO, ROME
Piazza del Popolo
The Tassi Family
Villa Medici
Castel Sant'Angelo
The Raso Family
The Moretti Family
Ponte Sant'Angelo
The Market
Church of San Girolamo
The Tiber River
THE ORTACCIO
N
W
E
S
San Giacomo of the Incurables
Tomb of Augustus
Ponte Sisto
Santa Maria of the Angels
Tiber Island

THE ORTACCIO
The Tavern
Giulia and Carmela's Apartment
Tofana Apothecary
The Santori Family
Maria and Laura's Apartment
The Butcher

EVERY THING IS POISON

Carmela slips inside the apothecary behind an ancient woman leaning on a cane so the proprietress, ever vigilant when the door chimes, might not notice her entrance.

She hovers behind a potted bay laurel as Signora Russo totters over to Giulia Tofana at the counter. When they are engaged in discussion of the old woman's medical maladies—kept private from Carmela's curious ears by the apothecary's discretion—Carmela slips deeper inside the cool respite of the narrow shop front.

There aren't many places to hide, but as long as the apothecary is occupied with a customer, Carmela will go unnoticed. She trails a hand along the dark wood shelving that runs from floor to ceiling, examining the endless bottles, dark glass, carefully lettered labels. Headache remedies, skin balms, love potions. She knows each one like she knows the wrinkles on her own mother's face, more every day.

She could locate almost any remedy in a flash. At least the ones that are ready-made, available in the shop front for a hurried customer to grab and go. She has never ventured back behind the counter, to the workshop where Signora Tofana does her real magic. Where she crafts cures specific to the patient and their needs. Where brazen Maria cackles loud enough to be heard out front, and silent Laura moves like a ghost, only occasionally floating past the archway dividing front and back.

That's where the real secrets are guarded, the potions made that can't be just as easily whipped up by one's grandmother. That's where Carmela would go, if she ever got the chance. Where she'd find what she needs.

But for now, these endless shelves of common remedies serve her well enough. Knowledge is dispensed a drop at a time, but she's nothing if not patient.

The shop bell rings and Carmela's eyes dart to the door as Signora Tofana sings out, "Ah, Violetta! How are you today?"

Carmela ducks around the other side of a cabinet full of pigments, oils, and resins, dusty with disuse since Rome's painters mostly live across the Tiber in Trastevere, rather than here in Campo Marzio. The cabinet's contents may be underused, but the cabinet itself will serve to hide Carmela. She mustn't be seen by Signora Tofana, but even less does she want to be seen by Violetta Raso.

Violetta Raso, who floats freely into any shop she pleases, head held high. Violetta, who enters most shops surrounded by chattering friends, none of whom would spare Carmela a glance if they spotted her there, lurking.

Violetta is alone today.

She glides up to the counter and engages Signora Tofana as though they are equals, as though Violetta, a silly girl without a thought in her head, is a match for this indomitable force of a person.

But once they're face-to-face, Violetta falters.

"No need to be shy," the proprietress says. "I keep secrets for half this town."

"It's only that my friend Penelope said . . ."

Signora Tofana waits, though Carmela recognizes the look on her face; the apothecary knows exactly what the girl is here for.

"There's a boy," Violetta finally says.

Signora Tofana smiles. "Ah, there's often a boy."

Carmela stifles a snort of derision. All the magic Giulia Tofana wields, and Violetta wants a love potion? Any boy in town would fling themselves at her if they thought they had a chance.

"I know he likes me," Violetta says. "I only want to help him admit it."

"That's exactly what our love potions are for." Signora Tofana's tone is the same rich, welcoming one she uses on most customers, gathering them in to her bosom without ever touching them. Assuring them the apothecary knows best, they can trust her, she will not lead them astray.

Violetta glances around, to be sure no one has heard. Carmela flattens herself against the wall on the other side of the cabinet.

Signora Tofana questions Violetta about her plans for the love potion, and for once the girl drops her voice low enough that Carmela can't hear. It doesn't matter. Carmela knows exactly how Violetta will use it.

She'll ensnare Davide or Marco or Filippo, it doesn't even matter who. One of the boys a few years older but not so old they could be her father. She'll sail from favored eldest daughter to newlywed, forever under the watchful eye of a doting man. Before you can say "love potion," she'll be back in here looking for a remedy for morning sickness.

And even though they were children together, jumping hopscotch and playing pretend—at least before they all got old enough to realize who Carmela really was, who her mother was—Violetta will continue to ascend through an entirely different world than the one Carmela will always be tethered to.

Violetta pays for her potion and thanks Signora Tofana, clutching it as though it is the answer to all her pious mornings spent in hard-backed pews.

When she turns away from Giulia Tofana, though, something unfamiliar flickers across Violetta's face. Some hint of insecurity, some glimmer of concern. Then the pretty girl smooths back a ringlet that has escaped her snood and hurries out the door.

"Carmela."

Her heart sinks at the tone of that voice from the counter, no longer warm, never welcoming, not here, never for her.

"How many times have I told you not to spy on my customers?"

Carmela emerges from behind the cabinet, but doesn't meet the apothecary's gaze. "I wasn't spying—"

"Lurking in dark corners where you believe yourself to be unseen? It comes to the same thing. Go home. It's getting dark."

Carmela scowls at the apothecary—the person, the place, conspiring to exclude her from all she's ever wanted. She sends one longing look through the archway back to the workshop, back to where Laura and Maria work, where the apothecary herself will join them when there is a lull in customers. But Carmela should have known better than to dream she might be granted entrance today.

"Yes, Mother."

The next time Carmela walks into Tofana Apothecary with any glimmer of hope in her heart comes some three months later.

It does not come because her mother, the proprietress, has decided in her benevolence to bestow wisdom on her only child.

No, it comes because once, years ago, when Carmela was ten or eleven, pleading to know when she would be allowed to learn all the apothecary's secrets, when she would inherit her mother's legacy, when she would become an apothecary herself, her mother had said, "When you are grown," and Carmela hadn't let that lie. Carmela stuck her finger in that hole and wiggled, endlessly, until her mother finally answered with specifics: "Sixteen. When you are sixteen. Until then, if I hear another word about it, I'll ship you off to a convent."

Carmela has held her tongue.

In the weeks leading up to her sixteenth birthday, it has been almost unbearable to remain quiet, not to remind her mother of her promises. Not to explode from the dual possibilities that all her dreams might be crushed and all her dreams might come true.

The morning of her birthday, Carmela rises with the sun. Easy, considering she barely slept. She can't bear to wait for Giulia to wake her with a tart she's fetched from the baker. Instead, she slips out of their apartment above the apothecary and meets Signor Amari in front of the bakery.

"Carmela? Is everything all right?" He unlocks the door and she follows him in.

"I'm here for my birthday tart."

"I haven't begun to make the tarts." He goes straight to the hearth to build up the fire from the banked ashes. "Is your mother unwell?"

"She's fine." Carmela examines the baskets of bread from the day before. "It doesn't have to be a tart. I'll take this." She holds up a hardened bun. "How much?"

Signor Amari shakes his head. "I'd pay you to drop those by Marcello's for his pigs!"

Carmela grins and takes a second hardened bun. "Thank you! Have a good day!"

"Happy birthday!" he calls as the door closes behind her.

The streets of Campo Marzio are quiet as the citizens of Rome's northern-central rione awake and prepare for their days. Carmela passes a young woman hauling water from the public fountain, and a merchant leading a donkey loaded with goods, but she keeps her eyes down. She does not want any chance interaction to ruin this long-awaited day.

Back in their apartment, her mother still hasn't woken. As Carmela builds up their own fire and heats water for tea, Giulia begins to stir. Carmela grabs the buns and rushes to her mother's bedside, sitting on the edge and placing a bun on her mother's bleary form before she's even opened her eyes.

"Carmela?" Giulia squints against the light from the curtains Carmela has opened. "Why are you up?"

"It's my birthday!"

"Yes, but . . ." Her mother sits up, taking in the day-old buns, her wide-awake daughter too impatient to wait in bed for her birthday treat. "Your tart."

Carmela waves her hand. She doesn't care if she never eats another tart again in her life, if it means she gets what she's been promised on this day.

"I don't need a tart. It's my birthday. I'm sixteen."

She waits. A beam of light from the window cuts between them, and in it the specks of dust dance an entire ballet in the time it takes Giulia to understand.

"The shop," Giulia says.

The floodgates open. "We were at Maria's house and Laura was there too, so they'll both remember that you said when I turn sixteen I can learn everything there is to know about the shop. I can go into the back room and learn to make potions and help customers and be a real partner. You said when I was grown, and you said that would be when I turned sixteen, and here we are, it's my birthday, I'm sixteen. And you said I couldn't say another word about it or you'd send me to a convent, so I didn't, even though I knew you never would, but I did what you asked and waited all this time and now I'm here. I'm ready."

Carmela studies her mother's face. Sleep-creased and beginning to wrinkle, but still as beautiful as ever. An elegance Carmela will never achieve.

Giulia purses her lips, and now the dust motes perform an opera, keening at Carmela that her hopes are about to be dashed. When Giulia finally speaks, she says only, "The water is boiling."

Carmela leaps from the bed to pull the kettle from the flame. In her haste, she fumbles the hook and nearly drops the kettle. Her face burns. It's only water. But in the apothecary, it could be a delicate potion, a remedy ruined by her carelessness.

Giulia rises from the bed, wrapping herself in her raggedy quilt, and settles next to the fire. "Happy birthday, darling."

Hope flickers as Carmela scoops her mother's favorite blend of morning tea into mugs, then pours the boiling water over the top, breathing in the aromatic vapors as the heat from the water releases the magic of the herbs. She sets her mother's mug in front of her, then sinks onto her own stool. "Please, Mother."

Giulia is silent for so long Carmela's heart breaks open, scabs over, breaks open again before she finally speaks. "I am a woman of my word," she says. "And I would be a poor excuse for a mother if I did not fulfill a promise made in earnest."

Carmela yelps, jumping up from the table to dance around and wrap her mother in her arms.

"All right, all right." Giulia laughs. "There will be limits, you know. Like any apprentice, you'll start from the bottom. You'll work harder than you've ever worked in your life. You'll listen to me, and to Maria, and to Laura. Or you'll be out. Just because I allow you to try does not mean I guarantee you'll stay."

Giulia's voice is stern, but her eyes follow Carmela around the room. They dance with her, two dust motes tumbling together through their own beam of light.

All Carmela wants is a chance, the chance that has been denied to her all these years, the back room closed to her because of vague dangers and things too complicated for children's ears.

Carmela is not a child anymore.

CARMELA WAS A CHILD. Six, maybe, or seven. The group of children ranged from five to ten, and Violetta Raso decided every game they played.

Carmela was tired of never having a voice. Carmela was tired of playing prisoner's base over and over because it was what Violetta chose, and no one dared speak against her.

"Let's play marbles instead," Carmela said.

Sides formed immediately. Children flocked to Violetta, whether or not they wanted to play prisoner's base. A few hesitated; they liked Carmela's suggestion. But they liked Violetta's favor more.

Only Nina was brave enough to speak her mind. "I have marbles," she said quietly.

All eyes turned on the small girl with a limp who was forever chosen as the prisoner and spent the entire game waiting to be rescued.

"Are you sure you really want to do that?" Violetta asked.

"Play marbles?"

"Play with Carmela."

And there it was. The turning point Carmela had never seen coming. The turning point that would mark a before and after in her life as sharp as any she'd ever experienced. Sharper, even. Her father had died when she was too small to remember a before and after she'd had two parents.

This was the moment Carmela would realize her mother's magic, her extraordinary gifts and powers, all she did for the people of this town were only one side of a deadly sharp blade.

"Didn't you know?" Violetta said to Nina, and all the other children hung on her every word. "Carmela's mother is a witch."

Some of the children laughed but sobered immediately when they realized Violetta wasn't laughing. When they realized Violetta didn't mean a witch of fairy stories.

Nina glanced at Carmela. They were friends. Her mother was a regular in the apothecary. But Nina was not foolish. It didn't matter whether she believed what Violetta said. It only mattered that Violetta said it.

Violetta wasn't content only to have said it, though. It wasn't enough that they were always certain to play her game and not Carmela's. That had never been in doubt, not really.

"Carmela's mother is a witch," she repeated, louder this time, loud enough that a woman passing on the street looked over in alarm. "And if you play with her, she'll turn you into a toad!"

The Witch

There is a woman
like Carmela's mother
but not

on a platform
in the northeast corner
of the Piazza del Popolo

some two miles north
of the apothecary.
Just go straight up Via di Ripetta,
you can't miss it.

This woman is not
from Campo Marzio or even Rome
but life brought her here
and ever since
she's never stopped longing for home,
for the place she was born, seen, known.
Here she was invisible
until she wasn't.

If she'd grown where she was planted
things might have been different
or perhaps
she was always going to die this way
on a platform in front of a jeering crowd
spitting judgment to mask their fear

if not here in Campo Marzio
then on some other scaffold
in front of some other crowd

always destined
for a length of rope around her neck
or the blow of rocks to her head
or the bite of flames licking at her ankles
and the whim
of an executioner.

Is she moments from death
because of some inherent,
inevitable wrongness
or is she
that woman
because the world
has always insisted
on seeing her

as other?

Someone shouts.
An apple core
glances off her shoulder.
She doesn't want to know
who threw it.

The executioner
positions the rope
around her neck,

tightens the knot
under her chin.

She tries to meet his eye
for one last moment
of human connection.
He focuses his gaze on the rope
even as he helps her step up
onto a wobbly stool
which is barely there
before he yanks it away.

The church bells toll
as her body jerks,
every ounce of her weight
now tugging on the rope
biting into her neck.

She isn't gone yet.
An instant death
is for one who deserves mercy.
No, this woman could still be saved.
In time, the rope's mark around her neck
might even heal, a phantom memory
of this sickening dance.

The long, gruesome minutes
it will take for her to die
convulsing on the end of the rope
are too much for some.
They begin to disperse.

But others stay
desperate for the certainty
that all is right in Campo Marzio
because this
                    other
has breathed her last.

The bells above the shop door tinkle, a faint echo of the ringing from the Piazza del Popolo as Carmela walks inside the apothecary with La Tofana herself. This time, Carmela doesn't hide next to the painting cabinet. She will follow her mother through the shop front to the back, where her life will begin.

Before that, though, Giulia reaches behind the counter and comes out with a broom. She hands it to her daughter without a word. Everything inside Carmela rebels, wants to scream out that she could have swept the shop front any time over all these years; that isn't what she has earned with her patience. But this is her mother, La Tofana, with eyes of steel and spine to match, and this is a test.

Carmela takes the broom and begins to sweep.

Loitering in the archway, where she at least has a view of the inner sanctum, would be too obvious. But Carmela lingers longer than necessary, perhaps, behind the counter, where the shelving opens up to the back, allowing a glimpse. Maria usually works to one side of the arch, and Laura to the other, and at Giulia's request, they hand things through to the front. But the shelves mostly obscure the customer's view of what happens in the back and Carmela doesn't manage to see much more than she has before.

By the time Maria and Laura arrive, the floor of the shop front is spotless. Carmela rushes over to check for any dirt they've dragged in. With her luck, they'll be followed by a steady stream of customers and Carmela will be sweeping all day.

But this is a test, she reminds herself. She will be the best shop sweeper a store has ever known. She will pass this test, and then the next.

"Happy birthday, Carmela!" Laura's voice is soft as always, but her eyes twinkle as she holds out a bundle wrapped in brown paper.

Maria says nothing, but squeezes Carmela's shoulder as she moves past her to her spot along the worktable.

Carmela glances to her mother at the counter, bent over the inventory book. Perhaps she should keep sweeping, save the package for later. But her mother smiles and nods. "Open it," she says.

Carmela sets the broom aside and tears into the paper, unable to stop the childish grin plastered across her face. The only gift she's hoped for has been this right here, this chance to be included, but now she's been given another.

Heavy green fabric unfolds into an apron like the ones Maria and Laura wear. But this one has beautiful vines and flowers embroidered along the edges.

"She's been working on that forever," Maria calls from the back.

Carmela trails her fingers over the beautiful needlework. "Oh Laura, it's beautiful!"

Laura keeps her head down, never one for compliments, and comes to help Carmela tie the apron on.

"You didn't have to do this," Carmela says.

"It's an important occasion," Laura says.

"Yes, but—"

The apron on, Laura looks Carmela up and down and nods. Then she moves through the archway to her regular spot.

"Wait, did you know?" Carmela follows Laura through the archway, almost without noting it, because now she needs to understand what's happened here. "How did you know I'd start today?"

Laura looks bewildered. Behind Carmela, Maria speaks. "It was decided that you'd start on your sixteenth birthday, wasn't it?"

"Yes, but . . ."

Carmela glances at Giulia, still bent over the notebook where she keeps her records of sales and inventories. She doesn't glance up, but a smile dances on her lips.

"I thought you'd all forgotten!"

Maria lets out a half laugh, half snort. "Well, we didn't. Here you are."

Here she is. In the back room of the shop, as though it isn't something she's been dreaming of since she could toddle around and be told no every time she drew near.

She takes in Maria's workspace to the left—a disastrous whirlwind of ingredients and bottles and implements Carmela can't make any sense of. To the right of the archway, the same ingredients and bottles and implements fill Laura's space, but all in perfect order.

Laura smiles. "We're very glad you're here."

Carmela allows herself a single, solitary twirl in her beautiful new apron. It's childish, but she's here now, and they can't take it away from her.

She drinks in the rest of the back room. More shelves upon shelves of bottles and crocks and containers of all different shapes and sizes, filled with powders and liquids and leaves and roots. Not uniform, carefully labeled remedies, like out in the front, but raw ingredients. Mortars and pestles and empty bottles and paper packets to fill with custom remedies, crafted to a patient's needs. A hearth with a fire Maria is coaxing into existence, a heavy cauldron on the kettle stand.

And everywhere, dried plants, hanging from every beam, making an upside-down forest Carmela wants to live in forever.

"It's wonderful," she says.

Maria grunts.

Giulia appears, inventory book in hand. She opens it to a list of ingredients and shows Carmela where to start. "Go through the inventory," she instructs. "Mark anything that's less than half full."

The shop bell rings, and Giulia turns away, as though that is all the instruction Carmela will need.

"But how will I know—"

"I have a customer," Giulia says. "Ask Maria if you have any questions."

CARMELA IS MADE OF QUESTIONS.

As customers flow in and out of the shop, she listens closer than she ever has before. She's not spying now. She's an apprentice. She's supposed to learn what to do when a customer complains of toothache or stomach pain or a sleepless baby. Not only the remedies for the ailments, but the questions to ask, the tone to take, how to make them feel at ease.

She's also supposed to check the inventory, which feels important at first, but quickly becomes drudgery. There are so many ingredients, and the writing on the labels is so tiny. Often they're smudged into illegibility or there are no labels at all. Her mother and Maria and Laura don't need labels; they simply open a bottle, take a sniff, and know what's inside.

Many are familiar to Carmela: lavender, sage, lemon balm, chamomile. But some give her pause: bone splinters, nail clippings, powdered mummy, crocodile dung. When she reaches sanguis pulvis, it's nearly empty. She pulls the jar from the shelf and peers inside. A dark red powder with a faint metallic smell.

She notes its low supply and starts to put it back on the shelf.

"Oh dear." Giulia materializes behind her, holding a hand out for the jar. "That's almost out."

"What's it for?"

Giulia's not listening. She's carried the jar to another corner of the workshop.

"Inciting the passion of a lover." More incongruous words have never flown past Laura's lips.

There it is: the line between what they do in here and what happens out there. Laura measures powder from a jar of sanguis pulvis, mixes it with whatever else a love potion contains, packages it, and Giulia sells it to a girl like Violetta, who then gets her happily ever after.

Giulia returns, frowning. "We've never run out before."

"Everyone wants a love potion," Laura says mildly. "I won't begin for another two weeks."

"Don't look at me," Maria says. But then she jerks her thumb at Carmela. "Have her courses started?"

Carmela knows her Latin well enough, but it takes a moment to make sense of "sanguis pulvis." Powdered blood. "We use our own?"

"When your time comes, wring your rags into that crock there." Giulia points beneath Maria's workspace.

"Couldn't you use . . . I don't know, pig's blood?"

Maria guffaws, but Giulia simply shakes her head. "Not unless you want to incite your lover's passions for a pig."

"If you ask me," Maria laughs, "most lovers need their passions suppressed."

"For the time being, Laura," Giulia says, "let's adjust the love potions? More rose water, a pinch more sorrel. Stretch the powdered blood."

Carmela looks from face to face, expecting an objection. Changing a recipe on the fly—and a popular remedy at that. "But how do you know it will still work? Have you tried?"

"It's a love potion," Giulia says. "The ingredients don't matter. It's hope in a bottle."

"That can't be true, though. They work! Everyone says!"

Giulia settles on a stool, amused, giving Carmela the rope to hang herself. But there is no way the love potions are a fantasy. People who must make the choice between buying meat or vegetables spend precious coins on the prized potions. People who wouldn't otherwise dare to cross La Tofana's doorstep risk it to get their hands on those coveted bottles.

"Nina Santori bought a love potion and the next day Sandro asked for her hand."

Giulia looks unimpressed.

"Penelope Strozzi says Victor was never going to speak to her again, and then the love potion melted his heart."

Carmela realizes she sounds like a child, precisely at the moment she's meant to be showing her maturity. But any citizen of Campo Marzio would object to the apothecary saying the love potions are worthless. It's not her fault if she's ignorant to the secrets of the shop. When there's still no reaction, she unleashes the most obvious argument of all. "Violetta Raso thinks you're a witch and still she came in here for a love potion!"

At that Giulia laughs. "Carmela, my love, everyone who walks through that door has said I'm a witch at one point or another. And none of those girls are your friends. Why are you listening to what they say?"

None of those girls are Carmela's friends *because* of what they say. Because they believe, like everyone else in the neighborhood, apparently, that her mother is a witch. That by spending time with Carmela they're doomed to become witches themselves. And yet they'll turn to the witch to solve their problems.

"If the love potions are worthless, why are you taking people's money for them? Isn't that dishonest?"

This time Giulia doesn't laugh. Laura stops grinding comfrey root to listen to her answer.

"When someone comes in here for hope in a bottle, I listen to them. I offer advice, if that's what they want, but most of the time what they're paying for is my listening ear." Giulia stands and busies herself restocking ingredients that are cluttering Maria's workspace. "And when they walk out the door with a pretty bottle that promises things will turn around, their newfound confidence is what makes it so. I think that's worth a few coins, don't you?"

Laura nods and turns back to her pestle.

"Then why do you bother collecting your monthly blood? If it's all pointless?"

"Because the blood also has other important uses." The front door chimes and Giulia dusts off her apron, the discussion clearly over. Though right before she sails through the archway, she says over her shoulder, "Besides, the blood gives the love potions the perfect blush of pink."

The Wife

There is a woman
like Violetta Raso
                                        but not

outside the dry goods shop
a stone's throw
from the apothecary

clutching a coin
she set apart ages ago
for a love potion
but hasn't summoned the nerve
to cross the threshold
and make it hers.

She keeps her head down,
tips her face away
from an approaching friend,
as though they would know
what the coin is for
and how would this woman answer
if asked why she needs a love potion?

She does not seek
to snare a husband.
That was done for her, long ago
and though it was arranged
it grew into a marriage of love.

Her heart galloped at the thought of him,
her breath caught at the sight of him.
She forgot her own name at his touch.

He felt the same.
She's almost sure.
It's hazy now, looking back
through the years of irritations and grievances,
shifting fortunes, changing bodies, children.

If she's not certain he loved her then
what is the point of ensorcelling him
to love her now?
What would that even look like?

A gentle touch, an encouraging word,
a light in his eyes when he looks upon her.
The certainty that he would look at all.

She might have asked for more
when she was young
but now those simple things
would be a bounty.

If she ever gets the love potion
she will tuck it under her pillow
safe from prying eyes
and when he lies
beside her sleeping
she will part his lips
and quench her thirst.

The daily tasks are endless. Sweeping, grinding, checking inventory levels. But the shop is never boring. There is always more to learn. As Carmela notes that juniper berries are running low, Maria explains what they're for. As she cleans the blood crock, Laura explains how she'll dry the blood. First it will simmer for hours, reducing the liquid until it forms a paste. Then that will be spread thin over a slab of stone and dried out over long, low heat until all the moisture has evaporated. Then it will be ground to powder with the mortar and pestle.

And the customers. They are a constant churn of need and pain and loneliness. Giulia spoke true: people pay for her listening ear.

"Giulia, darling!"

Carmela jumps at the booming voice out of a woman she's only ever seen in the market, accompanied by her husband. At his side, Signora Abate is nearly as timid as Laura. But here—

"You were absolutely right and I stand corrected: that rash cleared up with just a bit of sun. You are a treasure trove of knowledge, aren't you? Now my daughter-in-law, there's a silly twit of a girl. She tried to convince me to go to that other apothecary for some expensive remedy, when here you were, telling me God's own creation could heal it. And you were right!"

"I'm so glad," Giulia says. "God's own creation doesn't cost a thing, now, does it?"

"Amen." Signora Abate crosses herself and then reaches for one of the most expensive items in the shop. "Is this the cream Pia has been raving to me about? Says it makes her look twenty years younger!"

Giulia nods, modest. She wouldn't dare make such a claim, but she won't contradict a loyal customer.

Signora Abate pulls the remaining two jars of the cream off the shelf and plunks all three down on the counter. "I may need to simply bathe in the stuff!" She brays with laughter, and Carmela cannot fight a grin on her face as she heads back to restock three more jars of the expensive cream.

Signora Fontina is not nearly as jolly when she comes in, brow furrowed and hands worrying a handkerchief that will very soon be in shreds.

"Signora Fontina, what can I do for you?" Giulia asks, sliding a glass of calming tonic across the counter.

"It's decided," the middle-aged woman says with a wobble in her voice. "We're going to the New World."

"Oh my." Giulia strikes the perfect note between envy and compassion. And rather than jump in with all the questions Carmela would ask if she were trusted with the customers, La Tofana waits.

Maria grunts at Carmela and points at the mortar full of mashed something or other that she's meant to add to the remedy simmering over the fire; then she must wash out the mortar. Carmela moves slowly. She knows a voyage to the New World is long and dangerous, but she can't stop her imagination from filling in the land of milk and honey that awaits Signora Fontina on the other end.

"It's not mine to question," Signora Fontina says. "But starting over at this point in our lives? I'm a grandmother, for goodness' sake."

Giulia nods. "Is there anything I can do to help you prepare?"

Signora Fontina begins to rattle off her list: remedies for seasickness and insomnia to get her through the voyage; a private store of all of Giulia's household remedies, for who knows what will be available in the wilderness of that far-off place; and finally—

"Joint salve. As much as you've got. I'll fill a trunk with it."

"I'm sorry, we certainly don't have a trunk's worth. Carmela?" Giulia calls as Carmela is still dragging her feet to go wash Maria's mortar. "Could you bring out all the joint salve we have in the back?"

Carmela shoots an apologetic smile at Maria and does as she's told. She brings an armful of the salve out to the front and deposits it on the counter.

Signora Fontina tsks. "All of those," she says. "And I'll take three times that again, if you can have it ready by the time we leave."

Giulia struggles to keep her face neutral—that much joint salve will pay their rent for ages. "And when is that?"

"One month."

Someday, Carmela will be as trusted with the customers as her mother is. Perhaps it makes sense that Maria and Laura stay in the back. Maria is composed of sharp edges; life has forged her blades again and again until they can do nothing but cut. And somehow life has left Laura without any blades at all.

But Carmela likes people. She likes the fleeting glimpses into their lives. Sometimes they're not the most pleasant glimpses; she'd rather not know as much as she does about Signor Abate's digestive system. But when a woman who is already married comes in for a love potion, Carmela cannot help but wonder. Is she trying to reignite a flame? Or light a new one with a clandestine lover? Is she buying it for a sister? Is it something she'll keep on a shelf to remind her of what's possible?

How would Carmela use a love potion? Supposing they work, supposing they are more than hope in a bottle, would Carmela want love from someone who'd been magicked into their feelings? That's supposing the love potions create true love, though, not only a facsimile.

If somehow her mother has been able to defy the laws of nature and create something from nothing, so that where someone may have been indifferent or worse, now they are truly, deeply devoted: Carmela isn't sure she would want that love.

There's not a single boy in town who Carmela can imagine spending a coin's worth of love potion on anyway.

The door chimes again and Giulia's voice rings out.

"Ah Violetta! How did things go with the love potion?"

Carmela stiffens and knocks too much belladonna into the vial before her. Maria's gaze burns into the back of her head. The barest hint of belladonna in an eye drop and the pupils dilate into a doe-eyed appearance. Hence the name *belladonna*: Latin for "beautiful woman." But the amount Carmela knocked in will more likely lead to delirium, hallucinations, coma, and death.

She hesitates. If she adds more of everything else, she could get the proportions right and make a larger batch.

But Maria shakes her head decisively. "Bin it and start over."

Carmela sighs and carries the ruined mixture over to the waste bin. As she passes by the archway to the shop front, Giulia calls out.

"I need a calming tonic."

Carmela's irritation spikes. She's already behind now that she must remake the eye drops. But Violetta is apparently so worked up with excitement over the object of her love that she requires a calming tonic.

Carmela pours a glass from the carafe Laura makes faithfully every morning for cases such as this, and delivers it to her mother, pointedly not looking at Violetta. But Giulia doesn't take the glass. She waves Carmela toward Violetta and instructs her daughter to stay with the girl as she whisks away to the back.

Carmela holds out the glass, still not looking. "Violetta," she says coolly.

When Violetta takes the glass, Carmela can't help but notice her face is blotchy, her eyes red. Giulia would say something warm and kind. Even Maria would clap a hand on the girl's shoulder and mutter something well-meant, if clumsy. But whatever mess Violetta's gotten herself into hasn't earned her Carmela's pity.

"Not here for more love potion, then?" she says.

Violetta chokes back a sob.

Carmela's head snaps up. The Violetta she knows would have bit back that she's never had need of a love potion to get any suitor she wants. But this is a different girl altogether. An unmarried girl in great distress—and disillusioned with love potions, besides? Carmela has seen this in the apothecary a few times. She simply never had an opinion on the customer before.

"I'm surprised you came here," Carmela says. "Considering how you feel about us."

Violetta sniffles. "I didn't have anywhere else to go. Your mother—"

"Yes, my mother." Her mother, who Violetta would happily throw to the flames when it suited her, but now that she needs help only Giulia can give, here she is sniveling on their doorstop. "The one you call a witch?"

Violetta's splotchiness intensifies as her face pales beneath the patches of red. If she'll admit she was a beast, Carmela will soften. At least, that's what she tells herself. She'll somehow find it within the depths of her heart to show her mother's mercy for those who badmouth her, then expect her to save their lives.

Violetta glances over her shoulder as though Giulia might come to rescue her. "I don't know what you're talking about."

The little coal of resentment Carmela has kept burning all these years leaps into flame. "Are you truly going to deny it when you've said it to my face? And to all the others?"

"I was a stupid child—"

"Yes, and now you're going to have one of your own if we don't help you. Isn't that right?" Violetta's eyes confirm it, and Carmela can't stop herself from barreling toward the cliff. "How does it feel to be at the mercy of the witch?"

Violetta is completely drained of color now, no trace of life in her face. Maybe Carmela has some magic too.

"Answer me," Carmela says, "or I'll turn you into a toad!"

"Well." Giulia's voice cuts through the room. "I'd surely love to see that." She glares daggers at Carmela before arranging her face into one of a pleasant, neutral party and saying to Violetta, "Personally, I've never been able to manage toad transfiguration."

Violetta blinks, too dull or shocked to understand it's a joke. Or perhaps it's not. Carmela's mother has definitely not yet told her all the secrets of the shop.

"Mother." Carmela grabs Giulia's arm and pulls her away, though she doesn't bother to control her volume. It doesn't matter what Violetta thinks of them. "We can't trust her. The things she's said about you—"

Giulia shakes Carmela off. "If I didn't serve people who've spoken ill of me, I'd have no customers at all." She turns back to Violetta, though she is still speaking to Carmela. "It seems to me that Violetta is the one who must trust us right now."

Violetta's face looks anything but trusting.

"Do you trust us, dear?"

But it doesn't matter. She has no other choices. She gives the tiniest nod.

Giulia kneels before Violetta, and the single flame becomes a raging inferno at the sight of La Tofana kneeling before the likes of Violetta Raso. The only thing that keeps Carmela from yanking her mother to her feet is the knowledge that Giulia would surely banish her from the apothecary.

"Good. Do you need my help to end a pregnancy?"

Violetta's eyes flicker to Carmela. With that one glance, the flame sputters.

"I gather you and Carmela have history, but she is a crucial part of the running of the apothecary and you have my word that you can trust her." Giulia takes Violetta's hands. "Do you want our help to end this pregnancy?"

The naked vulnerability on Violetta's face in that moment extinguishes the flame completely. It doesn't matter if Giulia kneels before Violetta. It doesn't matter if Carmela must clear her dirty glass, which she sets in the basket of things to be washed, steeling herself to turn around and face Violetta again. She has the power in this moment, and it's as useless as a cold, hard coal.

She wants to help people, yes, she wants to have knowledge and share it and be looked to as someone with wisdom. But wanting power over someone else's body is like wanting to live inside their skin. This should be Violetta's decision. Carmela should have no part of it.

She busies herself straightening jars on shelves.

"If I'm found out . . . ," Violetta finally says.

"If you're found out, your troubles will be a family matter. Ending a pregnancy is not against the law. Not unless you've felt quickening. Movement. You haven't felt movement yet, have you?"

Carmela holds her breath. She has a general idea of how pregnancies happen, but the details beyond that are a mystery. She has no idea when a baby starts to move so much the mother feels it. Violetta doesn't yet look like she's with child, but her fashionable gown would easily conceal any changes to her form. There is a window in which one must make this life-changing decision, but not everyone has a Giulia to walk them through each step.

Giulia has turned away from Violetta, busying herself with an unimportant task. Perhaps she doesn't want to see Violetta's face when she answers this question.

"No," Violetta says. "I haven't."

"All right then." Giulia produces a packet she presses into Violetta's hands. "This contains a blend primarily of pennyroyal, but also with rue, juniper, black hellebore—"

"I'll drink it," Violetta says. "I don't care what's in it."

"You should." Violetta shrinks into herself at the sharpness of Giulia's tone. "You should always take care with what you put into your body."

"Yes, Signora."

Desperate to busy herself, Carmela takes up the branches of thyme she has been putting off garbling. Removing the tiny leaves from the stems is painstaking but mindless.

"As soon as you get home, you'll brew a strong infusion with one quarter of this packet. Drink it straight down, all in one go. No sipping."

Carmela removes leaf after leaf and etches the instructions onto her own brain. For herself, for someone else, she doesn't know. But it seems vitally important that she soak in this wisdom, that she tuck it carefully away so she'll have it to share with those who need it.

"It's going to cause terrible cramping, almost right away. I'd have you stay here to keep an eye on you, but once the cramping starts, you're going to be too sick to move. I expect your father would not take it well if you stayed out all night."

"No." Violetta's pretty face has begun to take on a vague hint of green.

"There's enough in the packet for you to brew four strong doses. Drink one every six hours. The cramping will be terrible. You'll likely vomit and pass clots of blood and tissue. You may spike a fever. You will feel like you are dying. Do you understand?"

Violetta's voice is so faint Carmela barely hears it. "Yes, Signora."

"But you are not dying. You are living. Repeat that back to me."

Violetta hesitates, but Giulia grabs her free hand and holds her gaze until she says, barely above a whisper, "I am not dying. I am living."

"Good girl."

"What about her parents?" Carmela doesn't mean to interrupt the maternal moment, but she doesn't not mean to either. Her flame of resentment may have died down, but she has her limits. Violetta has everything in the world. She can have Giulia's help, but she cannot have Giulia.

"What about them?"

"She won't be able to hide what you're describing."

Violetta nods a tiny shred of gratitude to Carmela for voicing what she must have been thinking herself.

"No," Giulia admits. "But you'll tell them you're having your monthlies. They won't ask any questions."

"Not even her mother?"

"Stepmother," Violetta corrects.

Either way. Giulia would notice if Carmela's flow was suddenly a violent, near-death illness.

But Giulia shakes her head briskly. "She won't ask what she doesn't want to know."

"All right." Violetta looks unconvinced.

"Good, then."

"But, Signora . . ."

"What is it?"

"I don't have any money."

The ground shifts again beneath Carmela's feet. Here she's gone from decade-long hatred for Violetta to the beginnings of compassion and now, after all of this, she reveals that she cannot actually pay. The cold, hard coal reignites.

Giulia's wisdom is invaluable. Even if she's willing to serve those who'd just as soon destroy her, she certainly won't do it for free. Now Carmela will see how the master of handling customers shows someone the door.

"That's all right," Giulia says.

"What? Mother, no—"

"Hush, Carmela. Violetta, you get yourself home and follow my instructions, and then you keep on living. That's all the payment I need."

"Mother, this isn't—"

"Carmela will walk you home." The protest on the tip of Carmela's tongue dies at the look on Giulia's face. Carmela has overstepped in her objections and she is not so secure in her place at the apothecary that she can push any further.

Carmela stalks to the door.

But Violetta lingers with Giulia. "I am so sorry, Signora, about anything I ever said. To the other children, or—"

"Hush." Giulia squeezes Violetta's shoulder and pushes her toward the door. "All you need to do right now is get yourself home safely, dear."

Outside, Carmela wages an internal war. The injustice of this—that Violetta Raso should deserve an escort home. That Carmela should be expected to provide it. That Giulia has given her wisdom and remedies and kindness and Violetta will pay nothing in return.

"You don't have to walk me home."

To spite her, Carmela follows Violetta. If she returns to the shop, she'll only face her mother's wrath all the sooner. If Violetta wouldn't pay in coin, Carmela will make her pay another way.

"Was it Antonio?" she asks.

Violetta flinches.

Carmela saw Violetta and Antonio flirting at the market, a whole volume of love poetry written in their furtive glances, shortly after

Violetta came in for the love potion. But Mother claims they don't really work.

"I heard he's engaged to be married."

"He wasn't when we—" Violetta stops, as though it is improper to speak aloud the thing they both know happened. "I thought he was going to marry me."

She sounds so pathetic Carmela doesn't strike. Maybe she's smarter than Violetta. In fact, she's fairly sure she is. But she also knows she's never really had the chance to make the same mistake. There's never been anyone in town who's ever made her feel like doing something risky, something stupid.

"He's a fool," Carmela says. No matter what she thinks of Violetta, making someone believe you love them and then getting engaged to someone else seems blatantly awful.

"He's not," Violetta says, and Carmela's hint of compassion dissolves. "You wouldn't understand."

"No, the witch's daughter doesn't entertain a lot of suitors."

Violetta stops. "I'm sorry about that. I apologized to your mother and I apologize to you too. You can tell Signora Tofana you walked me all the way home."

Then she turns and darts down the alley, heading toward bustling Via di Ripetta and her family's apartment.

Carmela was inside that apartment once, back before the other children turned on her. It was warm, and smelled of baking bread, and Violetta's mother treated all the children who came through her door like they were her own.

Then one day Carmela showed up at the apartment and a black cloth draped the doorway. An angry man told her to go back to the witch, and she never returned.

The Widower

There is a man
like Violetta's father
                                        but not

in a cramped apartment
all the way up off Blacksmith's Alley
but you can walk there from the apothecary.

This man, his wife has died
but she was just here
baking bread, consoling children, tending the hearth,
wringing laundry, going to market, wiping bloodied knees
and still had time to fret
over the sore on his back that refuses to heal.

Then, quick as the neighborhood cat
pouncing on prey,
she leapt from sick to dead.

It cannot be. He must be mistaken.
Any moment now
she will walk in the door
and laugh at him in her gentle way
that makes him laugh as well
and realize his error.

Any moment now
she will soothe the children
wailing in the next room,

she will tell him where he left his paring chisel,
she will bring him a balm for his wound.

For how else is he to go on?
Six children will not raise themselves.
One day he will be hungry again
and no one will know what he craves.
For the master of the household
it is remarkable how inept he is
of mastering anything in this domain.

His family offers help,
the sisters from Santa Maria of the Angels,
the neighbors endlessly knocking
not realizing when he opens the door
the only face he wants to see is hers.

He paces the small room
where they used to share a bed
and wonders how to take the first step
into the rest of a life without her.

Carmela meanders back to the shop, making each step take twice as long, though her mother will somehow know she didn't actually walk Violetta all the way home. Witch or not, Giulia has maternal powers.

Maria's the only one left in the shop when Carmela returns.

"Signora Valenti's labor pains have begun," Maria says without preamble.

"Laura went to her?" Laura is the perfect support for early labor: quiet strength, encouragement. Maria will make her way to the laboring woman in the later stages and bully the baby out into the world. "And Mother?"

"She said to tell you she'll meet you at home."

Carmela exhales and slumps onto the bench. Another beat before she has to face Giulia's lectures, then.

"You must trust her," Maria says as she packs a bag with her supplies for attending births.

"Violetta Raso? Not in this lifetime."

"Your mother. She knows what she's doing."

"Even when she hands out charity like a convent?"

"You may have the wrong idea what convents do."

"You've said it yourself, Maria. The shop is struggling. We're losing Signora Fontina to the New World. Signor Russo raised the rent last month. How can we afford to hand out remedies for free?"

Maria scoffs. "This isn't about money. This is about your childhood grievance with Violetta. So some children called you names. Boo-hoo. We raised you better than that."

Carmela bites back her protest.

"Now get on upstairs and go easy on your mother."

Carmela helps Maria reach the fennel tincture on a high shelf, and then kisses her papery cheek. "Thank you, Donna Maria."

She grunts. "For what?"

"For always being honest with me."

Maria shakes her head, baffled, and holds the door open for Carmela so she can lock it behind her.

The Laboring Mother

There is a woman
like Signora Valenti
                                        but not

who wakes to the bells
of Santissima Trinità
a few minutes east of the apothecary
just past Via del Corso

with a baby inside her
so insistent it presses its feet
against their shared wall of her belly
and she can count the toes.

She is enormous, a galaxy of a creature
all distended belly and pendulous breasts
her body no longer her own
nothing more than a vessel
for this life inside
alien and strange
floating in a mixture of their shared fluids.

She has been here before.

The first time
she longed for the baby to emerge,
wanting not only to count the toes,
but touch them, kiss them, watch them wiggle.

She ached to hold the child in her arms
but never imagined a world
where that child would emerge cold and blue.

The second time
she scarcely believed she was with child.
Her body had shown itself
incapable, after all.
But when she could no longer ignore
another foreign invasion of her self
her changing center of gravity
her insatiable appetites
her loss of control

she accepted
this was happening again
and began to pray
for the child
for herself.

When the pains began
she called upon Santa Margherita
patron saint of labor and childbirth.
Margherita was a virgin, but she knew physical trial.
When devoured by a dragon,
she escaped by piercing the dragon's insides
with her crucifix, emerging the bloody victor.

But when the second baby arrived
still and cold as the first

this perpetually heartbroken mother
discarded the amulet of Margherita
and refused to think of her again.

The third baby lived
for three hours.

Now she is here again
with yet another baby
about to leave the safety of her womb
for this cold, dark world
and no matter how dearly
she longs to hold it, to know it,
she also yearns to keep it
safe inside forever.

The apartment above the shop is cold. Carmela moves about the room, starting a fire in the hearth, putting water on for tea, slicing cheese and bread for supper. Time is already tempering her annoyance with her mother. Not erasing it completely, of course, but the things she wanted to yell at Giulia earlier have dulled into a rolling of the eyes.

When Giulia finally returns, time has worked the same magic on her. She smiles at the meager spread Carmela has prepared for them—for all Giulia has taught her, domestic skills are not among them, not least because Giulia has very few of her own. She takes off her boots and cloak, and sits quietly for a few moments, staring into the fire.

When she finally speaks, it's barely about Violetta.

"We help whoever walks in that door. However we can. The ones like Signora Moretti, with every ache and pain under the sun? Who mostly need someone to talk to and have the coin to pay for it? They cover the costs of the ones like Violetta. Like I was when Maria took me in. Do you think she could afford another mouth to feed?"

Carmela can almost hear Maria loudly interjecting how very destitute she was and how young Giulia almost ate her out of hearth and home.

"But she took me in anyway. We take care of each other. If anything should ever happen to me—"

"It won't."

"If anything should ever happen to me, you'd have Maria and Laura. They'd have you. We are so incredibly lucky. We take care of the people who have nowhere else to turn. Who have no Maria, no Laura."

No Giulia.

"There are so many who have no one else to turn to, even if you think you know otherwise. Even if it looks like they have a mother, a sister, a friend. Maybe there's a reason they can't turn to those closest to them. That's where we come in. That is the daily work we are here for. Giving women a choice over what happens in their bodies. Are we clear?"

Giulia is always clear. Except when she is opaque. But Carmela understands her now.

"Yes, Mother."

"All right then."

Carmela can't stop thinking about Violetta, no matter how violently she tries to shove the loathsome girl from her mind. She volunteers for the most hideous tasks—rendering the human fat delivered by the executioner, distilling the urine, or, as she has done this morning, harvesting the Greek White—for she'd rather focus on scraping the white crust off hardened dog dung than worry about Violetta.

Worry about Violetta! Of all the preposterous things for this job to make her do. It's one thing to accept that they must serve monstrous people who thrive on bad-mouthing La Tofana; Giulia said nothing about allowing one of them to plant a flag inside Carmela's mind. Why should she care if Violetta took the remedy yet, if it worked, if it caused her much pain?

Carmela squats in the alley, hunched over as she scrapes the white parts of the sun-hardened feces into a bowl. This is distasteful, but it's meaningful. It will help someone battling a sore throat.

A vivid memory from when she was eight or nine: Each time she tried to swallow, it felt like knives being forced down her throat and lodging there. She was certain she would never swallow properly again, and if she couldn't swallow, then she couldn't eat or drink, and she would die. It was logic. She sobbed, and her throat hurt even more.

Giulia made her an infusion, but Carmela refused to try it.

Giulia persisted, sitting with Carmela under a blanket with a bowl of steaming water and herbs, cajoling the infusion into her mouth sip by sip, wrapping her neck in a poultice of ginger and honey, and, finally, singing her to sleep.

This is what mothers do.

Violetta's mother had died. But her father had remarried soon after; she'd never wanted for someone to care for her. And there's Violetta again, elbowing her way into Carmela's mind.

If Carmela had so much as a heavier flow than usual, Giulia knew. Carmela cannot fathom parents who wouldn't notice the sort of pain Giulia described. The idea that Violetta's parents don't pay enough attention to recognize alarming symptoms needles at Carmela. She huffs in frustration, inadvertently blowing bits of dry dung into her face.

She stumbles backward, landing hard on her rear, spilling the precious Greek White back over the pile of dung.

"Aaaargh!!!"

"Carmela?" Laura leans out the back door, concern etched into her normally placid face. "Are you all right?"

Carmela gestures helplessly at the mess before her.

"Oh dear." Laura approaches to help, but Carmela stops her.

"You don't have to. I'm fine. Or not, clearly. I'm a mess. But I can manage."

Laura ignores her and kneels. "But you don't have to. At least not alone."

At first they try to separate the Greek White from the useless dung, but it's impossible. Now that it's been scraped off, the fine particles are indistinguishable from the dirt of the alley.

Carmela moans. "Maria's going to kill me."

Laura bites back a small laugh. "Do you know, I think dog shit is probably our easiest ingredient to procure?" She pats Carmela on the back and then stands, holding out a hand to help her up. "Maria will be fine."

Inside, Maria barely responds when Laura tells her there was a problem with the Greek White and they'll need to get more. Laura winks at Carmela as she washes up in the basin of water near the back door.

Carmela's hands are much filthier, not to mention all the dung spilled down the front of her. "I'm going to the fountain," she tells Laura and Maria as she passes through to the front of the shop. Giulia doesn't look up from where she's deep in conversation with a new but extremely frequent customer.

The nearest public fountain is a short walk from the apothecary—through a couple of alleys in the jumbled warren of streets known as the Ortaccio—the Bad Garden—and then she is there. Carmela skirts a group of women clustered in front of the fountain. Some are customers of the apothecary, some aren't, but they all look askance at her. Admittedly, she's covered in shit. She spots Violetta's stepmother and averts her gaze quickly, focusing on scrubbing her hands in the sun-warmed water.

The women explode in laughter over something, it doesn't matter what, and it stabs through Carmela, this kind of belonging she's never had. Oh she belongs in the apothecary now, with her mother and Maria and Laura. She wouldn't trade that for anything.

But they're family, even if they're not all blood.

What these women have is different. The natural, easy rhythms of their banter, the way they tease one or shush another. There's a music to it. A choir, and each one sings her part. It wouldn't delight the ear so much if a voice were missing.

But they'll reach the end of their song, and each go their separate ways to their homes, their families, knowing the music could be picked back up at any moment.

"What are you staring at?" Signora Stiatessi snaps at Carmela, as though she didn't purchase a flatulence remedy yesterday. Or perhaps because she did.

Carmela turns away, removing her apron and shaking the debris off it.

"Stay away from that one," Signora Stiatessi's friend advises her. "Doesn't she belong to La Tofana?"

Carmela stands taller. That's meant as an insult, but she does belong to La Tofana, and that's more than any of them can say.

BACK INSIDE THE SHOP, her mother is helping a customer, and a young man loiters, waiting his turn.

Young men are rare in the shop, which is the only reason Carmela pays him any mind. Is he here for himself, or has he been sent on an errand by a mother or sister or girlfriend? Carmela is trying to decide if he's a secret romantic in search of a love potion or a heavy drinker who's heard La Tofana has a remedy for the next morning's consequences, when the young man makes his move.

The customer has withdrawn her pocket from her skirts and holds the simple bag lightly at her side. When she leans across the counter to examine something, the young man cuts the strap that winds around her hand, snatches the pocket, and is out the door before anyone else reacts.

Carmela is closest. As soon as she realizes what just happened, she lunges for the door, ignoring her mother's cry behind her. She got a good look at the thief. She might not be fast enough to catch him, but she's observant enough to give a description, and maybe she can at least see which direction he goes.

She catches sight of him lunging into the alley between the butcher and the mercer. He's heading for the square; if he gets through it and out onto Via di Ripetta, no one will ever find him.

Some of the women are still standing together near the fountain. This time they look at Carmela with open disdain as she runs through the streets.

"Thief!" she calls. The women won't help her, but perhaps a man who feels like being gallant will heed her cry, or a sympathetic shopkeeper.

And then she spots him, Nicolò Tassi, haughty with the power he wields in Campo Marzio, exactly as he was years earlier when Violetta and her gang had stolen sweets from a vendor in the market. When they were caught, they claimed it had been Carmela's plan. The notary paid a visit to the apothecary. Carmela wasn't there, of course—she'd only been twelve or so—but her mother had told her all about it, and pointed out Notary Nicolò Tassi on the street so she could avoid him.

Giulia hadn't believed for a second that Carmela had been the mastermind of a child gang of street thieves, not because she held Carmela's integrity in such great esteem, but because she knew those children never included her daughter. She'd dispatched the notary easily, but she'd warned Carmela that a man who'd been made a fool of not only by a horde of children but, even worse, by a woman, was likely to hold a grudge.

Still, a notary is an officer of the law. He gathers evidence and presents it to magistrates, who charge crimes. Carmela has eyewitness evidence.

"Sir," she says, gasping for air. "There's a thief heading that way through the square—"

The notary steps back, not even attempting to mask his disgust.

She'd washed off all the dung, hadn't she? "Sir, he's a bit taller than you, and fairer. Maybe seventeen, eighteen, with a patched cap—"

He holds out a hand to stop her. "Enough."

"Sir, he stole from—"

"From the apothecary?" The notary purses his lips tightly. "Your mother's apothecary?"

"Yes, he was there, and then a customer—"

"I am here," Nicolò Tassi says, drawing himself up to his full, if unimpressive height, "to ensure justice for the residents of Campo Marzio. Not for the likes of you."

Carmela gapes at him. "I am a resident of Campo Marzio. We live above the shop!"

He turns his attention quickly to an approaching woman, the very customer whose pocket was stolen, her cheeks red from outrage or exertion. "Oh Signor, thank goodness," she says, looking between Carmela and the notary. "Have you caught the thief?"

The notary glares at Carmela as though she's given him faulty information.

"He stole my pocket," the woman pleads. "But I didn't see which way he went."

Without a word, Carmela points, and the notary takes off running. He is more the sort to shuffle papers behind a desk than to chase down criminals, so it is with grim satisfaction that Carmela watches him stumble before she turns back the way she came.

Carmela falls into the rhythm of the shop. She begins to anticipate the regulars. When Signor Conti comes in for his gout remedy, she has it waiting for him.

"There's my second-favorite girl," he says to her as he counts out his coins.

"Second favorite?!" Carmela clutches a hand to her heart in mock devastation. "Who's my competition?"

"Oh my dear," he says as he takes the bottle, "my heart belongs to the pretty lady in the back."

Maria makes a rude gesture as she passes by the archway and Signor Conti's laugh fills the shop.

When the bells announce Signor Conti's departure, there is a lull in customers. "What do you think, Maria?" Carmela says through the gaps in the shelves. "Signor Conti has one of the nicest homes in the Ortaccio."

Laura snorts out a tiny laugh.

"You hush your smart mouth," Maria scolds. "And bring me my gloves so I can strip these nettles."

Carmela looks to Laura, who points out Maria's gloves inexplicably on a shelf of herbal syrups in the front of shop. When Carmela brings them to Maria, she snaps them on with a glare and begins to pull the nettle leaves from their stalks. Carmela bends to pick up a stalk that's fallen, and Maria snaps, "Don't touch that! Why do you think I wanted my gloves?"

Carmela glares back at Maria and uses a stray rag to pick the stalk up. She examines the jagged-edged leaves, the fine hairs standing up on the pointy green.

"Stinging nettle," Maria says, her voice slightly less barbed. "Learn to identify it now so I don't pay the price later."

At Carmela's questioning glance, Laura shrugs.

"What's it for?" Carmela asks. "If you can't touch it—"

"You can't touch it raw," Maria corrects. "Or you can, but you'll be itching up a storm all night like I was when your mother gave it to me fresh in a poultice."

"What?! Why?" A grin spreads across Carmela's face at the completely foreign idea of her mother making a disastrous mistake.

"Why your mother does anything, I can't say." But then Maria relents. "She was still learning. She knew stinging nettle could be used for inflammation—when it's properly prepared, that is. It's good as a tea, or topically as a tincture. The heat of cooking undoes the properties that make it sting."

"But she gave it to you fresh?"

"She was an insufferable child, needed to know absolutely everything all at once and show off to the world that she did." Maria raises a pointed eyebrow at Carmela, who chooses to ignore it. "I had a rash. Barely noticeable. But Giulia sprung into action like it was the plague."

Carmela can picture it—her mother treating Maria like she's near death, Maria grumbling at her, but letting her practice her craft. "You didn't see what she was putting in the poultice?"

"We'd just gone over poultices for skin irritations! I assumed she wanted to practice what I'd taught her! I should have known she'd try to improve on my instructions without any knowledge to back up her confidence."

Of course Giulia wasn't always brilliant; Carmela knows this. But it's still hard to fathom.

"Next thing I know, she's slapped a poultice on me and my whole arm is on fire!"

Laura giggles, never looking up from her work.

"Oh you go on and laugh," Maria calls over to her. "I'd like to see how you feel about an armful of raw stinging nettles!"

Carmela giggles too and then Maria is laughing, loud and raucous.

"I can't believe she did that."

"I can't forget." Maria wipes her hair off her face with her forearm, careful not to touch her skin with the gloves that have been handling the stinging nettle all this time.

The shop bell rings and they each look through the gaps in the shelving to see a priest lurching through the door. Maria's smile disappears. "Go see what he wants."

Carmela frowns. Though the apothecary stocks some candles and anointing oils for churchgoers, she's never seen a man of the cloth walk through those doors. She turns to Laura, the only one among them who attends Mass. "Is he here for you?"

She gives a quick shake of the head.

"Father," Carmela says, heading out to the front. "Hello. Can I help you?"

The priest sways slightly on his feet; fumes waft off him like incense off a thurible. Carmela steadies herself on the edge of the counter.

"Good morning, Giulia," the priest says.

Carmela glances over her shoulder, hoping perhaps her mother has appeared to take over the transaction. But no, the man is simply addled enough to mistake her for her mother. And familiar enough to call her by her first name.

"I'm afraid she's not—"

"You look lovely today," he says, reaching the counter. "Very youthful."

Carmela could dissolve a solid in the menstruum of his breath. There is no point insisting Giulia is not here. The man will remember nothing tomorrow.

"Thank you," she says. "If you're here to invite us to Mass—"

He frowns, confused. "No, nothing of the sort." He glances around, checking for potential eavesdroppers. Carmela's shoulders relax slightly; many customers would rather not announce their maladies to whoever else might be standing in the apothecary.

But then he leans in, inches from Carmela's face and says, "I brought what we discussed."

There is no world in which Giulia could have discussed anything with this priest or any other member of the clergy. A vivid memory: Carmela returning home from learning that Violetta's mother had died.

"Where is she, Mama?" she'd asked Giulia after they were both tucked into bed.

"Who's that, darling?"

"Violetta's mother."

"Ah." Giulia was silent for such a long time, Carmela thought she might have fallen asleep. But finally she spoke. "I don't know."

Carmela waited for more explanation. On the very rare occasion that Giulia did not know the answer to a question, she made it her mission to find out.

"Nina says she's in heaven." The word tasted funny in Carmela's mouth. Giulia didn't respond to that. "Mama, is she in heaven?"

"I don't know that, either, love. I don't know what happens when we die. I only know it's our job to take care of Violetta and her father and the ones who are still living."

Carmela was quiet for a long time. "Nina says there's going to be a Mass tomorrow for Violetta's mother. Can we go?"

"No, darling. Go to sleep now."

"But Mother—"

"Sleep now," Giulia said more sharply, and this time Carmela did as she was told.

She'd learned not to ask why they didn't go to Mass like nearly everyone else in Campo Marzio. She'd learned—from the bitter twist on her mother's face whenever Laura mentioned church or customers spoke of services or even when Maria made a joke about priests—that the church was not for them.

"Father," Carmela says to the priest before her, "my mother isn't here right now—"

The priest grabs Carmela's wrist. "Listen carefully. Use extreme caution. This can't be traced back to me. The smallest amount will kill a man."

Carmela yanks her wrist away.

He draws a small packet wrapped in brown paper from the folds of his cloak and pushes it across the counter, using all his focus to approximate a straight line.

"One barleycorn should do it, you understand?"

The shop bell rings. Signora Moretti wafts in. She comes almost daily with an ache, a pain, a rash, a bruise. She has a litany of ailments, and though it seems none of the remedies help, she still continues to return and buy more.

The package of something deadly, at least according to this strange courier, sits on the counter like a beacon of guilt.

"I understand." Carmela grabs for the package and searches for a place to conceal it.

Perhaps he is mad and there is nothing more insidious than communion wafers in that square of cloth. But if it is truly deadly, it cannot be stashed anywhere it might be mistaken for something else.

"Where is Signora Tofana?" Signora Moretti demands right

before the priest crashes into her. Carmela seizes the gift of an extra few moments to figure out what to do with the package.

"Honestly!" the outraged woman huffs, staring after the inebriated man of the cloth as he finally makes his way out the door.

"I'm sorry about that," Carmela says. "He's . . . unwell."

"I'll say."

There is an awkward pause in which Carmela does not ask Signora Moretti what she can get for her, because they both know she wants only Giulia, and Giulia is not in right now.

Finally, "My mother's not in right now," Carmela says.

"How does she run a business when she is never here?"

Carmela bristles. "She is often here. Almost always, in fact."

"I have very poor timing, it seems."

"I suppose?" It is the wrong thing to say, though Carmela is at a loss for the right thing to say, and her mind cannot stop focusing on the illicit package that surely must be pulsing with a white-hot light from its current, not-at-all secure location. "Look, Signora Moretti, I really am qualified to help dispense nearly anything you might need. And whatever I can't help you with—"

Signora Moretti's eyes narrow. "Is that so? Anything?"

"Well. The more complicated things of course would require my mother's expertise, but with Laura and Maria's help we could surely at least make you comfortable until my mother's return."

Something shifts on the woman's face. In the space of a breath, she goes from skimming past Carmela when she sees her to realizing she might be useful. Young, yes, but that doesn't mean she has nothing to offer.

"All right then. What do you recommend for a tempestuous husband?"

Carmela blinks, startled that Signora Moretti has asked her a legitimate question. Not one she's received before, but she can make some inferences.

A tempestuous husband likely has an excess of yellow bile, so angelica and astragalus would balance that. Holy basil is very good for improving mood, and damiana balances aggression.

"I think I have exactly the thing."

Signora Moretti beams, and Carmela wrestles her own pride into submission. All these weeks this woman has spent endlessly seeking the solution to a problem Giulia hasn't been able to solve, and perhaps Carmela has done it.

In the back room, Carmela reaches first for the damiana tincture.

"What are you doing?"

"Getting this for Signora Moretti."

Maria's eyebrows shoot up. "Balancing aggression is required for very few female customers."

"It's not for her. It's for her husband. She said he's tempestuous, so I thought—"

Maria clunks her heavy mortar onto the work counter and heaves herself to her feet.

"What? Was that wrong?"

Maria doesn't answer. She heads straight for Signora Moretti at the counter. "Is there something I can do for you, Signora?"

Signora Moretti is startled but pulls herself together quickly, trying to look past Maria to catch a glimpse of Carmela. "I believe the young lady is gathering what I need."

"Yes, for your tempestuous husband, was it?"

"Maria—"

Signora Moretti shoots a glare at Carmela, who no longer needs to wrestle her pride into anything, for it's a deflated puddle at her feet.

"I thought one could assume a certain level of discretion in this shop."

"One can," Maria says. "For example, I will not be telling anyone besides Signora Tofana that you were attempting to wrangle from her child what you have been unsuccessful in getting from her."

"Well!" The woman's cheeks flame, eyes flashing. "See if I ever come in this shop again!"

Maria waves a languid hand. "See you soon."

From the back room, Laura laughs. Quiet, but clear.

When the bell rings behind Signora Moretti, Carmela turns on Maria. "What was that? I had it handled! You completely embarrassed me and lost us a frequent customer besides!"

"She'll be back. She hasn't gotten what she wants yet."

"I was trying to sell it to her!"

Maria takes the remedies from Carmela's hands and returns them to their shelves. "She wasn't looking to improve her husband's disposition."

"Well," Laura says. "In a manner of speaking."

Carmela turns to Laura. "What is going on? What am I missing here, Laura?"

Laura looks apologetic as she stands. "I need to see if Benicio has any mandrake to spare."

Carmela roars in frustration, but Maria pays her no mind. She may as well not be here at all.

The Tavern Mistress

There is a woman
like Signora Moretti
                    but not

serving drinks
at the tavern
around the corner
from the apothecary.

The crude, demanding customers
are flies in her ale.
With a husband like hers,
she barely notices pests like them.
Not after all these years.

Only fifteen the first time
a customer grabbed her ass
as she passed between the tables,
she whirled around and dropped a tray,
shattering glass and gathering ire
from her older brother, the tavern owner.

That lout put his hands on me!

        So? What did you think
        you were getting paid for?

She'd thought
her brother would protect her

like when a boy got out of hand
in the streets and her brother showed him
who was boss. But now he was her boss.

So she learned to take care of herself,
ignoring what could be ignored,
making herself scarce when certain men loitered
and by marrying the first man who claimed her.
Customers wouldn't
mess with another man's wife,
would they?

They would
and anyway
her husband is the worst of the lot,
especially when he's drunk,
which is most of the time.

Sometimes
she considers
packing up her things
and running away
to her sister's home in the north.

Sometimes
when he blacks out
she dreams he'll never wake.

The first time she heard of Acqua Tofana
she scoffed; she didn't believe
women capable of such a thing.

She'd seen brawls in the tavern,
men beaten and bloodied and sometimes dead
at another's hand. But a woman
snuffing out her husband's life,
cool and bloodless—unthinkable.

Until she tied her life to this unbearable man's
and lived with him year after year.
She was capable.

But the poison mistress
wouldn't provide what she was after.

Do you fear for your life?
Do you have another way out?
Is it possible to survive this?

Lies wouldn't work;
La Tofana knew the truth of a situation.

This woman, who even now
must grit her teeth and endure
the leers and hands and filthy mouths
of the customers between her
and her husband
on the opposite side of the tavern,
will survive this.

She will not end his life.
She will simply die a little
each time she serves his whims
and suffers his blows.

When Giulia returns from checking on the woman whose baby was delivered the night before, Carmela braces for Maria to tell her about Signora Moretti. She doesn't know what she's braced for: punishment or shame. She did nothing but try to provide the requested remedy.

The displeasure radiating off Maria has been impossible to ignore, especially as Laura has been out all morning and isn't there to balance Maria's temper with her own sweet one.

But Maria says nothing. At least not at first. "How's the baby?" she asks Giulia.

"Just fine. Mother too. Leticia said you and Laura were a great comfort."

Maria huffs and busies herself in the back. She wouldn't want to get a reputation as soft, but Carmela has seen her with new mothers. Maria can be soft. She can also reach out and squeeze a nipple hard to induce the contraction needed to expel the placenta. She probably does not need to worry about her reputation.

"Did Father Piero come by today?" Giulia asks from the counter.

Carmela pauses, glancing at Maria's back. She moves out front and keeps her voice low. "Who?"

"Father Piero. Never mind. Where's Laura?"

"Getting mandrake."

At that Giulia's eyes twinkle. Mandrake is for rheumatism cream. There's nothing delightful or scandalous there. But as always, there's another current of meaning pulling right beneath the surface.

"What?" Carmela asks. "What about mandrake?"

"Oh it's not the mandrake," Giulia says. "But rather the mandrake grower."

"Benicio?"

"Don't let Laura hear you talk like that," Maria calls. "She'll combust on the spot."

Giulia smiles as she moves toward the archway. "We don't know anything for certain," she says. "But Maria and I both suspect that Laura has a . . . special friendship with Benicio."

Carmela glances at Maria, who waves her arm like there are flies around her head. "You heard nothing from me!"

Laura, who keeps her head down and never speaks to anyone outside of these three women. Carmela's not sure she's ever seen her speak to a man. Her life is lived between the apartment she shares with Maria and the shop. She never ventures farther out, except—

"She is always the one to make pickups from Benicio," Carmela realizes.

Giulia nods. "And stays longer than she should. And always comes back flushed."

"It's a long walk," Maria says.

"Not that long."

When the shop bell rings and Laura steps in, there is no hiding the fact that they've been speaking about her. But Laura isn't flushed this time—at least not with happiness. She is pale, and agitated fingers worry at the handle of her empty basket.

"Signora Tofana," she says, "I'm so sorry, but I couldn't get the mandrake."

Giulia's face remains impassive. As abrupt as she can be with

Carmela and Maria, she always takes special care with Laura. "Was your botanist not in?"

"He's not my— He was in. But he wouldn't give it to me."

At that, Maria emerges from the back. "Lovers' quarrel?"

Laura ignores this, speaking only to Giulia. "He was changed. Beside himself. He was babbling about the mandrake's use in poison."

"We use it for rheumatism!" Giulia says.

Carmela frowns. Mandrake isn't even kept on the top shelf, with the most dangerous ingredients. (Except the one in her cloak pocket.)

"That's what I told him." Laura's voice wobbles. "He gave me this."

She hands Giulia a leaflet.

PARIS, FRANCE

FEBRUARY 1651

Geneviève Laurent, a humble washerwoman turned Lady of Death, has been executed for the murders of over 1,200 men.

For the last six years, she has operated under the noses of local officials, peddling her poisons to greedy, vengeful women who seek to execute their defenseless husbands and take control of their fortunes.

In some cases, the household servants used the diabolical poisons to bring low their rightful masters. In all cases the poison was odorless, colorless, tasteless, completely untraceable.

The madwoman's laboratory was a chamber of horrors unfit for description in print. Like Catherine de' Médicis and Lucrezia Borgia before her, Madame Laurent has proven that men everywhere must beware the vengeful women in their lives who can no longer be brought to heel with the back of one's hand.

It's horrifying, but Carmela can't figure out what it has to do with the mandrake for their rheumatism cream.

"But this is ridiculous." Giulia tosses the leaflet onto the counter. "Benicio gave you this?"

Carmela picks it up and studies it. Twelve hundred men killed by a single woman. She shivers; if someone like that ever got access to the ingredients in the apothecary, she could take out half of Campo Marzio.

Carmela's mind glances off the package still in the pocket of her cloak.

"Can you imagine?" Giulia is laughing. Actually laughing, joined by Maria. "Twelve hundred men in six years? That's what . . . four a week?"

She looks to Laura, their numbers expert. Laura isn't laughing, but she nods.

"Four men mysteriously dropping dead every week in the same neighborhood, with no apparent cause? They'd burn all the women as witches before the first month was up!"

"Not to mention the nonsense about untraceable poison," Maria says, shaking her head.

"If that were possible, I'd have done it."

Carmela's head snaps up. "So it's not true?"

Maria and Giulia exchange a loaded glance.

"No," Giulia finally says. "It's most certainly not true."

Still looking disturbed, Laura returns to her work.

"Without that mandrake, there's no way I can finish Signora Fontina's remedy before she leaves," Maria says. "Should we tell her? Give her a chance to order from someone else?"

Giulia shakes her head. "Not yet. Perhaps I can pay Benicio a visit. See if he'll listen to me."

That's what's bothering Carmela. "If this is so obviously a ridiculous fiction," she says, "why would Benicio be so troubled? And why would it prevent him from selling us mandrake?"

Maria takes the leaflet and tosses it in the fire on her way back to her worktable.

Giulia puts water on for tea. Carmela waits for her mother to formulate her response.

Finally, she says, "Just because we see it for what it is doesn't mean your average citizen will. Especially your average citizen who is comfortable in his position of power and wishes to stay that way."

Benicio the botanist has an extremely modest property on the eastern edge of Campo Marzio, with a few greenhouses where he grows his wares.

"How much power does a botanist have?"

"Well, that's exactly it. Obviously, the wealthy fear losing power. That's the story of every uprising, right?"

Carmela nods, remembering nights at the kitchen table after her mother came home from a long day at the apothecary, exhausted, but still determined to teach her daughter to read, to understand the world she lived in.

"But men like Benicio," Giulia goes on, "they have their own little dominion. Even if it's over one powerless woman. If they're to believe a woman could simply slip something into their drink and get away with it unpunished? Their very foundation crumbles."

Carmela looks at Laura, working industriously as usual, but there's an air of distraction. Spills aren't immediately wiped. She and Benicio aren't married or even betrothed, but still he has power over her.

Giulia retrieves her cloak. "I'm going to see if I can change his mind."

They watch her leave. Then Laura returns to her work. Carmela retrieves the broom.

Maria bangs around the back room, spilling more than usual. Maria was married once. A butcher, Carmela is almost certain. Nothing much is said about him. He's not mentioned with either fondness or malice. She wonders how much power he could have had over a force like Maria.

The Miller's Daughter

There is a girl
like Maria
                but not

at the mill
on the eastern edge
of Campo Marzio,
far enough you'd really need
a horse and cart to get there
from the apothecary.

Fifteen when she meets
the baker, broad-shouldered and twinkly-eyed.
She is covered in flour
helping her father with the mill.

        More than helping.
        The mill would not run
        without her.
        But he is the miller.

Are you the lady of the house?

The baker's tone is light, precise.
In jest, but not.

The girl's father snorts.

        Call your brothers
        to help load the cart.

The baker is young and strong,
fully capable of hoisting the sacks of flour
onto his back, if it weren't for the sling on his arm.

The girl ignores her father
and leaves her scrawny brothers to their idling.
She hefts the largest bag over one shoulder.

I would be much obliged
if the young lady would accompany me
to help unload in town.
I'll pay for her trouble.

The miller only grunts
and collects his payment.

Riding into town
the baker asks the girl questions.
She stares at her hands, flour in every crevice,
deep under each nail and one with her cuticles.
She wonders if he's mocking her.
He wouldn't be the first.

She doesn't mind
if it gets her away
from the mill for a spell.

But once she has unloaded the sacks of flour
he is busy with customers.
He can't leave the shop unattended.
Surely her father will understand?
He'll take the blame.

It seems to me
you deserve a day of peace.

She fidgets on a bench by the door
until she can no longer stand inaction.

When the baker struggles to refill his crocks
from the great bags of grain with only one arm,
she rushes forward, grateful for something to do.
When a customer comments
on his pretty young wife
the baker winks at her
and plays along.

No reason
to contradict
a customer.

The girl works as hard that day
as she does every other day at the mill.
But she never realized how much more enjoyable
it is to work hard when no one is berating her, belittling her.

It will be at least a month
before the baker calls her

an ignorant cunt.

Giulia hasn't returned by the time the shop closes.

"You go on home," Carmela says when Laura is wiping the counter for the fourth time and Maria is pointedly drumming her fingers.

"We can wait," Laura says.

But Carmela knows Laura doesn't like to be out in the streets after dark, even if Maria's with her. "I'm fine. I'll wait here for her."

Or Carmela could go upstairs and start the fire. But she likes the idea of being alone in the apothecary.

"All right." Maria needs no convincing. Laura hurries after her, still off-kilter from the events of the day.

Carmela follows them to the door and flips the sign in the window to closed. She leaves it unlocked for Giulia. There is a back door, but they hardly ever use it, opening as it does into a dark alley filled with refuse.

She stands in the center of the shop and takes a deep breath, the scent of the herbs as familiar to her as the scent of her mother's skin. Even when she wasn't allowed full access to the apothecary, the smell of the herbs wafted up through the floorboards to their cozy apartment above.

There are less enticing ingredients, of course. But Giulia keeps the various types of feces and animal parts tucked away in a back corner, carefully sealed. Healing doesn't always come from fragrant blooms, but Giulia understands her customers and how to make the shop inviting.

Carmela straightens bottles and tidies Maria's work area. She opens ingredients she hasn't had cause to use before and sniffs, trying to identify each one. She looks at the records, in Laura's precise handwriting. The money out, the money in, the money due.

Finally, Giulia returns, empty-handed and stormy-eyed.

"What happened?" Carmela asks.

Giulia sighs. "He was evasive. He tried to claim he'd had a poor crop, but I could see a basketful right behind him."

"What about the leaflet?"

"I asked him about that. He became flustered and said he was only sharing interesting news with Laura."

Carmela can imagine how intimidated the botanist must have been when La Tofana swept into his greenhouse. Even a man with a small dominion is no match for her mother. "If he's going to refuse to sell you something, he should have the guts to tell you why."

"Indeed." Giulia raises an eyebrow at the open record book before Carmela. "Anything to report here?"

Carmela closes the book and replaces it on Laura's shelf. "I was only trying to learn how the records are kept."

"As you should," Giulia says. "When the shop is yours, you will need to know every facet. It was nice of you to wait for me, but let's go upstairs, yes?"

Giulia pulls Carmela's cloak from the hook, but then she pauses, noticing the rustle of paper, or perhaps feeling the rhythmic beacon of *poison poison poison* that had been emanating from the cloak since the priest's visit.

She withdraws the packet and holds it up. "What is this? Where did it come from?"

Carmela is a child with her hand in the lozenge jar. Except she never wanted that packet. She didn't ask for it. "It's not mine."

Giulia throws the cloak onto the bench. "Father Piero did come by, didn't he?"

"I guess so? Maybe he put that in your cloak?" She's grasping at nonsensical excuses; she knows that, but it doesn't stop her tongue. "He was drunk."

"It's not my cloak, it's your cloak and I can read you like a recipe. Stop lying."

The injustice of being accused flares up in Carmela. "He thought I was you! That's how drunk he was. And then Signora Moretti came in and I didn't know what to do—"

"Giving it to me would have been a start. Telling the truth when I asked if he'd come! You've been holding on to this all day? What was your plan?"

"I don't know! I was confused. Someone else was always there, and—"

"There are no secrets from Laura and Maria."

"Even poison?"

Giulia flinches, but recovers swiftly. "Even poison."

Carmela refuses to ignore that opening. "What is it? What's it for?"

Giulia's eyes flash. "Just because you know how to mix a sleeping draught does not make you privy to every aspect of this business, little girl."

"I know how much of that powder it takes to kill a man. I'm feeling pretty involved!"

Giulia sinks onto the stool and buries her head in her hands.

The silence is oppressive. Carmela waits for her mother to tell her that poison is not meant to kill a man.

Finally: "I was planning to tell you when I thought you were ready."

Carmela isn't ready. She isn't. She's barely gotten to know the secrets of the shop, the ones she could handle, the ones she could fathom. She knows how to mix a sleeping draught and a calming tonic and drops for dry eyes. She is here to help people.

Like her mother.

But her mother is clutching a packet that contains a quantity of poison deadly enough to kill every man in town, and that knowledge is infused with Benicio's reluctance to sell them mandrake, and his concern about the washerwoman turned Lady of Death who killed over a thousand men.

"Ready to know that you poison people?"

She doesn't believe it, even as the words come out of her mouth. Her mother keeps the people of Campo Marzio alive. She soothes their pains and delivers their babies, and eases their passage out of this life. There is no world in which she harms a soul intentionally.

Giulia sits up. Her eyes are steel, as ever, but there's a different quality to the steel.

She begins.

GIULIA MADE HERSELF SMALL. If she was small, perhaps her father wouldn't notice her. Perhaps she wouldn't anger him, and they would get through a day without the thud of flesh on flesh, without a gaping wound in need of bandaging.

But that was a child's daydream. For she was a child, even if her monthly flow had begun and her shift had started to fill out with curves that echoed her mother's.

"Where's Costanza?" he roared. "Where's my dinner?"

That's the kind of night this was going to be. No preamble where everyone playacted a happy family. No fraught moments of tiptoeing through broken glass, attempting to cross the room without drawing blood.

Straight to the fury.

"Answer me!"

The trouble was, the only correct answer would have been *She's right here, and your dinner is exactly what you wanted, ready on demand.*

"At the apothecary." She braced for the fury. Giulia's mother was only allowed her work as an assistant at the apothecary as long as she was always home in time to feed him a hot meal. The trouble was, there was never any telling what time he'd show up, hungry.

Giulia looked from the cold stew in the pot to her father, already waiting at the table, expectant. She could make him wait while she heated it up, or serve it as it was.

She made the wrong choice.

"It's cold, you stupid bitch!" He stood up from the table and shoved her out of his way.

Giulia fell, crashing into the cauldron. The iron blazed and the flames licked her skin before she could change her momentum and collapse away from the fire.

Her father grabbed his cloak from the hook and left, slamming the door behind him.

Giulia held the burned arm close to her body, the skin puckering as she watched it, not yet aware of the pain that would soon explode. Right now she was learning what happened when an arm is plunged into a fire. What happens when a girl burns.

Her mother would know what to do. From her own burns, but also from her work at the apothecary. Giulia's mother would know which herbs to plaster over the angry welts on her arms to keep them from growing infected. To ease the pain. For it was blossoming now, the pain, inexorable. Giulia welcomed the familiar friend. She rode its waves, drifting in its inevitable wake until finally footsteps sounded.

Too gentle to be her father.

"Oh no! Oh Giulia!"

The instant her mother was there, the pain crested. No longer gentle waves but a violent tempest that would drown her but not before tossing her against every rock on the coastline.

"Your arm. Let me see."

The slightest shift sent screaming pain through Giulia's entire body.

"Is it broken?"

"Burnt," she managed, between the sobs that flowed freely now.

Anyone could fall into a fire. But Giulia's mother knew this had been no accident. "The monster," she cursed as she hurried to her small private store of remedies. "I'm so sorry, darling. I didn't think he'd be home . . ."

Giulia didn't blame her mother. Costanza had shielded her as a child, but Giulia was growing now. She was old enough to share the burden of his rage. They were in it together.

As her mother pressed a poultice of herbs to the worst of the burn, Giulia cried out, but almost immediately the plants worked their magic and the pain melted into a dull ache. Much more painful was the anguish on her mother's face.

"It's all right," Giulia said, even though they both knew it wasn't. "If it hadn't been me, it would have been you."

"That's not acceptable." Her mother stroked her hair, desperation in her eyes.

"Neither is what he does to you."

"It has to stop."

But it wouldn't. Not without the intervention of some outside force. But there were no white knights here.

"We could run," Giulia offered.

"To where? With what money? Oh Giulia, I wish . . ."

Giulia's life was lived within these walls. Her father had made sure they had few people to turn to. But there had to be someone, somewhere, who would help them.

"What about the church?" They attended sporadically, when her father was sober enough to pretend they were a happy family.

"No," Costanza murmured as she cleaned the congealed stew from the tiles around them. "No, I don't think so."

GIULIA DRIFTED IN AND OUT of a troubled sleep, her mother there one minute and gone the next, doors opening, closing. A thud.

And then her mother's hand on her shoulder, shaking. "Giulia, wake up. We have to go."

"What? Where?" Giulia peered at the pitch-black windows. Her father's cloak had returned to the hook by the door, but she didn't hear his snores.

"Come, hurry." Her mother had already packed a bag, and Giulia still wore the clothes she'd worn when she fell, for there was no removing her dress over her burn.

Her father was slumped over the table, eerily silent.

"Mama, what's happening?"

"Love, I need you to trust me. Can you do that?"

Even when all else was shifting ground, that was one thing Giulia knew she could always stand upon: she could trust her mother.

They hurried through the dark streets, and Giulia didn't know where they were headed until they arrived on the steps of the church of San Girolamo. "You were right," Costanza whispered, arm tight around Giulia's shoulders. "The church will help us. San Girolamo taught women no one else would, did you know?"

Inside, the incense-heavy air and candlelit warmth enveloped them. These stone walls were made to hold secrets, to protect the vulnerable. This was safety. Not all fathers would shove their child toward the fire.

Giulia's mother set her on a pew, positioning their hastily gathered belongings as a pillow beneath her head. She was sleepy, but the poultice was wearing off and the pain lanced through her arm, keeping her awake, shifting uncomfortably in search of a manageable position.

"What is it, my child?"

Giulia peered over the edge of the pew to see an angelic young priest, concern etched across his face. When Giulia replayed this night for years to come, she would always remember how he was younger than her mother but called her child.

"Sanctuary, Father." Giulia's mother knelt before the priest as though he were holy himself.

He reached out a hand and helped her up. "All who confess their sins are welcome here."

Giulia's mother followed the young priest to the confessional, and Giulia took a cautious breath. The first full breath she'd taken since her father struck her into the flames.

He'd struck her before. But never in the presence of her mother, for if Costanza were there, she was his target. It occurred to Giulia then that if he had truly realized his power, he would have struck Giulia in front of her mother. That would have wounded Costanza far worse than any broken bone or split lip.

But he saved his petty violence toward his daughter for when his wife was out, and he never left a mark. Whether he took care to do this, Giulia didn't know, but it was a small blessing. She'd shielded her mother from the knowledge that he hurt her too. At least for a time.

Giulia jerked upright at the crashing sound of the confessional door bursting open.

"But you said we were welcome!" Costanza cried, in a voice more desperate than she'd ever used with her husband. She closed the distance between herself and her daughter in seconds, throwing her body between Giulia and the priest.

As though a man of God would ever hurt her. Giulia shook her head to clear it.

"She is welcome." The priest flung an indignant hand toward Giulia. His voice was transformed, completely different from that of the gentle young holy man who'd greeted them. "You are a wicked, vengeful woman! A murderer!"

She was dreaming. She had to be. Any moment she'd wake up and the priest would be kind and welcoming. Better yet, they'd still be in their apartment, for no matter how bad her father had been, he had never made her mother's face look like this.

"You don't understand, Father. He would have killed us both!"

"Then you would have gone to your eternal rest rather than the damnation that awaits you now!"

All sleepiness evaporated. Perhaps Giulia would never sleep again. Her pain was irrelevant as her focus closed in on her mother. "What is he saying?"

The priest backed away from them, as though afraid of what this beaten-down wreck of a woman and her terrified child would do to him, then bolted toward the doors leading out to the street.

"You have to understand," Giulia's mother said, turning her attention to her daughter. The priest was beyond convincing. "Your father never would have stopped."

Out in the street, faintly, came the voice of the priest, shouting for help.

"If I'd had more time," Costanza said, her face drained of all color. "But this was the only way."

The priest's voice, closer now, leading an officer of the law into the sanctuary. Sanctuary. Sometimes a place of safety and rest. But sometimes it's only a building. "This wicked woman killed her husband."

Even hearing the words, Giulia could not connect the pieces in her mind. Her father dead? At her mother's hand? How could that possibly be?

The officer shifted uncomfortably under the gaze of the saints all around him. He looked to Giulia first, confused.

But the priest grabbed Costanza by the arm and shoved her forward.

"Mother!"

Now it was real. Now everything clicked into place with jarring force. If her mother had killed Giulia's father—Giulia's father was dead?—they would take her away and Giulia would never see her again. Not unless she attended the hanging.

"I'm sorry, darling." Was her mother apologizing for killing the monster who terrorized them both? Or for getting caught? "But he'll never touch you again."

"Mother, no!" Giulia pushed past the priest to wrap her arms around her mother, tight.

"Go to Maria," Costanza whispered in her ear. "I love you so much."

MARIA WAS THE MIDWIFE who had brought Giulia into this world. Nothing shocked a woman whose work was literal life and death. When she opened her door to find Costanza's daughter, a mess of tears and weeping wounds and horror, she knew. Enough, anyway, to open her door wide, usher in the girl who had been thrust into adulthood in one evening, and mourn the friend she'd never see again.

Maria's husband, the butcher, was a different kind of monster. He didn't rage, like Giulia's father. He had kind words, gentle caresses. He praised a well-made meal. He was proud of Maria's work, and her esteem as the midwife every woman wanted present at her birth.

He was kind to Giulia, an extra mouth to feed, an unexpected, sudden member of their family. Even when she lashed out, angry and confused at her sudden change of circumstances. So it was a special kind of shock when he blamed Giulia for a billing error they'd both watched him make.

"She's not the brightest," he'd said quietly to the customer as he'd rectified the error. "But she's dear to Maria, so she's dear to me."

Giulia thought she'd misunderstood. His face still seemed so kind. But when she asked him about it later, there'd been the briefest flash of ugliness in his eyes and he'd insisted so convincingly that it had been Giulia's error that she began to question her own memory of things.

Giulia began to keep on her guard, like she had with her own father. It felt silly, when the butcher never raised a hand to her, when he was so beloved by the customers who came into his shop.

When he began to call her their daughter, while continuing to undermine her own reality, she blamed herself. She'd intruded on their happy lives. Perhaps she deserved his slips of temper, his incisive cruelty.

But she watched more carefully and saw him do the same to Maria. Maria, who seemed so tough that nothing could cut through her exterior, who softened only for the butcher, and then when he had the chance, he'd twist the knife in. Quick, deep, always followed with loving care and a bandage that could not contain the gaping wound.

So there were all sorts of monsters.

Giulia began to catalog them. The monsters who threatened and intimidated. The ones who cajoled and wrangled pity. The ones who grabbed a handful in the marketplace and the ones who watched and said nothing.

She began to understand what her mother had done. It wasn't that all the monsters deserved to die. But there were some who could clearly be stopped by no other means, who would destroy their wives or children if no one took action.

Her mother's only mistake had been the sloppiness of her poisoning. She'd been hasty; she'd known her methods would be obvious and she had no other choice but to seek refuge somewhere she would be forgiven. Or at least believed she would.

If only there were a subtler poison, one that wouldn't immediately incriminate the woman who served a man his meals and ale. If such a thing existed, then women like Giulia's mother would have a way to protect themselves and their children. How would their lives have proceeded if her father had simply succumbed to an apparent illness, and they'd lived out their days as widow and daughter?

Giulia began to listen and learn. She drifted away from the butcher shop and instead made herself useful at the apothecary. They wouldn't pay her, but they also hadn't replaced her mother and they needed the extra hands.

If the shop's proprietor noticed that Giulia asked more questions about belladonna, antimony, cantharidin, and Spanish fly than she did about nettle and yarrow and hawthorn and rose hips, he never said. In fact, he seemed to take a special interest in teaching Giulia all he knew about the darker ingredients and their possible uses. Even if he'd cared nothing for Giulia, it became clear that he'd have done anything for her mother, if he'd been given the chance.

"Everything is poison and nothing is poison" was his constant refrain. Giulia had no idea what that meant, but she kept listening. It would come clear eventually.

When she had grown a bit older and proven herself, the apothecary offered her a job. A paid position, the one her mother had held. Giulia was thrilled. Finally, she could contribute more to Maria's household than being a witness when the butcher was cruel.

The butcher, however, was displeased.

"No daughter of mine will work for that charlatan," he said.

But Giulia was no daughter of his.

I sound monstrous," Giulia says.

Part of Carmela agrees. Her mother set out to discover the best way to kill a man without getting caught. Wasn't that monstrous on its face?

But she knows her mother. And she knows Maria. She knows monsters too. Some will kill by a thousand cuts and far too often there is no one to tend the wounds. Giulia learned that the hard way when they tried to take refuge at the church.

"Your father was the monster," Carmela finally says.

And the look, oh, the look of hope on Giulia's face that she might not have lost her one precious thing in this world, her only daughter, her Carmela: it erases any doubts Carmela might have had.

Whoever her mother has killed, it was the only way.

"Truly," Giulia says. "My father, and Maria's husband, monsters both."

"Maria's husband. Did you . . . ?"

Giulia pauses. "I should let Maria tell you that part." Giulia has been avoiding Carmela's eyes, but now she grabs both her daughter's hands and looks at her urgently. "I need you to understand that sometimes there are no other options. The authorities are certainly no help. The church . . . My mother died protecting me. I wasn't going to let that happen to anyone else's daughter."

Carmela nods. "So you developed a poison to help those women."

"Yes. To be distributed very sparingly, you understand—only in cases of the utmost terror. Cases where there were truly, absolutely no other options and the woman would die if her husband weren't handled."

"But how . . ."

"It took time. The apothecary grew old. He had no heirs. Maria was never going to run a business, but he was fond of me and I had a mind for it."

Something sick turns over in Carmela's stomach. "Wait. My father?" He is only the vaguest memory, gone before Carmela was speaking full sentences, and she doesn't know if it would be worse to find out her mother had killed him, or to find out he had been a monster who needed vanquishing.

"Simple consumption!" Giulia's eyes are wide, face open in a moment of rare earnestness. "I promise. I wish he'd lived longer."

And there it is, the third possibility. There had been a good man and her mother had found him, but he had been taken from her too soon.

"Did you love him?"

Carmela can't imagine her mother in love. She's never seen her in anything but control.

"I did. He believed in me and the shop. He made us respectable. And most of all, he gave me you."

"Did he know?"

Giulia falters. "Know what?"

"Did he know about your poison? What it was for?"

"He knew how my father died. I think he understood, to a point."

Carmela absorbs this. It is a lot to consider. It will take some time. But nothing about who her mother is has changed.

"I'll never ask you to be a part of this," Giulia says. "I only ask that you don't stand in my way."

Carmela wouldn't stand in Giulia's way if she were setting out to poison the entire water supply of Rome. If her mother felt it had to happen, Carmela would see her way to understanding.

Giulia reaches behind her neck and unclasps the locket she has worn every moment of Carmela's life.

"I want you to have this," she says.

Carmela steps out of reach. This feels wrong; like a goodbye. She did not expect to ever wear that locket until the day Giulia left the earth—and even that is unfathomable, that Carmela could outlive her outsized mother.

"It belonged to my mother," Giulia says. "She gave it to me right before we were parted. I always thought I'd give it to you when I could tell you about what she did for me. Without her sacrifice, Carmela, I wouldn't be standing here today. You wouldn't be here. We wouldn't be doing this work."

Carmela allows Giulia to approach and fasten the locket around her neck. It's nearly weightless, but Carmela feels it there, pulsing so close to her heart, this remnant of the grandmother she never knew.

Another Wife

There is a woman
like Giulia's mother
                                                but not

just down the way
from the apothecary
in the northwest corner
of the Ortaccio,

            the Bad Garden,
            a ghetto, once upon a time,
            for women who lived by their bodies
            until the authorities realized
            there were too many such women
            to contain them within walls
            and they spilled out
            onto every street in Rome.

This woman
doesn't live by her body
doesn't work in an apothecary
knows nothing of poison

but she too
grew up with a father
who frothed and raged
who controlled with his fists.

The first time her husband struck her
it was inevitable, familiar.
She was home.

It has never occurred to her to seek help.
For what, from who?
Perhaps it is a mercy
she doesn't unburden herself
for it would only hurt more
when no one lifts a finger to help.

There is no way out for her.
She will endure the beating and belittling
until either he kills her or
by some miracle she outlives him

and spends the rest of her days
a hollow, terrified husk of a woman
jumping at shadows
never able to enjoy her well-earned peace.

Now that Carmela truly knows all the secrets of the apothecary, there is no longer any reason to speak in code.

While Giulia and Maria fret over how to obtain more mandrake for the rheumatism cream, Carmela asks outright, "Is it used in Acqua Tofana?"

For that is the name of her mother's poison. Rarely dispensed, but often enough that it bears her mother's name.

Maria and Giulia look at her in shock. It's Laura who says, "No, it's truly for the rheumatism cream."

Giulia says, "Rheumatism cream keeps the doors open. Everyone has achy joints eventually. Acqua Tofana doesn't register in our finances."

"Literally." Laura looks up from the financial ledger she's balancing. Carmela wonders then what is recorded when a customer buys Acqua Tofana. What do they charge?

What is it worth to rid the world of a monster?

"What's in it, then?"

"The rheumatism cream?" Giulia asks.

But Maria knows what Carmela means. "Do you want to learn to make it?"

Carmela's heart stops. "No."

"Tough," Maria says. "Bring me the jar of belladonna, and some antimony."

"Maria."

"She has to learn sometime."

Carmela knows where the belladonna is. Even when she makes eye drops, she must wear gloves, for the slightest contact with her skin and it flares up in a rash for days. Antimony is rarely dispensed, but she's seen it on the top shelf; her mother uses the silvery powder in a remedy to deworm animals.

"And the ingredient Father Piero brought?" Carmela has not stopped wondering about the inebriated priest's involvement, but her mother has opened so many doors in so little time, she is careful not to push.

"I'll get that," Maria says.

They meet at Maria's workstation, where she brandishes a dark jar that now contains Father Piero's contribution. "Arsenic," Maria says. "Some apothecaries offer it freely; there are those who use it sparingly for all manner of ailments. And painters use it in pigments. But a shop already under extra scrutiny from those who might call the women who run it witches? Better to be cautious. You've seen how they are about the mandrake."

"So how did Father Piero become Mother's supplier of arsenic?"

Giulia has busied herself in the shop front; if she hears the question, she gives no sign.

"It's a long story," Maria says.

"I have time." Carmela would much rather sit and listen to a story, however strange and twisted, than open that jar and mix a lethal poison into a so-called remedy. The very word *remedy* indicates it is meant to right a wrong. Ending a life, no matter how monstrous—it's hard to wrap her brain around how that can be right.

Even if she does trust her mother with her own life.

"You're stalling," Maria says, readying the workspace. "I don't know all the details anyhow. Only that Father Piero had the contacts and owed your mother a debt—"

"For what?"

"How should I know? Perhaps she cured an infected boil on his ass."

Carmela recoils, and Maria laughs. Across the table, Laura shakes her head.

Maria opens the jar. "We make only a single vial of Acqua Tofana at a time. As your mother has explained, it is very rarely dispensed, and for safety's sake, better not to have a surplus of inventory sitting around the shop. One vial contains thirty-two drams—"

"And that's the dose to kill a man?"

"Not all at once. The secret to Acqua Tofana—"

Giulia appears in the archway, glaring. "Must we lay bare all our knowledge at once?"

"If she knows, she knows. Better that she know everything."

"She's not going to be dispensing it—"

"She should know." Everyone turns in surprise to Laura. "I didn't like learning the details either," she tells Carmela. "But it actually helps me to have all the knowledge. Otherwise my brain fills things in for the worst."

Maria turns triumphantly to Giulia, who sighs. "Fine. But this is purely an intellectual exercise."

That's more than all right by Carmela. She still isn't sure she wants to know about any of this, but Laura makes sense. Better to know as much as she can, and be governed by truth rather than speculation.

"So one dose is thirty-two drams?" Carmela says.

"One vial is thirty-two drams. But the secret to Acqua Tofana is how it is doled out a little at a time. So it's gradual."

"And painless?"

Maria hesitates. "Let's settle for gradual."

The shop bell rings and Carmela looks up, eyes wild, sure the world will know she's making a poison meant to end a life.

Signora Moretti's laugh drifts into the back room. For someone in constant pain and despair, she does laugh a lot with Giulia, and keeps coming back, no matter how rude Maria is in Giulia's absence.

Maria lowers her voice ever so slightly, though there's no way any customer could hear them over the laughter out front.

"The dosing instructions are key," she says. "A woman is to give her husband one drop the first night."

"How?"

"In his ale, his stew, straight into his slumbering maw. It's amazing how trusting men are when they believe their wives are powerless."

"Can they taste it?"

"No. It's such a minuscule amount. Of course, I've never tried it. But we haven't had complaints."

Laura snorts.

"He's a bit sick the next day. Perhaps she expresses her concern to a neighbor, even stops in to another apothecary for a remedy. A guilty woman wouldn't be telling the world her husband is ailing, would she? That night, she dispenses two drops. The next day he's really quite ill. A physician is called. Only an innocent woman would call a physician to examine her husband."

"The physician can't tell there's poisoning involved?"

"It's too subtle. Headaches, mild upset stomach. The third night, three drops. By the next day he is gravely ill. The physician has been unable to help. The priest is called, and the clearly dying man has time to repent of his sins, so those who care about such things don't have to worry that they're damning the monsters to hell."

Carmela doesn't know what to say to this.

"It's more mercy than they deserve, if you ask me, but your mother is a better woman than I am. Now, no more stalling. Weigh out sixty-four scruples of the arsenic." Maria sets the scale to balance when it reaches the desired measurement and sits back.

Carmela takes a deep breath. She opens the small jar and peers inside. The gray powder looks the same as any number of powders on the shelf. But it's not.

"I don't know if this helps," Laura says, "but you've handled poisonous ingredients before."

"Belladonna," Maria says. "Mandrake, mercury, hemlock, aconite, castor beans."

"Turmeric, fenugreek, clove," adds Laura.

"Wait, what?" She regularly adds cloves to spiced tea.

"Everything is poison, love." Giulia has finished with Signora Moretti and leans in the doorway. "Too much garlic will cause a rash. Too much fenugreek can bring on premature labor. Excessive cloves can cause seizures. In fact, the very air we breathe could smother us in excess. It's all about dosage."

Strangely, Carmela does find this comforting. She scoops the tiniest amount of arsenic out of the jar and onto the smallest scale. Two scruples.

Maria laughs.

Carmela's indignation flares. "I'm afraid to put in too much."

"Why? Are you afraid you'll kill someone?"

"Maria." Giulia waves Maria away and takes her place. "If you put in too much, the scale will show that, and we'll take some out. That's why we weigh each ingredient separately."

Carmela adds more of the gray powder and the scale inches closer to balanced.

"That's it."

"Oh sure, she listens to you," Maria grouses.

Giulia smiles fondly at Maria, then Carmela. "I'm her mother."

The shop bell rings, and Maria peers out through the archway. "It's that Moretti woman again."

"Wasn't she just here?" Carmela asks.

"Hush." Giulia plasters on her dangerously docile face, the one that says she's never had any ambition in life more dear than meeting each and every need of Signora Moretti's.

Signora Moretti, who asked Carmela for help with a tempestuous husband. Who Maria chased out of the store for the request.

"Wait," Carmela says quietly. "Is she here for . . ." She indicates the arsenic on the scale.

Maria grunts. "Most likely."

"But didn't you say her husband is an advisor to the governor?"

"One of the reasons your mother hasn't given her what she wants yet."

"How does someone even know it's an option? It's not like Mother advertises."

"No." Maria's quiet for a moment. "But when you need something badly enough, you do whatever you can to find it."

But then what? Suddenly Carmela understands Signora Moretti better. Coming in here constantly, making up every malady under the sun to ingratiate herself with Giulia, hoping the apothecary will eventually give her what she needs. Talking endlessly about her awful husband.

What a trap, then, if she is informing him of her every move. If Giulia says, "You know, I have something that could help you deal with that husband of yours," and then she could act shocked and horrified, as if she'd never implied her husband was anything less than a paragon of virtue and Giulia would meet the same fate as her own mother, despite all the care she's taken.

"That's our girl," Maria says as the scale finally balances at sixty-four scruples. "Now into the mortar."

Carmela tips the small mound of powder into the heavy stone bowl.

"I'll grind this, while you wash the dish."

Carmela already knows how important it is to avoid contamination when measuring and mixing ingredients, but how much more important now, when the ingredients are so deadly. Even if they say that any ingredient can be poison, she'll never have the same concern when she's washing a dish that's only held lavender.

She scrubs so long, Maria calls her back, finished with her own task before Carmela deems the dish immaculate.

"It's clean," she says, without even looking. "Get back over here."

The arsenic, which was already powder before, is now a powder so fine it would feel slippery between Carmela's fingers, if she were willing to touch it. Which she is not.

"Does it dissolve?" she asks. "What's the menstruum?"

She loves the sound of that word in her mouth, loves knowing terms specific to this line of work that educated people outside of it would never recognize. *Menstruum: a solvent; the liquids used to extract an herbal preparation.*

Arsenic isn't an herb, but some of the ingredients for Acqua Tofana are.

"Alcohol," Maria says. "And no, it won't dissolve any further, which is why you need to grind it as fine as possible. We'll add an emulsifier, which will help suspend the particles throughout the tincture so there's not a sludge at the bottom."

One by one the ingredients are weighed out on the scale. The arsenic together with the other minerals goes into the bowl first. Then they add the tinctures from the plants, like belladonna and oleander. Finally, the emulsifier.

And there it is. A tiny vial filled with Acqua Tofana. Six drops to kill a man without a trace.

THE BUTCHER WAS CRUELER than Giulia ever knew. Maria could bear each casual cruelty, each belittling subversion of what she knew to be true, each careless chipping away at the girl she'd been when she first walked into his life, but she couldn't bear the sum total. She couldn't face it, and she certainly couldn't articulate it to someone else.

Each time he sliced her open she convinced herself it was an isolated incident. Each lie to herself undermined what she knew to be true in her gut.

She began to see him more clearly when Giulia entered their lives. Not because she was bracing for him to seduce the girl and then convince Maria she was out of her mind when she called him on it. That had happened before.

No, Maria began to see the butcher for what he was, the monstrous total of it, when she watched him use the same tired tricks on Giulia. The sweetness and affection, the turn of a knife. The twinkling eyes and almost-shy smile, the lacerating tongue. One face to the world, and another to the women in his home.

The more Maria grew to love Giulia, the more she began to understand the grace and complexity and generosity of real love. The more she began to dream of a life without the butcher. The more she wondered if one day she might turn his own cleaver against him and end everyone's misery.

As it turned out, she didn't have to.

Something else came for the butcher, a cancer not unlike the one at the very heart of him, only this one he couldn't hide from the rest of the world. He grew sicker and sicker, and as his health fell away, so too did any inclination to rein in his cruelty, to strike only in the most vulnerable places.

The weakened man who lashed out at anyone and everyone was

a relief to Maria. She was not alone now. She had not provoked him. Everyone could see what he was. He would shout obscenities and Maria and Giulia would share a look, or apologize to the customer.

"He's not well," they would say, and he would rage further, and it felt like justice.

One night when he'd raged himself to sleep, Giulia sat with Maria next to the fire and showed her a small vial.

She wasn't certain of course—she'd tested it only on animals headed for the butcher's block—but she believed she had created a formula that would end a life without a trace. Doled out slowly, it could be exactly what her mother had needed. What her mother hadn't had time to do properly.

She'd need to try it on a human, though, before she ever considered dispensing it to a woman in need.

They both looked to the snoring monster in the bed across the room.

He was sick already. No one would be the wiser, even if the poison didn't work as Giulia believed it would. But these two women knew this man who'd abused them so thoroughly for years. When they gave him the first drop, they noticed the stutter in his steps, the delay in his attacks. When they gave him the next two drops, they noticed the headaches and stomach pains beyond what the cancer was already doing to his body.

They called for the priest then. His illness seemed to be progressing.

When they gave him the final drop, they were free.

Carmela wends her way between the market stalls as she gathers the things her mother has sent her out for.

Signor Abate nods to her gravely and she does not ask him if his digestion has improved—the secrets of the apothecary remain safe within its walls. But when Signora Russo's face splits wide with a smile at the sight of her, Carmela says, "It's good to see you out and about, Signora. Are you feeling well?"

"Never better!" the old woman crows. "Thanks to your mother."

When a boy crashes into her and doesn't excuse himself, Carmela shrugs it off. She would never ever use it, but since learning to make Acqua Tofana, she can't help feeling she wields some bit of power. She is not completely vulnerable in these streets.

She double checks the list her mother gave her: eggs, onions, cheesecloth, lard, tea. All accounted for, except the eggs, which had run out when Carmela arrived at the vendor's stall.

She nearly trips over a black cat darting across her path, so much smaller than the humans moving around him, the carts and stalls towering above him, but he moves with all the confidence in the world.

Carmela can be a street cat.

When she turns down the row of shops toward the apothecary, her newfound confidence falters. For heading toward her on the other side of the street is none other than Notary Nicolò Tassi.

Carmela struggles between wanting to charge at him, tell him off for how he disrespected her the last time she saw him, how he didn't pursue the thief until a more respectable woman requested his help. She is not weak; she knows how to kill a man now.

But she also knows that right inside the shop, on a tall shelf in the very back, behind the various types of feces, is a vial of Acqua Tofana made by her own hands. It could kill a man, yes. It could also bring down all the women in Carmela's life. Her family.

It's foolish to worry about. There's no way he could know. He could go inside the apothecary right now, tear everything off the shelves, and still he'd have no idea what was contained in that vial.

Carmela's heart pounds, faster every second. He must not enter the apothecary. As though she has willed it, he turns to slip between two shops back toward the square.

Only then, "Don Tassi!"

They both turn to see Violetta Raso calling out to him, beckoning him over.

Carmela freezes. She mustn't stand here like this, gawping at them, giving them the satisfaction that they've unnerved her. Still, she cannot move.

The notary reaches Violetta and greets her politely. She speaks urgently to him, and they both glance over at Carmela.

Cheeks blazing, Carmela hurries into the apothecary.

"Finally," Maria grunts as the door swings shut behind her.

Carmela ignores Maria, turning to peek out the window at Violetta and the notary.

"What's wrong with you?" Maria barks. "I'm waiting on that cheesecloth."

Carmela waves her basket toward Maria, not turning from her spot. Violetta and the notary continue to speak, continue to glance toward the apothecary.

"You teach a girl a few things and suddenly she's putting on airs, suddenly she doesn't feel the need to listen," Maria rants, and Carmela doesn't realize Maria is approaching until she's there, looming over Carmela's shoulder to see for herself what has Carmela's attention.

"Maria!" Carmela tugs Maria away from the window, even though there's no chance they weren't noticed.

"Well, why didn't you say what you were looking at?" Maria snaps. "How long have they been out there?"

"Who is it?" Laura's eyes dart between them.

"Violetta Raso," Carmela whispers, as though they'll hear.

"And that plague sore Nicolò Tassi," Maria adds.

Laura's eyes widen.

"Just since I came in," Carmela says.

"What is going on?"

Carmela and Maria both whirl around at the sound of Giulia's voice.

"Maria, shouldn't you be straining the chamomile? And Carmela, that shopping took you twice as long as it should have."

Maria recovers herself and jerks her head at the window. "We've got an audience." She heads to the back while Giulia strides forward to assess the situation. She only glances out the window, then takes Carmela firmly by the arm and steers her to the back.

"Ow!"

Giulia shoots a skeptical glance at her. Her grip is firm, but it doesn't hurt; it was more the surprise, the injustice of the treatment. Carmela is trying to protect them all.

"He's a notary," Carmela informs her as Giulia shoves a broom into her hands.

"I know he's a notary. Sweep."

"She's not wrong to worry," Maria grumbles as she sits down at her workstation.

"And how does it help anything for you two to stand there worrying?" Giulia snaps, her voice rising. "Does it get us any closer to finishing Signora Fontina's order?"

"Well, that's not happening until we get more mandrake." Maria stands to meet Giulia's gaze. "So unless you've figured that out, I've got plenty of time."

They exchange glares, and Carmela's stomach turns over. They snipe at each other from time to time, but Carmela rarely sees any real bite.

"I'm sorry about Benicio," Laura says quietly, as though it is her fault the botanist has turned against them.

All the bluster deflates from Giulia and Maria as they turn to Laura. "It's not your fault he's an imbecile," Maria says, sitting back down. Giulia smiles and squeezes Laura's shoulder as she moves past her to resume stirring whatever's simmering in the cauldron.

"Is Laura's friend really the only one who sells mandrake?" Carmela asks.

"He's not my friend anymore." Color rises in Laura's cheeks.

"There are other suppliers," Giulia says. "But we can't be caught buying it. Not with the extra scrutiny."

Other vendors have gotten skittish and more than one has brought up Geneviève Laurent, washerwoman turned Lady of Death. Giulia has managed to charm them all into cooperation so far, but one wrong move and the apothecary will be in more trouble than they already are.

"Wait, but we only use it for rheumatism cream. We can't be caught buying it? If there's concern, couldn't we show them how we use it?"

"They wouldn't believe us," Maria says.

"And," Giulia adds, "we really don't want to invite anyone to snoop around in our inventory. Not everything is as innocuous as mandrake."

Carmela's eyes drift to the dark bottles on the top shelf. All apothecaries carry poisons, for all sorts of purposes. And they can't be the only apothecary that uses poison in the same way. Perhaps in Campo Marzio, but surely not in Rome, or beyond.

"Maybe we shouldn't keep the arsenic in the shop anymore," Laura says. "Since we need it so rarely anyway. And there's already a finished vial of Acqua Tofana."

The one Carmela helped make, ready should a husband become too tempestuous.

Giulia nods. "Yes, that's a good point. But I don't want it in any of our homes, either."

"There's a shed—"

Giulia cuts Maria off with a sharp hand. "Tell me later. I'd rather leave Carmela out of it."

"Out of what?" Carmela is on her feet, and she doesn't bother beseeching her mother. Maria is her only hope now. "Donna Maria, I won't be kept on the outside anymore."

"You are an apprentice," Giulia says. "You are learning, but I do not owe you every morsel of information."

"Information like where you'll hide the arsenic that was handed directly to me?"

"Precisely," Giulia says. "Do you want to know why? Of course you do. Because the fewer people who know a deadly secret, the fewer people can be tortured into revealing it."

"You don't trust me?"

Giulia's eyes blaze. "No, Carmela. I don't want my only daughter disfigured by the magistrate's lackeys under pain of death! Is that all right by you? Am I allowed to be your mother anymore, or am I only your Apothecary Master now?"

Carmela struggles to find her breath, thrown more by the tears in Giulia's eyes than her harsh tone.

Maria stands and puts an arm around Carmela. "Giulia, I understand. Truly. But you know that you and I would both be too conspicuous on the church grounds."

Giulia lets out an angry huff as Maria lets slip the secret location, as though Carmela can narrow down where they might hide a single vial on the sprawling grounds of the Church of San Girolamo. She's not even certain that's the church they mean, though it's the closest.

Maria glances at Laura, but there's no possibility that the meekest among them might undertake a clandestine mission. "But more importantly, Carmela is right. She knows enough about Acqua Tofana that she's already at risk, whether she knows where we've hidden it or not."

Giulia slams an angry fist on the counter and then winces, cradling her hand.

"Mother!" Carmela flies to Giulia, who will not face her. She retrieves what she needs for an arnica compress and returns to her mother's side. She wraps Giulia's hand while speaking like her mother used to when she woke with nightmares. "You faced far worse when you were younger than I am now. I have you, and Maria, and Laura. And everything you've taught me. I understand the risks and I want to share the burden."

Carmela is not certain the words are true, even as she says them. But they must be.

Giulia dashes a tear from her face with her free hand and scowls. "Fine. Maria will tell you where to hide it. Laura, I want you to look into what would be required for us to grow our own mandrake." She takes a deep, shuddery breath. "And in the short term, I'm going to travel to Tivoli."

"Tivoli?"

"In another town I won't call attention to the shop, but I can get what we need. It's not a practical solution in the long term, but it will help Maria finish Signora Fontina's order before she departs."

"I just don't understand why you should have to travel all that way for a crop that's common here." The look on Giulia's face says Carmela has won enough concessions for today, but she presses on. "There must be other suppliers in Rome who would work with us."

"Even if that were true—which it is not, but heaven forbid you trust I know my business—we do not have the time for me to find them, assess their trustworthiness, build relationships. In Tivoli, I'll be a solitary herbwife buying supplies at the market and never seen again."

Rome is vast. Surely the same could be done at a market on the opposite side of the city. But Giulia is an unstable potion, one wrong scruple away from combusting.

"All right. Fine," Carmela relents. "I'll go with you. I'll hide the Acqua Tofana, and then—"

"No, love." Giulia's tone is final. "I need to leave right away and I'll be less memorable on my own. Besides, I need you to be here to tend the shop."

Carmela looks pointedly at the empty shop front, but says nothing.

"Neither Laura nor Maria are good with customers," Giulia goes on, already pulling her cloak from its hook.

"She's right," Maria says.

"We're not," Laura adds.

"And who could ever suspect us of anything untoward when they walk in and see your sweet, innocent face?" Giulia pats Carmela's cheeks like she's a toddler.

"Ugh, fine." Carmela twists away, trying to hide the hurt in her eyes. They've managed the shop for years without her. Giulia simply doesn't want Carmela's company. "How long will you be away?"

"Three or four days. You'll barely notice I'm gone."

Carmela feels like a petulant child, even as she's a grown woman with an important position in the apothecary. She shouldn't throw a temper tantrum because her mommy's leaving.

"She'll stay with us," Maria says. "Won't you, Carmela?"

"Maybe." If she's so grown, perhaps she should stay in their flat above the shop, just in case.

"It's up to you," Giulia says. "But during shop hours, I'm counting on you to keep the doors open."

"Yes, Mother."

Giulia gathers a few things, and then she's gone, as though it costs her nothing to leave.

"All right then." Maria retrieves the bottle of arsenic and wraps it in brown paper. "Should be secure, but if there's a place to tuck it up and off the ground, it would probably be safest for curious creatures."

She walks Carmela to the front door, out of Laura's earshot, and quietly describes the location of a ramshackle shed on the church property. "Off you go," she says, patting Carmela's hands. "Stealthy like a cat."

THE STREETS ARE TEEMING with everyone finishing their tasks for the day, or heading home after closing their shops.

Carmela weaves between these people she's known all her life, these people whose ailments she tends, or her mother does, but who do not meet her eye as they pass.

That's all right. She's on a clandestine mission. Better to be invisible.

The packet of arsenic in her cloak pulses its presence, never letting her forget. A black cat crosses her path, and Carmela stumbles to avoid tripping. Some might see the cat as an uneasy omen, but not Carmela. She knows what it's like when people assume you're something you're not.

The bells of the Church of San Girolamo ring out as Carmela approaches. The doors are open, as though anyone is welcome.

But you said we were welcome!

Carmela doesn't turn past the immense stone building into the alley that leads to the back of the property; that feels too risky. There is a reason Maria thought she and Giulia would be too conspicuous here. Of the apothecary's women, only Laura is a churchgoer. That in itself causes talk. If one of them was seen lurking around the building, who knows what wild stories the Campo Marzians would invent.

Instead, Carmela makes her way past the glover and the cobbler, rounds the corner, and then turns down an alley that will lead to her destination.

The church property is sprawling, one of the biggest in a neighborhood where churches seem as plentiful as the pox. Behind the building itself is an open-air courtyard with benches and statues, the tinkling of running water somewhere. It would be peaceful, if one could be at ease so near a church.

Even before Carmela knew her grandmother's story, she felt the oddest unease around churches—an inherited trauma she couldn't have articulated, the bone-deep betrayal passed from mother to child. Since learning the truth, she has quickened her pace every time she passes one, especially this one, as though all these years later some hands might reach out and snatch her, deliver her over to the magistrate for her misdeeds.

Normally this is absurd. Today, however, she is truly trespassing on the church property with ill intent. Her presence would be noticed, questioned. If she were searched . . .

The cat is underfoot again, strutting through the church grounds with all the confidence Carmela doesn't have. She follows him, something to focus on. When he slips inside a shed, Carmela believes for the slightest moment that he has led her to the hiding place Maria described. But then an unfamiliar priest appears and steps inside the shed behind the cat. Carmela ducks behind a statue of San Girolamo. The saint reads from a book, his arm propped casually on top of a skull that sits at Carmela's eye level.

Moments later the priest emerges from the shed with a spade and strides off in the opposite direction. Carmela waits another beat, and then edges toward the door and peers inside. Maria called it an abandoned shed, but this is clearly in use. Orderly rows of tools and garden supplies, a clean-swept floor, very tidy. A cat, somewhere in the darkness, unless he slipped out through a gap in the siding. This can't be where she's meant to hide her package.

She moves carefully around the outside of the shed, and then she sees it: a dilapidated collection of rotten boards in the vague shape of a shed, if she squints.

Not even the black cat would enter that dubious structure. But Carmela will, to keep the women of Tofana Apothecary safe. She will brave whatever waits inside to find refuge for the package in her pocket.

There is no discernible door. Only a space where the boards create an opening large enough to make her way through. In full daylight, the cracks and gaps would provide as much sunshine as shadow, but in the waning light, Carmela's eyes need a moment to adjust. She does not want to stay inside any longer than she has to, but neither does she want to place her hand into a rat's nest or a decomposing animal. Both possibilities seem equally likely.

For such a dilapidated structure, there are a surprising number of things inside, but they are all covered in thick layers of cobwebs and grime. It has the feel of a place where those with something to hide knew they could squirrel it away. Perhaps in Maria's childhood. But those items seem to have been forgotten by time, which makes this a perfect spot for the apothecary's purposes.

She nudges a wooden bucket on the top shelf—"shelf" being a generous description of the rotting board upon which things are piled, but they have held this long and Carmela's package is very light. The bucket moves slightly to the side, and Carmela tucks the small jar into the corner. Praying to all the statues in the yard outside that she doesn't touch anything unexpected, she inches it back, out of sight.

Her hand returns, mercifully unscathed, and Carmela memorizes the spot so she can tell the others. She suspects this will become her job; retrieving the arsenic when it is needed, but like all other things in the apothecary, they always make sure at least two people know any given fact.

Top shelf, left corner, between the wooden bucket and the wall.

She climbs carefully out of the pile of kindling, darts toward the nearest exit from the church's property and finds herself face-to-face with a priest. She jumps back, startled, as though he is holding a skull, not a spade.

"My child, are you well?"

"I'm— Yes, I—" Carmela's eyes cast around for a way to explain herself, a way past this man who is not her father and has no right to call her child.

"You are not a regular parishioner. Where do you attend Mass?" When she has no answer, his eyes narrow slightly. "What were you doing on our grounds?"

"My cat!" she blurts, catching a glimpse of black tail rounding the corner. "I—I saw him come this way. I was trying to find him."

The priest shakes his head a little bit as he moves to the side for Carmela to pass. "It's a fool's errand to try to contain a cat."

The Cat

There is a cat
that wanders
from the Piazza Monte d'Oro
to the Church of San Girolamo,
and around the Palazzo Borghese.

He has owned these streets
for centuries—nine lives and all that.
He circles the tomb of Augustus
nodding to the ghosts of those interred there.
He notes the absence of Julia,
Augustus's only child,
barred from resting eternally
with her family because she dared
act upon her desires.

A cat acts upon every desire.

When Pope Pius V wished
to outlaw prostitution but couldn't
because those women paid good taxes
he tried instead
to enclose their business
within the Ortaccio

but this cat moved freely,
hopping up onto walls,
lithely stepping through windows,
loitering in arched doorways.

He avoids the Palazzo Zuccari
where a monstrous visage is carved,
a gaping maw prepared to devour
those who cross the threshold.
He is the monster in these streets;
he'll abide no challengers.

This cat has no home
and his home
is every stone
on these cobbled paths.

The apartment Maria and Laura share is right around the corner from the apothecary. When Maria's husband died, she and Giulia lived there until Giulia married. When Giulia and her new husband moved into the apartment above the apothecary, Maria's niece Laura came to stay with her.

It's cozy. Carmela can imagine how that coziness became cramped when Giulia was young, infringing on Maria's husband and the life he had grown accustomed to.

It is above the butcher shop, and the current butcher graciously allows Maria to continue to live there. At least, he reminds her how gracious he is every month when he collects the rent, never mind that he has nine children and his family could never fit in the tiny space.

Carmela is used to the smell of blood soaked into the walls, the floors, the very air around them. But after the cramped mustiness of the shed, she notices the smell in the stairway as she makes her way up to Maria's. Sharp, mineral. Not so unlike the garden shed, actually.

"There's our girl." Maria sits with her feet up while Laura moves about preparing a simple meal.

Laura looks up and smiles. "All well?"

Carmela nods. It's the first time she's been to Maria's apartment since learning what became of her husband. How her mother and Maria made a poison here, tested it on a man, saw the possibilities.

She waits to feel a horror in the walls.

"Why are you just standing there?"

Carmela shakes off the strange unease and removes her cloak. She helps Laura slice polenta and set it out with olive spread and beans.

What is Giulia eating this night? Where is she sleeping? Will she hire a horse or will that make her too memorable? Will she walk all the way to Tivoli in search of an ingredient that surely can be bought within Rome's city limits?

Maria and Laura don't seem concerned. Giulia has traveled before. But now that Carmela has so much more knowledge, she feels it differently, her mother's absence.

The Traveler

There is a woman
like Giulia
                but not

crossing the Tiber
at the Ponte Sisto
due south of the apothecary.

She travels alone,
carrying all she needs
in one small bag
for when she assessed the home
she'd built for decades
she realized she'd already lost
everything that mattered.

The children, off and married.
The husband, dead and gone.
She survived by her body, no different
from the ones they call courtesans
who flaunt their wares in church
and fetch a high price for the same transaction.

The high-priced girls
offer charming conversation
music, culture, class
but that's not what the clients want, really.
This woman gives them what they want
with no other distractions.

Occasionally she declines
if a man is too rough
or demands pieces of her
she is not willing to give.
Once, because he smelled
exactly like her husband.

But then along came the notary.
His position didn't bother her;
his hands around her throat, however, did.
The next time he loitered in her doorway
she didn't let him in.

She cringed at his racket,
the shouts of
whore and cunt and witch.

Her neighbors understood
when clients came and went
but disturbing their peace wouldn't stand.

The next night the notary
returned with friends.
Drunken men screamed for hours
outside her window; bottles smashed
against the door. When she emerged
in the morning, she choked on the stench
of shit and piss coating her threshold.

A neighbor stepped out
then quickly disappeared inside

but not before a shaming glance at this woman
as though she had soiled her own front door.

The third night she decided
as they continued their siege
she would leave at dawn.
Perhaps she shouldn't back down.
Perhaps she should stand up for herself.
But she had no energy left to fight.

And so she crosses
the Ponte Sisto
with a few belongings
and just enough hope
to make it to the other side.

In the morning, Carmela is awake long before dawn. She has spent a restless night, sharing Maria's bed. It's not Maria's company, or even her snores. It's the uncertainty of Giulia out there, on her own, now that Carmela fully understands what she does, and how the outside world perceives it.

When her mother was called a witch before, it was absurd. Carmela could scorn the children as fools and the adults as bigots. But it's more complicated now. If someone whispers that Giulia might be a poisoner, well, they're not wrong, are they?

She may not do it often, she may do it only with very good reason, but the fact remains. She is traveling alone as a woman in a world that hates her, even before they discover she has killed men, on purpose and without remorse.

Carmela pulls herself from the bed and quietly makes her way to the hearth. Laura is a light sleeper, and she doesn't want to wake her. But the extra kindness of an already-crackling fire will be worth it, if she does stir.

Carmela scoops the banked ashes into the bucket in near silence. When she pulls a small log from the pile by the hearth, Laura rolls over. More carefully, Carmela coaxes another log into position, encouraging the hot coals to ignite the fresh fuel.

"You didn't have to do that," Laura whispers.

"I'm sorry I woke you."

"I was awake," Laura says. "I never sleep."

Carmela wonders at that. What specters accompany Laura in the night? Laura never speaks of her life before she came to live with Maria. Maria calls Laura her niece, but Maria—who speaks voluminously—has never mentioned siblings.

"Get some more rest." Carmela wraps last night's remaining bread in a cloth and sets it to warm on the stones. When she has left things so that Maria and Laura will have an easy morning, Carmela slips out.

It is far too early to open the shop, and there's no point going home to a cold, empty apartment. She meanders through the streets, enjoying the hazy light, somewhere between night and day. She waves to the baker as he unlocks his shop.

"Is it your birthday again already?" Signor Amari jokes.

She smiles. "Not quite."

A little ways past the baker's shop, the scrawny black cat crosses Carmela's path again, or rather, he plants himself in Carmela's path. The same cat she followed into the churchyard, she's almost sure. His green eyes bore into her, disconcerting.

She considers turning down an alley to avoid the cat. But her mother is out traveling alone through who knows what dangers; how absurd to be afraid of a cat. She steps slightly to the side, for she is not willing to kick the animal and he is truly directly in front of her.

He yowls as she passes and then—she knows without looking, she can sense him, she can sense those green eyes—he follows her.

She's coming around a corner when she hears a familiar voice, but a completely unfamiliar tone.

"I'm sorry, it won't happen again!"

"See that it doesn't, you little slut."

Violetta Raso stands in the street outside the chandler's stall, clutching a pile of rags to her chest. A vile woman towers over her, the one Violettta's father married immediately after her mother died.

"I know what you did and I know who helped you do it."

"I'm sorry—"

"If you don't want your father to know, you'll mind me like your life depends on it. Because it does." The woman storms back into their building, leaving Violetta shaking in the early-morning light.

Carmela is frozen; she mustn't move until Violetta has, or she'll be seen.

Then the woman's voice comes again, this time out the window. "And don't bring those back until they're spotless!"

Carmela shrinks into the alley. She hears nothing and decides Violetta must have gone the other way down the street. But the second she steps forward, she collides with Violetta.

The pile of rags in her arms falls to the ground between them, a bloody mess.

"I'm sorry—"

"Were you spying on me?" Violetta snaps, trying to hide the shame of the rags, as though Carmela doesn't bleed on rags every month herself. Though this looks like an awful lot of blood.

"Yes, I somehow divined that you and your mother would be making a scene in the street before dawn and positioned myself here for the entertainment of it."

"She's not my mother." Violetta hurries down the alley. But her heart's not in it and, as soon as she's past Carmela, her shoulders begin to shake.

Carmela mustn't take pity on this girl, who huddled outside the apothecary with the notary, telling him God knows what about them. But also: *We take care of the people who have nowhere else to turn.*

"You need salt!" Carmela calls.

Violetta looks back with an expression of absolute perplexity. "What?"

"You make a paste with salt and water, and scrub it into the stains. Let it sit for half an hour before rinsing it out."

Violetta's face is unreadable. "You think that woman is going to hand over her salt jar?"

Carmela sighs. She should leave this impossible girl to struggle in the public fountain with stains that will never come off. But then someone could notice and wonder at the amount of blood. "Come to the shop."

She spins and heads to the apothecary, not waiting for Violetta to catch up. She'll come; she has no other choice. Maria has the keys to the front, but Carmela knows how to jiggle the back door in the exact right way to make it open, and by the time she has, Violetta has caught up.

She leads Violetta through the dark workshop—"Careful," she growls when the shaken girl bumps into something—out to the shop front. This would be better done in the back, but if Carmela wasn't allowed to set foot there for sixteen years, Violetta's certainly not getting a chance to poke her nose around.

"Sit there."

The face of the apothecary fetches a crock of salt, a scrub bush, and a basin of water, then brings the supplies out to the counter. She creates a paste with the salt and water, showing Violetta the right consistency, then she reaches for the first stained cloth.

"These are dried," she says. The stains would be much easier to remove if they were fresh.

"Yes, I—I drank the tea the day your mother gave it to me."

Carmela waits. That was ages ago. "And?"

"And . . . I hid the cloths under my mattress."

Carmela makes a face.

Violetta turns away as color rises in her cheeks. "It was a lot of blood. Like you said, I didn't think that witch would believe it was only my monthlies."

Carmela raises her eyebrows. "You are fond of that word."

"'Monthlies'?"

"'Witch.'"

It sits between them for a loaded second. Then Violetta turns her attention to stirring the paste as though it is a very complex activity. "Sorry. I just . . . I hate her. So much. But you don't care about that. So I scrub this into the stains?"

"We have to soak them first, since the stains are dry. Help me haul in water."

Without a word, they each carry a bucket to the public fountain, fill it, and haul it back in. Once the cloths are soaking, Carmela sets about starting the fire in the hearth.

"Can I help with something?"

Carmela laughs. "Want an excuse to investigate? Gathering evidence?"

Violetta falters. "What?"

"I saw you with the notary. You saw me see you. You weren't exactly subtle."

"With the . . . Don Tassi?"

"You were very cozy. What I don't understand is why you would risk him finding out your own business here."

"I didn't! I wouldn't!" Violetta looks wildly to her cloths soaking in buckets, looking for all the world like she wants to grab them back out, drenched, and run away as fast as she can.

"Really? Then what were you talking about?"

"Dinner that night. He wanted to know what Carla had planned, because he hates when she roasts lamb. I was warning him so he could fake sick."

Carmela blinks at her.

"Don Tassi is my stepmother's brother."

"He's your uncle."

Violetta shrugs. "I guess? Not really. Whatever."

"And you weren't talking about us? Then why did you keep glancing at the shop? At me?"

Violetta's cheeks flush. "I didn't want you to tell him. About me. About my . . ." She trails off, looking miserable.

"Why would I do that?"

"Because you hate me!"

"I don't hate you!" Perhaps Carmela hated Violetta once, but the edges have dulled to distrust and irritation. "You're a customer," she adds. "We won't disclose your secrets."

A stricken look crosses Violetta's face. "Are you expecting me to pay you for the washing help? Because—"

"No. I'm not expecting you to pay."

She didn't mean it the way it sounded, like Violetta never pays for anything, but Carmela lets it lie. She's doing this kindness for some reason she can't articulate. Perhaps her mother's noble sentiments about helping those who have nowhere else to turn, although Violetta has a town full of friends she could have turned to for help, with the pregnancy or anything else.

"Do your friends know?" she asks.

Violetta looks confused.

"About Antonio," Carmela says. "And your . . ." She waves vaguely in Violetta's direction as she retrieves the broom.

"No, and they can't! I mean, they know we were . . . talking. A couple knew we were . . . that I thought we were . . . None of them know I've ruined myself."

Carmela freezes. "The remedy shouldn't have done any lasting harm. You can still get pregnant."

Violetta looks around the totally empty shop as though the stones themselves might have heard. "I meant . . . losing my purity."

This thinking is so foreign it takes Carmela a minute to land on Violetta's meaning. And another minute to absorb not only her meaning, but her beliefs around it.

"Do you remember our wedding?"

"What?"

"I mean, if anyone should be upset, it's me. You did marry me first."

"What are you talking about?"

Carmela examines Violetta's face to see if she truly doesn't remember. Violetta has had so many friends over the years. Long after Carmela became the daughter of the witch, Violetta would have played pretend with countless other children too, taking hands, exchanging rings fashioned from flower stems, processing around the public fountain to the cheers of other children. Perhaps with some she took it further—playing house as loving parents, doting on a cat who yowled like the baby he represented against his will.

"Never mind." Carmela unclasps the hands of the carefree children in her memory. Such foolishness must be addressed head-on. "The point is, you haven't lost anything."

Violetta scrubs a stain with a particular fierceness. "My stepmother says I can only give my flower once and after that no man will ever want it."

"Then how does she explain your seven siblings?" Carmela asks.

"Carmela!"

Violetta's cheeks match the stains on her cloths.

"Or the courtesans of Venice," Carmela goes on, enjoying the girl's horror. Violetta spent a childhood making Carmela uncomfortable, after all. "Men travel from all over to sniff their flowers and they're not exactly fresh blooms."

"How you talk!"

"I'm only honest."

Violetta smiles a little, shaking her head.

"Your mother doesn't care?"

"About what?"

"Your . . . bluntness."

Carmela grins. "Where do you think I learned it?"

The truth is, she learned most of it from Maria, but Giulia has never objected to Maria's frankness. She knows Carmela will inherit the shop eventually. She can't do that as a complete innocent.

The Groom

There is a boy
like Antonio
                    but not

in a tavern
right up the road
from the apothecary

not so far from home
but also a world away.

Here no one nags
or reprimands
or demands anything
besides another round.

Here he can forget
that soon he'll be married
with responsibilities
and also a wife
to keep him fed and clothed

though he already has a mother
so he's never had the chance
to want for care.

The marriage bed, though—
soon he'll be able to bed his wife
without sneaking, without assuaging

her guilt, without thinking
of that one girl,
his first love,
the one his parents called

a poor match
with narrow hips besides
for marriage will erase her
from his mind

won't it?

When Laura and Maria arrive, Violetta is scrubbing the last cloth, while Carmela wrings the moisture from the ones they've already cleaned.

Laura's eyes grow wide at the sight of Violetta, but she says nothing. Just gives the tiniest nod and slips past to the back.

No such luck with Maria, though. "Signorina Raso," she says. "To what do we owe the pleasure of . . . doing your laundry?"

"I'm sorry, Donna Maria." Violetta looks to Carmela, panicked, as though they have been doing something illicit.

"Don't worry about Maria," Carmela says. "I'm only sharing some stain-removal tips, helping someone who had nowhere else to turn."

Carmela's glare is enough to soften Maria slightly. "Yes, well, be sure to clean up thoroughly. The shop needs to open."

Violetta is half the girl who normally rules the streets as she hurries to gather her things together, shoulders hunched, attempting to disappear into the walls.

"Wait," Carmela says. "You haven't gotten that last stain out."

"But your grandmother said we need to clean up—"

"She's not my grandmother, and she's not my boss, either. In fact"—the boasting words tumble out before Carmela can stop herself—"I'm the face of the shop in my mother's absence." Then she hears what she's said and busies herself scrubbing the last remaining stain, hoping Violetta won't have heard, won't think to ask—

"Where is your mother?"

In the back, Maria coughs.

While Carmela searches for an explanation, Laura appears in the doorway. "Violetta, would you like to take some ginger tablets home to your stepmother? I understand she's expecting again."

Violetta's about to decline, but Carmela takes the package. "For a peace offering," she says, pressing it on the flustered girl. "Not that she deserves it."

Violetta gives a tiny nod and takes it, then gathers the rest of her things. "Thank you. I don't know what I would have done without your help."

Carmela recognizes it then, the feeling her mother must get when she helps someone—truly helps them—with something they couldn't have managed on their own. Carmela has been working in the shop for weeks now, but only doing what she's been told, dispensing the remedies Giulia or Laura or Maria point her toward. This time she saw a problem and guided someone toward the solution. It's everything she wanted throughout all those years of longing to be let inside the apothecary's secrets.

"You're welcome," she says without looking up as she wipes down the counters. "Now get those tablets home before she pops out another baby."

Violetta lets out a startled laugh and leaves with her head held high.

"What?" Carmela demands before she even turns around to see Maria and Laura watching her. "I only did what my mother would have done."

Maria frowns. "We can't let anyone know where your mother has gone."

"I know, I didn't." Carmela shouldn't have brought up her absence and she can't defend herself for that error. It was foolish. She was caught up in her own importance.

"I thought you despised that girl," Maria says, returning to her task.

"I do."

"You seemed awfully friendly to me."

Were they friendly? Well, that doesn't make them friends. Carmela is simply getting better at setting aside her personal feelings in order to help a customer. That is all.

AND THERE ARE SO MANY CUSTOMERS TO HELP. The shop is never packed, but a steady stream of people come in throughout the day.

Old Signora Russo hobbles in and announces that her husband told her not to come here, but that she doesn't care if the lot of them are witches, because Giulia is the only one who can do a thing about the boils on her bum.

Carmela keeps a straight face until the door chimes closed on the old woman, leaving with her precious remedy.

"And what are you laughing at?" Maria gripes. "Boils on the bum are no laughing matter, believe you me."

A young man Carmela hasn't seen before comes in, looking over his shoulder to make sure no one saw him enter. "Excuse me," he whispers. "Do you have anything for stomach upset?"

"Of course." There are many causes, and therefore many remedies, for stomach upset. But it is one of the more delicate areas to ask questions about. Carmela considers how her mother would proceed. "Is this a chronic condition, or something more acute?"

"Uh, I would say chronic." His face is vaguely green.

"Is it . . . constant? Or do you notice anything in particular that triggers an episode?"

He hesitates.

"Oh!" Carmela speaks so sharply he jumps and jostles a display of electuaries. "Sorry. I realized I should have asked. Is this for you? Or someone else? Your wife?"

If the stomach upset is his wife's, it could be related to menstruation or pregnancy, a rather important detail Giulia would not have forgotten. But the question unnerves the man further. "What? My wife, nothing to do with her, nothing at all!"

Laura emerges and wordlessly sets a mint tea blend on the counter.

"All right, well, let's start with this." Carmela gives him instructions on how to prepare the tea and drink it after meals to ease indigestion. He pays double and leaves in a cascade of thanks.

"How did you know what he needed?" Carmela asks Laura. Stomach upset could be related to nerves or elimination or other nearby organs. The tea would only work for digestion.

"I know his new wife," she says quietly. "She's a terrible cook."

The highlight of the day is little Serafina, who comes in clutching a coin like it's a crown jewel. "My mama sent me for her uwirany remedy," she proclaims, or at least that's the best Carmela can make out.

"Her what?"

The little girl repeats the same words, as though she was told exactly what to say and had been practicing it all the way to the apothecary.

When Carmela is at a loss, the little girl scowls. "She said you'd know what that meant."

How would Giulia handle this? Not many children come into the apothecary alone, but when they do, Carmela has noticed (sometimes with a bit of jealousy) that her mother treats them with respect, as though they are no different from the adult customers.

"Do you know," Carmela asks, careful not to condescend to the girl, "what her symptoms are?" At the girl's confusion, she simplifies slightly: "I mean to say, do you know what's wrong with her?"

Serafina's face lights up. "She says there's fire in her pee-pee!"

This time Carmela can't hold back her laughter. The girl doesn't seem to mind; she's relieved that her message had been relayed, and her coin can be exchanged for the proper remedy. She leaves with a skip in her step.

Carmela straightens the items on the counter and delivers the day's coins to Laura for safekeeping.

Maria stands and stretches. "We may as well head home."

Carmela glances out the window. "The shop stays open until dusk."

Maria glances at Laura. "There are no customers and we're done with our work. Your mother wouldn't mind."

"I mind," Carmela says. "And I'm—"

"The face of the shop. Yes, you've mentioned that."

"It's fine." Laura crosses her hands at her perfectly immaculate worktable in front of her. "We can stay."

"You go," Maria tells her. "Get home before dark. I'll stay with the face of the shop."

She's irritated, but no more irritated than she gets with Giulia sometimes. It's strange when the child one's raised grows into their power.

"You don't have to stay either." Carmela winces at how lofty she sounds, as though she could truly compel Maria in either direction. "But I'm going to. It's important to me."

It isn't that it would be the end of the world if Signora Strozzi should stop by right before closing for more mullein oil and had to wait until the next day. It isn't even that Giulia might find out things hadn't been run exactly as she would have run them. It's more that Carmela likes the responsibility. She also wants to be worthy of it.

Maria considers her. It's not long before the shop closes. Either of them could easily cave. But Maria watched Giulia go through this phase of trying on her responsibility, testing its flexibility, its limits. She knows how this goes.

"All right," she finally says. "You know how to lock up?"

"Yes."

"And you'll come back to our place when you're done? I don't know how I'll possibly sleep without your bony elbow in my back."

"Yes, Donna Maria." Carmela may have responsibility and she may like it, but she knows who her elders are and what they've gone through to get her here, where she can be a young woman minding a shop on her own. "Thank you, Laura," she says as they head for the door.

"Good night."

And then Carmela is alone in the shop.

She feels a bit silly, for there is truly nothing she can do, and there are no customers. She has made her stand for no reason at all. Carmela is reaching for her cloak when the shop bell rings. Her principles weren't in vain! There's someone she can help, and she will be able to tell Maria so in the morning.

But then she sees the customer: Signora Moretti.

"Oh hello, Signora." Her heart sinks. "My mother's not—"

Signora Moretti reaches the counter and lifts her face for the first time, revealing a terrible gash slicing through her right eyebrow to where her eye is swelling up.

"Oh Signora!"

"Can you fetch her?" There's nothing haughty in the woman's voice, nothing demanding. Nothing but pure desperation.

"I'm so sorry, she's not . . ."

Carmela no longer likes responsibility. She no longer wants to prove anything to anyone; she is not ready for this. "What happened to you?" she blurts, but the look in the woman's eyes tells her. Enough, anyway, to know she shouldn't ask that again. "Never mind, I'm sorry, here, sit down." She leads the shaking woman to the bench. "Let me get you some tea."

"I'm beyond tea."

Carmela is too. No calming blend of herbs will get her through this. Tea is a ritual, a way to slow down and buy time, but time is not going to solve Signora Moretti's problems.

Carmela can't solve Signora Moretti's problems either. But she can take things one immediate step at a time. She can stop the bleeding.

"All right, yes. I'm going to get some cloths to clean you up. And then a yarrow poultice for your eye." Signora Moretti doesn't care, doesn't need to know what Carmela is doing, but it helps her to list the steps, to say them out loud, to feel there is a procedure to follow.

"You're a good girl," Signora Moretti says as Carmela gathers her supplies. "I've never been able to have children. Perhaps that's why my husband treats me as he does."

There it is: her husband. The man who came into the room with her, indeed has been with her every time she's come in here, seeking a way to stop him, to stop exactly this from happening. She is not a spy for an advisor to the governor. She is a woman with nowhere else to turn. How many times has she come into this shop, irritable and irritating, with fresh bruises blooming beneath her fine garments while they judged and assessed her motives?

"That's no excuse." Carmela gently dabs a cloth to the edges of the gash. She barely touches her, but Signora Moretti flinches.

"I didn't even want children. Do you know, I've never said that out loud to anyone? But I tried, for him. My body simply couldn't."

The blood seeps into the cloth when it meets the moisture, spreading through the fibers like this man's presence in Signora Moretti's life, inextricable.

"I don't want children either." Carmela's never really thought about it before, but now that she says it, she knows it's true. She doesn't want anything but the work she's doing now.

"In your world," Signora Moretti says, "that might be all right."

But they both know that's not precisely true. It's all right inside

Tofana Apothecary, but Carmela lives in Campo Marzio, Rome, the Papal States, Europe, the world. There will come a day when she will have to make difficult decisions.

Outside, a man's shouting voice approaches and all color drains from Signora Moretti's face. "My husband—"

"Hide." Carmela presses the poultice into the woman's hands and runs to the front door, where she throws the bolt. She is all adrenaline and instinct, a wolf kit who grew up watching what her mother did when danger approached, suddenly faced with her own danger and no alpha to protect her. She hurries back to Signora Moretti, still frozen on the stool. Carmela pulls her from the shop front to the sacred back room, where they crawl under Maria's worktable.

Signora Moretti recites a prayer, the words unfamiliar to Carmela, but soothing in their rhythm.

A brutal fist pounds on the door. "I know you're in there, woman!"

Carmela assesses the weapons available to her. Fire poker, knives, iron cauldron.

Outside, a cat yowls in outrage.

"He's going to kill me," Signora Moretti moans.

"He's not." Carmela wraps her arms around the shaking woman. Something crashes against the window and they both startle. "I won't let him."

"You're a child."

But she's not. Not anymore. Perhaps she was still a child playing responsible adult when Maria and Laura left for the night, but now she is here, drowning in responsibility with no choice but to learn how to swim, and fast.

"Tonight," Carmela says, "I'm La Tofana. We take care of each other. It's what we're here for."

The Women

There is a woman
like Patrizia Moretti
                                        but not

and another
and another
and another
and another
and another
and another
and another
and another
and another
and another
and another
and another
and another
and another
and another
and another
and another
and another
and another
and another
and another
and another
and another
and another
and another

and another
and another
and another
and another
and another
and another
and another
and another
and another
and another
and another
and another
and another
and another
and another
and another
and another
and another
and another
and another
and another
and another
and another
and another
and another
and another.

To list them all
would be to use
all the ink in the world
and still have stories to tell.

Life carries on, profoundly different and exactly the same. Carmela knows now what it is to hold someone's life in her hand. But also she returns home to Laura and Maria. She opens and closes the shop. She dispenses remedies, listens and nods.

Signora Moretti does not come into the shop in the next few days, but Carmela tells herself the woman is all right. She did everything she could to help her. There's nothing more she can do now, unless she comes in and asks for a remedy, a tincture, a listening ear.

When Maria gets up to leave early a couple days later, Carmela doesn't object. Neither does she insist on staying in the shop herself. But Maria isn't abandoning her duties. "Head out of the clouds, girl," she snaps at Carmela as she bustles around.

"What?"

"You're coming with me to the Santori birth."

Carmela blinks out of her stupor. Giulia rarely attends births and neither does Carmela intend to. Births are Maria's domain—a piece of her earlier life she's never completely shaken—and she has trained Laura to assist her.

"I'm not—"

"Laura's feeling unwell and I suspect it's twins. I'll need help. Your mother would come with me if she were here, you know she would."

Carmela glances at Laura, who indeed looks ill. "All right."

The moment she stands, Maria shoves a bag full of supplies into her hands and heads for the door.

"Good luck," Laura calls. "Just help her remain calm!"

Whether she means Maria or the expectant mother, Carmela isn't sure.

IT ISN'T UNTIL THEY'RE ON THE DOORSTEP that Carmela registers the name Maria gave—the Santoris.

Giada Santori is older than Giulia, with six children already. At least the ones who've lived. She has done this so many times she could do it without any help. Except: twins, Carmela reminds herself. Even the most seasoned mother would need assistance to do the whole ordeal back to back.

But Giada Santori meets them at the door, distinctly unpregnant. She grimaces when she sees Maria; likely she had been hoping for Laura. Most women in town would, despite the fact that Maria has brought hundreds more babies into the world than her sweet-natured niece.

"Come on through," Giada says wearily. "Good luck to you, for she certainly won't listen to a word I say."

Carmela doesn't connect the pieces until she follows Maria into a dimly lit room filled with the moans of someone in labor, hair plastered to a sweaty brow, tears streaking her face.

"I can't," wails Nina Santori di Alonso.

Nina Santori, who tried to defy Violetta all those years ago. Who dared express her desire to play marbles with the witch's daughter, even if in the end she went off to play prisoner's base with the others.

"None of that," Maria barks. "Of course you can. Most natural thing in the world."

Do the women who Maria bosses through labor know that she's never done it herself? Perhaps it doesn't matter.

"Let's get you off that bed, to start," Maria says.

"I told her she should be up and moving," Nina's mother offers from the doorway.

"Right you are. Could you bring us all the clean cloths you've got?"

Giada disappears, likely relieved to be given a task that isn't hauling her caterwauling daughter off the bed.

Maria jerks her head at Carmela to come take half of the moaning Nina's weight and together they move her into a squatting position, leaning on the side of the bed.

"Strip the blankets," Maria orders, which is when Carmela notices the bed Nina has just left is a sodden mess. At the expression on Maria's face, Carmela does as she's told, trying not to watch as Maria unceremoniously shoves her hand beneath Nina's shift.

"You're very close," Maria tells her. "When did your waters break?"

Nina doesn't answer; she doesn't seem to be entirely on the same plane of existence. But Giada has returned with blankets and rags.

"Not more than an hour ago," she says, snapping a blanket open and tossing half to Carmela to help smooth it over the pallet. "She's moving fast, this one. Like always."

"Let's get a fresh shift, hmm?" Maria whips Nina's soiled one over her head and the girl makes no objection, despite the fact that she now crouches entirely naked in front of them all.

Carmela doesn't know where to put her eyes. Nina's mother supplies a fresh shift and Maria begins to coax it over Nina's head, but the girl waves it away. She will remain naked, then. No one else objects, so Carmela tries not to stare at Nina's strange, heaving shape, her pendulous breasts with their dark brown nipples, the globe of a belly that shifts with the movements of the alien life forms within.

She has ceased moaning and rests her cheek on the clean blanket before her.

"There now," Maria says, with what passes for her comforting tone. "Rest up until the next wave comes." To Carmela, she says, "Distract her."

Then Maria goes to confer with Giada about something and Carmela is left with this girl who was once a peer but is now a whole other species.

"Do you think it's a boy or girl?" she asks feebly.

"One of each," Nina manages, a little color returning to her cheeks now that her muscles have stopped contracting for a moment. "Donna Maria says it's twins. Mother doesn't believe her, but I do. All the way through, I've gone back and forth thinking boy, then girl, then boy again. Makes sense that there's one of each."

It could just as likely be two boys or two girls, but Carmela doesn't introduce this possibility. It doesn't seem the time for logic.

Maria sets a stool in the middle of the room. "All right, Nina, while you're still between pains, let's get you moved over to the stool—"

"I don't want to move," Nina says.

"And I don't want to clean up your shit, but that'll surely happen before the night is through. Squatting will help the first baby's head descend into position. Babies are coming whether you're ready or not. We might as well make it as easy as possible for them, hmm?"

Nina doesn't respond, but neither does she object when Maria and Giada haul her over to the stool.

It's not a stool, precisely, Carmela realizes. Or rather, it is, but the seat part is mostly an open hole, for the baby to drop through. They lower Nina to squat over this sketch of a stool right as the next wave overtakes her. Carmela watches the muscles of her bulbous form contract. The whole engorged swell of her changes shape and it's no wonder she cries out like she does.

"Take this hand," Maria instructs Carmela, moving from her spot at Nina's side so she can squat in front of her and feel for the baby's head.

Carmela moves into position, holding one of Nina's hands while

Giada holds the other. Nina grips Carmela's hand so hard she thinks her bones might splinter into a thousand pieces, but it's clearly nothing compared to the pain Nina is enduring.

Giada recites prayers, and Carmela is struck by a memory of Nina confessing to her, when they were very small that she didn't believe in God. It was years ago, likely a childish impulse, and Nina may well be as devout as her mother now. Just in case, Carmela decides to give her something else to think about.

"Which do you think will come first? Boy or girl?"

"Boy," Nina says, her face tightening with the next impending wave of pain.

"What'll you name him?"

"Sandro wants to call him Sandro, but I like Matteo."

"Matteo's a good name," Carmela says as Nina's eyes go glassy and there is no more conversation while she rides this wave.

Carmela does not blame her mother for avoiding births. It's not only the messiness and unrelenting agony. It's the intimacy of it, sharing in this moment when Nina is laid completely bare, literally but also in every other sense. She does not have the energy to hold back anything she feels. She grunts and moans like an animal, and all Carmela can do is sit with her.

This only strengthens Carmela's resolve not to bear her own children. It's not the pain; that's temporary and Carmela could endure it if she had to. But the vulnerability, to go through this in the presence of other people, and then to usher into this world this piece of yourself that is no longer kept safe within one's womb: that is its own vulnerability.

When Nina's grip on Carmela's hand loosens and her eyes refocus, Maria speaks. "The baby's head is in position. When the next wave comes, you're going to feel like pushing. Trust that instinct and push as hard as you can." To Carmela, she says, "Make sure she breathes."

How? Is Carmela to reach inside this primal girl as Maria does and ensure the inflation and deflation of her lungs? Carmela is fairly certain that Nina's body is going to do exactly what Nina's body wants to do.

Which, in a way, is a comfort.

The wave builds again. This time, Nina's eyes don't go glassy. Instead, Carmela sees fear, the same fear she saw in Patrizia Moretti's eyes as her husband pounded on the apothecary door. Only this time, Carmela can't shield her. It doesn't matter how much the women of Tofana Apothecary have Nina's back. She must go through this on her own.

"Breathe," Carmela says. "Your body knows how to do this."

The sound that emerges from Nina is different than all the sounds she's made before. It shakes the foundation of Carmela's very view of motherhood. Her own mother did this to bring her into the world.

Nina howls and leans her weight into Carmela's side as she pushes and pushes, her face red, her entire being given over to this task. No thought to her nakedness, her dignity, her comportment.

"Good girl," Maria says, the most warmth in her voice since they arrived. "Good, strong girl. You're getting there."

Getting there? All that effort and the baby isn't here?

Carmela looks in horror to Maria, sure something must be wrong, but Maria is tranquil, the expression on her face no different than if she were grinding plantain leaves.

The wave of pain passes and Maria instructs Nina's mother to get her something to drink.

"Another few pushes like that and the head will be out," Maria says.

"My legs," Nina complains.

Maria nods. "Carmela, get under her arm and help support her weight. Nina, after this next push we'll move you into a different position, to give your legs a break, okay?"

And then it's happening again, but this time Carmela is bearing most of Nina's weight and hoping with all her heart that she doesn't stagger to the floor and bring mother and unborn babies down on top of her.

Nina pushes and yells, and Carmela takes long, loud breaths, encouraging Nina to do the same. Giada continues her litany of prayers and Carmela is struck by the idea of a god who would deliver babies into this world because they have been prayed for, but would leave the heathen children forever inside their mothers' wombs to rot.

"Good, strong girl," Maria says again as it passes. She instructs Carmela and Giada to shift Nina forward so she is on her knees, with Carmela knelt before her, taking the weight of Nina's arms over her shoulders. Maria positions herself behind Nina's backside, Giada with her to catch the baby when it comes.

This means Carmela is the only one Nina can see. Their faces are so close, the intimacy almost unbearable.

When the time comes to push again, Nina buries her face in Carmela's neck as she grunts her animal sounds. Carmela feels the weight of this girl who once tried to take Carmela's side, if only for a second, and knows she would bear the weight even if it were Violetta. She knows now what Maria meant about petty childhood grievances. So some children called her mother a witch. So what, when there are new lives entering the world, nurtured and born by women who perform a miracle in delivering them from the world of the womb to this one.

When it passes, Nina collapses even more weight onto Carmela's shoulders.

"Good girls," Maria says. At least Carmela's almost sure she says "girls," and if she didn't, she'll choose to hear it that way, Maria encouraging them both. "The head is out. The next push and baby will be here."

"I can't," Nina whispers, only loud enough for Carmela.

"Of course you can," Carmela says. "Do you remember when you stood up to Violetta Raso as a child? I thought you were the bravest girl in the world."

The next time, Nina only has to push for one primal burst and then Maria and Giada are busy at the other end with a wriggling mess of gooey, bloody limbs.

"That's it," Maria says, "you've got a boy."

Nina crumples to the side, drained of all energy. Carmela catches her and lowers Nina's head onto her lap. She curls on the floor on her side, her belly still enormous, as though nothing has changed. But it has. There's a baby, Carmela can see him. There were four of them in the room, and now there are five. Maria is cutting a pulsing purple rope and Giada wraps the baby in cloths.

"You did it," Carmela says, stroking Nina's damp hair off her face.

"Let's get you more comfortable." Maria takes the baby from Giada and wipes its face, thumps it on the back. "Onto the bed now."

As Giada and Carmela move the exhausted heap of girl, a reedy cry fills the room. Nina doesn't react, but Carmela's heart seizes. That is the first noise that human being has ever made, and she is here to hear it.

With Nina settled, Maria brings the wailing bundle to her, then pulls Carmela away so the three generations of Santoris can have their moment.

"Help me clean up here," Maria says quietly. "We need to be ready for the second one."

The second one.

Carmela had forgotten there are to be two babies. Going through all of that again is unthinkable. Carmela looks at Nina, who doesn't even have the energy to hold her first baby. Her mother cradles the child and coos at it. Nina looks half-dead.

"She can't go through that again."

"Yes she can." Maria's tone brooks no argument. Nina needs every person in this room, except for perhaps that tiny being who is wondering what this cold, bright place is, to believe that she can and will do it all again, with ease.

When the pains return, Nina moans and refuses to be moved from her place on the bed. Giada takes the baby, leaving Maria and Carmela to get her daughter through this second round.

"All right, Nina," Maria says. "Your body knows how to do this. That boy over there is proof."

Nina's eyes despair, but this time she doesn't say she can't. She might feel it, but she isn't going to contradict Maria, or that child in her own mother's arms.

This one comes more quickly, small and still. Carmela tries to mask her face, but Nina is present enough to notice her flinch.

"What? What is it? Is she all right?"

"Nothing to worry about." Maria whisks the cold, blue thing away.

Nina grips Carmela's arm. "What's wrong with her?"

What is Carmela supposed to say? Surely not, *She looked dead to me.* And not, *This is my first birth.*

She settles for "I don't know," remembering how Giulia is always honest with her customers at the very least. "What's her name?"

Carmela isn't even certain the second baby is a girl; it all happened too quickly. But that doesn't matter right now.

"Giada," Nina says, "for my mother."

Her mother doesn't respond to that; she's distracted hovering next to Maria.

"Please," Nina says. "Will you find out what's wrong with her?"

Carmela isn't sure she can even stand. If she should find out the answer is that the child Nina has borne all these months is dead, there is no way Carmela can be the one to tell her that.

But Carmela has barely stood on shaky legs when another cry fills the room. Fainter than the first one. Carmela looks to baby Matteo, whose tiny rosebud lips are closed.

"She's fine," Maria says over her shoulder, where she's rubbing the second baby's limbs far more roughly than Carmela would have thought prudent. "Small, but she's got some lungs on her."

Nina releases a sob. Then: "Bring her to me. Bring them both to me."

The night is not over. There are still the placentas to deliver. What an indignity after all that, after bringing two brand-new human beings into the world, to be expected to spare yet more energy to expel not one, but two veined, red-purple masses of sinew and tissue.

Maria treats them as though they are as precious as the twins. "The placentas sustained those babies throughout the pregnancy." A more sentimental thing, Carmela has never heard her say.

Carmela grimaces as Maria wraps each one lovingly in a clean cloth.

"They may want to keep them," Maria says. "But if they don't, we'll take them with us."

Normally full of questions, Carmela doesn't want to know the possible uses for these spent messes of tissue. She puts them out of her mind and focuses instead, as she helps Maria clean and pack their things, on Nina on the pallet, her two new babies in her arms. Giada hovering, Nina's husband, Sandro, entering and weeping at the sight of his children, his wife, who just performed not one miracle, but two.

The Infant

There is a newborn
like these twins
                                        but not

a short walk
from the apothecary,
just on the other side
of Palazzo Borghese.

Of course this brand-new human
has no conception
of the Palazzo
or Campo Marzio
or Rome.

She only knows
that one moment
she was enveloped
in safety and warmth
a steady whooshing dreambeat
linking her own self
to her host self
not quite sure where one began
and the other ended

but then the gentle caress
turned on her
the walls around her suddenly enemy
constricting

forcing her out and away
as the dreambeat faded
and other sounds encroached

the familiar voice
through all these months
in agony, and this infant
would have made her own wails of distress
if she were able to fill her lungs
but she was stuck in a horrid in-between

no longer gently held
not yet able to draw breath

unaware that her first lesson
had already begun:

over and over and over
she will learn
how two things can be true
how there can be no good choices
how she has no way through but to survive

and then finally she emerged
from the safe, warm place
and as awful as the constriction was
its absence is worse, for there is nothing
holding her together, nothing reminding her
she is linked to another

and the light that still glares
even when she squeezes her eyes shut

and the noise all around, harsh and foreign
and the jolt as something smacks against her back
and her lungs expand, the air rushing in all at once
almost smothering her, and the sound that explodes
from her throat snags the inside, rough and unrepentant
but she'll need that voice because

there is no going back.

Carmela returns not to Maria and Laura's apartment that night, but to her own. There is a thrumming in her veins that will not subside. She has walked so close to both death and life in the short time her mother has been away. And now two new souls have entered the world, with her help.

The apartment above the shop is cold and the banked ashes have long since burned out. Carmela must start a new fire from scratch, but she is glad of a task on which to center her mind. She retrieves the flint and steel from the mantel, the bucket of dried thistledown nearby. Giulia always makes a spark on the first try, but Carmela is not so lucky.

It doesn't matter. She is still warm from walking home, and she can use the practice. It is something she should know how to do well. After all, Nina is her age and she's now the mother of two children.

After a few strikes she achieves sparks, but they die before she can ignite the thistledown.

She could go downstairs and retrieve a coal from the banked ashes in the shop. But she won't relent so easily. She strikes again and again until a spark ignites the clump of thistledown. She blows softly, feeding the tiny flame with the fuel of oxygen. Too much and it will extinguish, but exactly the right amount and the flame grows. It consumes the thistledown and she gives it more. Once the flame is strong enough, an infant who has released a primal wail, she sets it in the hearth and arranges a pyramid of kindling atop it. There are only a few pieces. If the flame goes out now, a coal from the shop won't even help her until she can gather more kindling.

But the flame doesn't go out. At first it seems to burn around the kindling, but then, finally, the wood darkens with scorch marks. Once the fire is roaring, it's gotten so late Carmela really should bank the coals and collapse into bed. But she can't bear to smother the fire, even though she knows logically that all her work won't have been a waste. In the morning, it will be simple to reawaken the buried coals.

But she is a taut wire, thrumming with everything she has seen and done and learned. And all while her mother was away.

Carmela drifts to sleep in front of the roaring fire and jerks awake at the sound of the door opening. For a second it's Signor Moretti, here to seek vengeance on her. But then her mother's hand is cool on her forehead.

"The fire's about to go out, darling."

"Mother! You're back! Did you get mandrake?"

"I did. I'll tell you about it in the morning. For now I'm exhausted. Bank the ashes and come to bed, love."

The Women, Part 2

There is a woman
like Giulia
like Maria
like Laura
like Carmela
                        but not

across the Tiber
to the northwest of the apothecary
in the servants' quarters
of the Castel Sant'Angelo
who has been on her feet
for sixteen hours
and still her day is not done;

by the Porto di Ripetta
in a tiny bed in a tinier apartment
west of the apothecary
lying back and thinking of the Holy Roman Empire
for though she has given of her body all day
to nursing babies and tugging toddlers
her husband has his needs too
and it will be easiest for everyone
if she gives in to him;

in the parlor of the notary's home
to the northeast of the apothecary
waiting up long past the hour
she used to retire, eyelids heavy

candles burned down and out
and still she sits, waiting
for her husband's return, knowing he will
eventually walk back through those doors
even if he never looks at her again
the way he did once;

in the hallway outside the finest bedroom
in the grandest home on Via del Corso,
close enough to walk to the apothecary
every day until she finally procured
this tiny bottle
and still is unsure of using it
but then he calls her name in his sleep
and if the tone had been slightly different
perhaps she would have tucked the bottle away
but the strangled moan is both demand and reprimand
and she uncorks the bottle as she steps inside.

Giulia has procured enough mandrake to finish Signora Fontina's order and plenty more besides. They tell her of the Santori birth and everything else she missed in between customers during a busy morning in the shop.

Nearly everything.

Carmela is minding the front when Father Piero bursts in. His cheeks flame, but not from drink, judging by his clear eyes and sure step.

"I must speak with Giulia." He barely looks at Carmela. "Giulia!" he calls toward the back.

"She's in the middle of a rather delicate—"

"I must speak with her now!"

Carmela's heart beat accelerates. He shouldn't be a threat. But his raised voice and squared shoulders, the fire in his eyes ignites a small panic.

"I'll see if she'll come."

Giulia rolls her eyes when Carmela ventures into the back; everyone in this shop and the next heard Father Piero's voice. "I'm not expecting him," Giulia says. "Give him whatever he needs."

Carmela draws in a steadying breath and turns back to the archway. Maria is heaving herself to her feet, ready to face off with Father Piero if necessary, but neither has a chance to offer their help before he pushes his way into the back room.

"Father!" Giulia says sharply. "What in heaven's name? I would never barge into your confessional—"

"We both know you are doing quite the opposite of absolving sins here. I must speak with you now. In private."

Giulia holds his gaze for a tense moment. Then she nods to Laura. "Would you take over for me? I'm waiting on a boil, at which point the skullcap must be added immediately and the heat lowered."

Laura nods and takes Giulia's place. Father Piero heads for the back door, but Giulia stands her ground.

"Speak freely, Father. We are all in confidence here."

Father Piero's face grows still redder. "The way Patrizia Moretti was in your confidence?"

Giulia freezes. "What are you talking about?"

Carmela's stomach turns.

"I'm talking," Father Piero says, his voice deadly, "about your customer, whose husband was recklessly poisoned last night."

No. That's not how it was supposed to go.

Giulia draws herself up to her full height. "I don't know what you're implying. I haven't given Patrizia Moretti anything but commonplace remedies."

Carmela grips the worktable, lightheaded.

"Are you sure about that?"

"Of course I'm sure," Giulia snaps, showing an edge to Father Piero that she never shows to anyone beyond the women in this room. "Do you think I could forget who I dispense Acqua Tofana to?"

Bile rises in Carmela's throat.

"You're leaving me with no choice." Father Piero strides out of the back room toward the front door. "This kind of recklessness is not what I was promised. If I confess to supplying you with the arsenic now, there's a chance I won't hang—"

"Father, wait!" Giulia and Maria are already on his heels. Carmela isn't sure her wobbly legs will carry her, and she can feel Laura's curious eyes on her.

"You must believe me," Giulia says, in the voice she uses on churlish customers. "We're in this together. In fact, as I recall, we've been in this together since—"

Through the archway, Carmela watches Father Piero spin to face her mother, every muscle in his body coiled to spring. "You cannot forever hold that over my head! I paid my penance long ago!"

Carmela, too, must take responsibility.

"You, on the other hand, wicked, vengeful woman—"

"I gave it to her," Carmela blurts, stumbling through to the front.

Laura gasps, but Giulia doesn't even face her. "Carmela, stay out of this."

"But I did." Carmela finds her footing, draws even with her mother. "When you were away in Tivoli. She was here. She was desperate."

"Maria?" Giulia turns, as though Carmela's word can't be trusted.

"This is the first I'm hearing of it," Maria says slowly.

"It was when you left early and I closed up," Carmela says. Giulia glares at Maria, as though she is to blame. "She'd been beaten. Her husband came pounding on the door. Throwing bottles, smashing things. He was going to kill her. He was."

But was he? Carmela was certain in the moment, but now it sounds so feeble. Her words, those shocked faces, the memories of that night and Signora Moretti's desperate pleas for help already growing hazy around the edges.

"Father, please." It is too late now to wonder if she did the right thing. "I was trying to help her. We have each other's backs. We take care of those who have nowhere else to turn."

Something shifts on Giulia's face. She moves to stand next to her daughter, so they're facing Father Piero together. "Isn't that right,

Father? Our duty is to those who have nowhere else to go. We both know the consequences when they're turned away."

"Enough!" he roars. "You will never grant me absolution for a youthful mistake, but when it's your own daughter—"

"All right." Maria steps in between Father Piero and the Tofana women. He would not actually strike them, Carmela is almost sure. But he was tottering on a very fine line. "Things are bad enough right now without bringing up the mistakes of the past."

Giulia and Father Piero glare at one another. Laura appears in the archway, taking in the tense scene.

"Maria is right," Giulia allows. "We must deal with the here and now." She turns to Carmela. "I need every bit of truth, this moment. You dispensed Acqua Tofana to Patrizia Moretti?"

"TONIGHT," Carmela had said, "I'm La Tofana. We take care of each other. It's what we're here for."

She had not known how to care for this woman, how to shield her from the monster outside, but she had known there was no other option.

They waited together, holding one another, Signora Moretti murmuring prayers while Carmela tried to breathe and think through what her mother would do in this situation. The man was a monster, that much was clear. Signora Moretti was terrorized; that was clear too. She said he would kill her, and Carmela believed her.

Finally the pounding and smashing and shouting subsided, though Carmela wasn't certain if he'd gone, or if he'd changed his tactics and lay in wait.

Carmela disentangled herself from Signora Moretti's arms and, despite her protests, went to look out the front window. If she didn't see him, there was a chance he'd gone around to the back and they should leave out the front.

But he hadn't gone. He'd passed out on their doorstep, surrounded by broken glass from the bottles he'd smashed.

"We have to get you out of here now." Carmela pulled Signora Moretti to her feet. She considered the apartment upstairs, but when he came around again, it seemed like an obvious place for him to check and Giulia wasn't even here to charm him away.

"I can take you to the convent," Carmela said, considering the walk to Santa Maria of the Angels. She wasn't certain she could make it there and back by morning. Perhaps she should go by Maria's first to get her input.

"No," Signora Moretti says. "No, I have to go home."

"Home? But . . ." Carmela's gaze trailed to the front door. On the other side was slumped a monster. A monster who would wake and return to that same home.

"Why should I be the one to run?" Signora Moretti's voice was tremulous, but her eyes flashed. "I've built that home. I've built that life."

"I don't understand. You said he was going to kill you."

"He is. Eventually. Which is why I've been trying to convince your mother to give me Acqua Tofana."

Acqua Tofana. She'd heard her mother and Maria say it. Laura too. It sounded different coming from another's lips. This thing that was almost mythical made real by a flesh-and-blood person before Carmela, asking to hold the vial from the top shelf. To use it. Carmela knew exactly where it was. She had helped make it.

"Acqua Tofana must be dispensed gradually," Carmela said slowly, well past pretending she didn't know what Patrizia was talking about. "It takes three days to . . . take effect. Even if I gave it to you, he would have time to harm you before—"

"It's not like that," Signora Moretti said. "He's not planning to kill me. When he wakes up in a drunken stupor in the streets, he'll be ashamed. He'll come home with his tail between his legs and want me to assure him he's a wonderful man. As long as I don't set him off in the time it takes . . ."

That seemed like an incredible gamble to Carmela. But Giulia had always stressed women should be in charge of what happens to their bodies.

"What are you looking for?" Carmela had asked Giulia.

"Terror," Giulia had said. "A woman who will not survive if her husband lives."

Signora Moretti, head gashed open, soul laid bare, was exactly who Acqua Tofana had been created for.

Carmela retrieved the vial. "You have to listen carefully," she said. "I can write it down if you want."

Signora Moretti shook her head. She likely couldn't read; Carmela didn't press the point. "A single drop the first day. It can go into anything he eats or drinks. He won't taste it. He'll start to feel ill."

Signora Moretti nodded, never taking her eyes off the vial.

"Two drops the second day. He'll be much sicker. You should call for a physician. They won't know what's wrong with him. Three drops the third day. You'll call for a priest. He'll have time to repent and set things in order. No one will suspect you of anything. But you must follow these instructions exactly, do you understand?"

Signora Moretti nodded and held out her hand for the vial. It was no longer shaking. "I understand."

Carmela had led her out the back door on the slightest chance that Signor Moretti roused enough to catch them leaving. She walked the woman all the way to her grand home, the life she'd built, that she was willing to risk everything to keep.

"I can come check on you tomorrow," she'd said.

"No, child. You've helped so much already. All will be well."

When Carmela returned, the monster was gone. She swept the

broken glass and wiped away the streaks of something foul he'd used to write upon their windows: *witch whores*.

CARMELA KEEPS HER EYES on her mother as she recounts these events. Giulia's steady gaze buoys her through the storm of Father Piero's huffs of indignation, Maria's grunts of agreement, Laura's faint sighs.

Carmela tells it like a bedtime story, real and not. If she keeps telling it, she can forestall the inevitable, when Father Piero explains why he's here, why he's so angry and scared he's willing to turn himself in for providing the apothecary's arsenic. For even though Carmela took every step she'd been taught to take, gave every instruction, made absolutely certain that Patrizia Moretti would not survive if her monster of a husband was allowed to live, somehow things had not turned out the way they were supposed to.

"You see, Father," Giulia says when Carmela has finished talking and it is clear she has nothing more to say, no further explanation to give. "Everything was done as it should be."

"It certainly was not! Signora Moretti dumped the entire vial straight into his mouth as he slept. Left the empty vial in plain sight. Left him to limp to the front steps with the most obvious of poisoning symptoms in front of all their neighbors."

Giulia's steady gaze falters. She turns away, covers her mouth as though she might be ill. Laura gasps and Maria lowers herself to sit on the bench.

Carmela's mind is a blank fog. Nothing makes sense. She did everything exactly as she was meant to.

"I told her, Mother," she says, her voice barely audible. "He was going to kill her."

At that, Giulia nods. Still turned away, but she says quietly, "I know, love."

The Priest

There is a man of the cloth
like Father Piero
                                    but not

inside the confessional
of Holy Trinity Church
to the east of the apothecary
off Via del Corso

without a confessor
to hear his myriad sins:

how he has broken his parishioners' trust
how he has broken his vows

of obedience
to the scripture
in nearly every way

of chastity
in his heart
if not his body

but only because
the object of his love
is so pious
he knows
she would be repelled
by his attention

so when she sits
on the other side of the screen
and recounts her trivial transgressions

    all excusable
    even if God were not so gracious

he imagines how her lips might taste
and her curves might feel
beneath his hands,
he imagines how their bodies
would fit together

and he hates himself
even as he professes
God's love for her.

There is no end
to his sins.

It looks bad," Maria says when they've flipped the sign in the window to closed. "But there was no label on that bottle. No way to trace it back to the shop."

"You weren't even in town," Laura points out.

"People don't know that." Giulia paces, wearing a groove into the floor.

"They do," Maria says. "Carmela told Violetta."

Carmela longs to defend herself at the shock on her mother's face, but if her slipup might help throw suspicion away from the shop, she'll bear it.

Instead, Giulia turns on Maria. "I don't want the suspicion off me."

There is a long silence. Maria has understood, but Carmela trails behind. "She could have gotten arsenic anywhere, couldn't she?" Carmela says.

"She could have gotten it straight from Father Piero," Maria grumbles.

"But she was in here so often," Laura says. "And the vial."

"Yes, but none of that matters. They'll believe what they want to believe," Giulia says. "And when they turn their heads our way, I need to be the one in their sights. How much did you tell Violetta?"

"Nothing!" Carmela's mind races. "Only that you were gone and I was . . . in charge." In the resulting silence, Carmela dies a million deaths.

Finally, "Will she believe you were lying? Trying to seem more important than you are?"

And still another death. "Yes. I think so."

Giulia nods. "You'll tell her that. But not before suspicion turns our way; no sense reminding her if she's already forgotten."

Father Piero stands abruptly from where he had settled into a morose silence. "I'll find out what I can. But you'd best prepare for the worst."

Carmela's heart lurches as Father Piero strides out. He could be on his way to turn them in this very moment.

Giulia stumbles to the back room and retches.

Carmela stands frozen. Maria squeezes her shoulder as she heads to check on Giulia. Laura stays in her spot on the bench, her face pale.

"What have I done?" Carmela would never voice such a self-indulgent question to her mother or Maria. But Laura will humor her.

Laura sighs. "I don't know."

ALMOST NO ONE COMES INTO THE SHOP for the rest of the day. A coincidence perhaps, but it's impossible to ignore the sense that word has spread: The women of Tofana Apothecary are murderers. They're dangerous. Witches all along.

In the late afternoon, Maria and Laura gather their supplies to check in on Nina Santori and her new babies once the shop has closed.

"Go ahead," Giulia says, waving them off early. "We'll close up."

Carmela retrieves the broom and sweeps as Giulia banks the ashes. Carmela waits for a word of comfort from her mother. An assurance that she understands, that she would have done the same thing, that Carmela was in an impossible situation.

It doesn't come. Giulia doesn't scold or say she blames her, but it's in the air between them, thick and heavy, clotted blood.

The Loiterer

There is a woman
like any other customer
                                        but not

loitering at the costermonger
on the north end of the Ortaccio,
down the road
but always with an eye
on the apothecary's door.

If she should catch a glimpse
of someone she knows
crossing the threshold,
someone her husband respects,
she will have her excuse.

Signora Valenti was there, she could say.
I wanted to be sure she came to no harm.
Or *Signor Abate accompanied me.*

Any reason to go inside
and buy the tincture she needs,
the one that dampens the blazing headaches
that slice her open, pain beyond enduring,
until she can do nothing but writhe on the bed
in the quietest, darkest room she can find.

She used to be afflicted constantly
until Giulia Tofana's teas and tinctures

delivered her from the vicious pain.
Her husband objected at first.

She's a witch. I won't hear of it.

But even he couldn't deny his wife
the relief La Tofana brought her.
Until Claudio Moretti died
at his wife's hand.

I cannot fathom
why they haven't burned her already.
You're not to go in there again, do you hear?

This woman finds it impossible to reconcile
the warm apothecary who listened so well
and brought so much relief
with one who would
craft a poison so diabolical
a little slip of a thing like his wife
could bring him stumbling
out their front door
crashing to his knees
on the threshold
retching and clutching at his throat
as he fights for his final breaths.

For that matter, she finds it hard to imagine
Signor Moretti's elegant wife as murderess.
She would have had to be under a spell.
But whose? Surely not Giulia Tofana.

Perhaps it was the older one.
She has the look of a witch about her
although this woman's husband always says
you can't tell by looking,
which is what makes
those women
so insidious.

The quiet one, then.
Or even the young one.
Nothing like this ever happened
before she began to work in the shop.

But even if
they are all in league with the devil
this woman will chance it.
She will cross that threshold
and hand over her coin

for another headache is coming
and without that tincture,
like every time before
she met Giulia Tofana
the blazing pain
will overcome her so entirely
she will wish for a fatal poison
of her own.

Father Piero doesn't come the next day, but neither do the notary or the magistrate's thugs. A few customers trickle in, but Carmela thinks they're quieter than usual, jumpier.

By unspoken agreement, Carmela is kept in the back. Giulia handles the empty front of shop. Maria and Laura pile endless menial tasks on Carmela—to distract her or keep her out of trouble, she isn't certain. When an errand is required that would normally fall to Carmela, Laura stands.

"I need a breath of fresh air," she says. "I'll go."

Carmela doesn't object. They're right not to trust her with the secrets of the shop.

WHEN THE BELL JINGLES SOME TIME LATER, Carmela hears Giulia's startled yelp and races to the front. Have the authorities come?

But it's Laura. Or a shadow Laura, face agonized, body covered in refuse.

"Mother of God!" Maria says when she sees her. "Carmela, fetch water and all the clean cloths you can find."

When Carmela returns, Giulia and Maria have sat Laura on the bench.

"What happened?" Carmela asks as Giulia motions for her to

bring a bucket. She and Maria pick bits of eggshells and potato peelings and meat gristle off Laura.

Carmela dips a cloth in water and wipes Laura's face free of a foul-smelling sludge. Only when she can safely open her mouth does Laura speak. "I can't go to market anymore. I can't leave the shop at all!"

"It'll be all right." Giulia wets another cloth and wipes Laura's hands.

"No it won't! There've always been whispers, but it's more than that now!"

Giulia nods to Maria, who wordlessly retrieves a calming tonic.

"I don't want your tonics!" Laura shrieks, her voice louder than Carmela has ever heard. "I don't want any of this!"

"All right." Maria unties Laura's soiled apron. "Why don't we get you all cleaned up, first things first?"

"Maybe upstairs?" Carmela suggests with a glance at the shop door. Laura nods, grateful. The shop may not be overflowing with customers, but she has suffered enough humiliation for one day. No reason to risk a customer walking in while Laura stands exposed in only her shift.

Carmela expects her mother to make her stay to tend the shop, but instead she flips the sign to closed, locks the door behind them, and leads the way up to the apartment. Maria guides Laura by the elbow and Carmela brings up the rear with a glance over her shoulder.

Inside the apartment, Giulia bustles about, gathering garments that will fit tiny Laura. Carmela stokes the fire and gathers another bowl of water and cloths, while Maria gently removes Laura's clothing. Even her shift has been soiled, up at the neckline. That comes off too, and then Laura is standing completely vulnerable. She is safe here, with these women, this family, but still she trembles.

Maria gently wipes at the last bits of residue clinging to Laura's skin, and then Giulia pulls a fresh shift over her head. Laura looks so small, standing there, a child in her sleepshirt. But she's not a child. She's a woman who ought to be able to go to market without fear of an assault.

Carmela busies herself with the fire, so as not to gawk while Giulia and Maria help Laura into an underskirt, an overskirt, a bodice. She only turns back once Laura is curled into the chair by the fire.

Giulia puts water on to boil, and they all sit down. "Is there any chance this could have been an accident?"

It would be a valid question under normal circumstances. Any stroll through the streets of Rome includes the risk of a citizen tossing refuse out an upstairs window.

"They yelled that I should burn."

Maria shoves her chair back and begins pacing. Giulia takes a deep breath. "Start at the beginning."

"There's no story. One minute I was at the chandler's stall, and the next I was covered in trash."

"The chandler's stall?" Now Carmela stands. "That's Violetta's apartment. I'm going to strangle her!"

"Hush," Giulia says. "You don't know it was Violetta."

But Carmela feels the certainty in her bones.

"Could have been," Maria says. "Sometimes the ones we help are the first to fan the flames."

Giulia shoots Maria a look.

"Sorry," she says. "Poor choice of words."

Carmela grabs her cloak. She's heading for the door. There are very few people in the world who require Carmela's protection; she'd die for her mother and Maria both, but they don't need her. Laura, though? Laura is all soft parts and beating heart, and tears well up at the thought of her apothecary sister being attacked without Carmela there to stand up for her.

"Carmela, stop," Giulia orders. "You're not going anywhere."

"After what we did for Violetta? She's not getting away with this!"

"Sit. Down."

Carmela doesn't. She's not a child anymore. Too much has happened in the last few days. If she must bear the brunt of life and death, she'll feel this anger and express it too. "Her family should know. If they hate us so much, they should know that we—"

"If you betray Violetta's confidence in us, you will never set foot in my apothecary again."

Carmela may not be a child anymore, but neither is she in charge. Giulia turns back to Laura. "I hope you understand, Laura, that I condemn what happened to you in the strongest possible manner. If it was indeed Violetta—"

"It doesn't matter." Laura sniffles.

"Of course it matters!" Maria is on her feet, and Carmela is fairly certain her mother couldn't stop Maria if she decided to give Violetta a piece of her mind.

"But it doesn't," Laura says. "If it hadn't been Violetta, it would have been someone else. Before, the apothecary was the only place I felt safe, but now—"

"Laura." Giulia takes her hands. "I hope you know you're under no obligation to keep working in the shop."

Carmela's knees buckle.

"Of course she knows that," Maria says with a huff, dismissive.

But Laura considers Maria, then Giulia with a new look in her eye. "It isn't that I'm not grateful for all you've done for me—"

Maria's hand flies to her throat. Instinctively, Carmela moves closer to the older woman.

"Of course," Giulia says, in her warmest voice. "You're family!"

"I just . . . I just . . . I can't anymore!"

Laura stands abruptly, knocking her chair over. Without stopping to right it, she runs from the room, her steps clattering down the stairs as the rest of them look on in shock.

The Cobbler

There is a vendor
like the chandler
                                        but not

along Via del Corso
just north of the apothecary

minding his cramped stall
from sunup to sundown,
hunched over worn-out shoes
patching soles, picking stitches
haggling with customers
over the worth of his labor

and watching the ebb
                                                  and flow
of Campo Marzio's residents
its visitors and immigrants
everyone needs shoes, candles, eggs.

When he first began
he'd get distracted by the sights
and then whipped by his grandfather
for shirking his duties. But now
he is in charge. He is the one
who counts the coin at the end of the day
and if his attention strays he has only himself
to blame. Which is how he has grown accustomed

to the casual violence of the city
the mistress backhanding a servant
the child shoving someone weaker
the knives drawn, slurs spat, garbage thrown
the men thrusting hands where they aren't wanted
and girls jostled into alleys against their wills.

The cobblestones of Campo Marzio
are soaked in blood, if you look close enough.
Which is why he doesn't.

When he was younger
he considered intervening
when an innocent was targeted
but his grandfather squashed that impulse.
Now he understands. He may be free
to watch, but if he abandons his stall
to right every wrong, no one
in Campo Marzio would have shoes.

Laura showed up on Maria's doorstep when she was fourteen, barefoot, a single bag in hand and not a word on her lips. Maria wasn't entirely certain who she was, only that she clearly needed somewhere to stay. Unlike when Giulia had shown up, there was no man of the house to consult. Maria made up a pallet for the girl, and a calming tonic.

It wasn't that she seemed agitated. On the contrary, she moved through the apartment in a muted haze, silent. But something needed calming, Maria was certain, even if it was very deep inside the girl.

Over time she came to understand that Laura was her half sister's cousin, but by the time she did, it didn't even matter. Laura had become a fixture in her life. Nearly always silent, but endlessly helpful. The first time Maria left her in the apartment for a few hours, she came home to find everything in perfect order, bread baking, and laundry done.

Since Laura liked helping, Maria asked her to run to the market for something one day, and Laura panicked. Without being able to articulate her reaction, she began packing her few meager belongings.

"What on earth has gotten into you?" Maria raised her voice for the first time as she grabbed for Laura's sack. When Laura flinched away from her, Maria understood. At least, she understood enough.

The next day, Maria took Laura with her to the apothecary. There was only so much to clean in their small apartment, but Laura clearly wanted to be of use. She didn't mind walking through town with Maria at her side, though she did startle at sudden noises.

When they entered the apothecary, Giulia was in a state. Something was amiss in her records and she couldn't reconcile the numbers.

"Well don't look at me." Maria settled Laura on an empty stool and began her daily tasks.

The shop bell rang and Giulia glided out to the front, removing all traces of frustration from her face. While she was helping the customer, Laura edged her way to the record book and took up the quill.

By the time Giulia returned, Laura was sweeping the workroom.

"You don't have to do that, Laura," Giulia had said. She didn't want the strange girl poking around her apothecary. But having been taken in by Maria herself, around the same age, she wasn't about to make Laura leave. Giulia sat back down with the records book, scowling. "If I don't figure this out . . ."

She trailed off, examining the page. Then she looked up sharply at Maria. "Did you make these changes?" she asked.

Maria snorted. She very nearly prided herself on her lack of education.

Then they both turned to look at Laura. She had the same panic in her eyes as when Maria had raised her voice at her.

"It's all right, Laura," Maria said, like she might speak to a frightened kitten that refused to come out from underneath a bed. "It would simply be better if you didn't—"

"No, she fixed it." Giulia looked in puzzlement from the page to Laura. "You fixed it, didn't you?" Laura nodded. "You're good with numbers."

Laura said nothing, but the truth of Giulia's statement was evident.

Laura became the record keeper, and also kept Maria's disaster of a work area cleaner than it had ever been. Slowly, Giulia began to teach her other parts of the business, until she became as indispensable as Maria or even Giulia herself.

But now they would have to learn to go on without her.

The Novitiate

There is a girl
like Laura
                    but not

at the convent
of Santa Maria of the Angels,
far to the southeast of the apothecary
beyond the curve in the Tiber
where the land turns to hills.

The habit of a novitiate
covers her head
as she learns the prayers,
finding comfort in the routine

if not the constant rules
and reminders of her unruliness
for even in a place without men
there are power structures
and she never seems to be
the one on top.

She bows her head,
makes the sign of the cross.
She is married to Christ
                though she doesn't believe in him.
Not so different
from her own parents' marriage.

She envies the girls
who are here out of devotion,
fulfilling their purpose.
She simply exists.

She wasn't forced into this life,
not like the ones whose parents dumped them here.
She chose it
        if you can call it a choice
                when you have no other options.

Sage?" Carmela says.

"Fine," Maria reports.

"Chamomile?"

"Fine."

"Lavender?"

"Fine. All the herbs are fine. And easy to grow ourselves if the supplier gets skittish."

Giulia appears in the archway from the front. "Perhaps we should get started with that now, just in case. What are we low on?"

"Mandrake, after the Fontina order. Spanish fly. Sanguis pulvis."

Giulia sighs. Without Laura, their supply of powdered blood will not be enough to keep up with demand.

"Sulfur and mercury too," Maria says. "All the minerals, really."

"Because we lost the supplier, yes. He also supplied our nitric acid and mercuric chloride, yes?"

"He did."

All three startle as the shop bell rings. Carmela leaves the others to deal with the crisis of inventory and heads to the front to help the customer.

But it's Father Piero again.

Giulia returns to the shopfront. "Father."

"I've come from Sant'Angelo."

Giulia says nothing. If he has been to visit Patrizia in her prison cell, he surely has more to tell her. But she won't grovel for the news.

"Patrizia Moretti is being held there until her execution."

Carmela's heart constricts. Signora Moretti is to be executed? For the crime Carmela helped her commit. It could just as easily be Carmela herself.

But this wasn't justice. Her husband could have killed her at any time and he never would have been executed for it.

"Giulia—" The tone in Father Piero's voice snaps Carmela out of her self-pity. She has never heard the priest call her mother by her first name. "She named you."

The air turns brittle around them.

"To you?" Giulia says carefully.

"There were guards present."

"Goddamn it!" Giulia pounds her fist on the counter, where an array of love potions rattle.

"Signora!"

"Oh I think we're both a bit past blasphemy, Father." Giulia freezes. "She named me, though? Not Carmela."

Father Piero nods, his glance flitting toward Carmela and away, as though he doesn't want to linger too long on her stained soul.

"Good," Giulia says. "Good. That's good."

But it's not good. It's not right. If someone is to blame here, it is Carmela. Perhaps they'll show mercy because of her youth, her ignorance—

"I suppose she didn't give you any of the blame?" Giulia asks Father Piero.

"She doesn't know I had anything to do with it! And supplying a single ingredient that could have been found in any painter's studio isn't quite the same, is it?"

Giulia and the priest glare at each other, neither willing to bend.

Carmela considers slipping out the back door and running to the prison, confessing her guilt, and exonerating them both.

"This visit right now is the last kindness I do you before I go to the monastery and lead a life of quiet—"

"At least until you want another drink," Maria interrupts from the archway. "Though I suppose you religious types always keep plenty of wine around."

Father Piero ignores Maria. "I suggest you do the same," he says to Giulia.

"What's that?"

"Take refuge at Santa Maria."

"You cannot be serious."

Carmela replays the scene in her mind, the one that has lived there since her mother first told it, Giulia as child, with her own mother, taking refuge in a church that immediately turned Costanza over to be executed.

"They will not turn you away." Father Piero does not look Giulia in the eye when he says it.

"You dare make me that promise?" Giulia's voice is as deadly as any vial of Acqua Tofana.

"I cannot change what's past, child. If I could, there would be no end to the things I would do differently. Your mother is but one of the penitents who haunts my dreams, who deserved better from me."

Giulia glares at Father Piero. His regret changes nothing.

"But the Mother Superior," he goes on, somehow standing up under the weight of Giulia's fury, "she is far wiser than I have ever been. More compassionate."

Carmela would give anything to understand the unsaid truths roiling beneath the surface of their words. She expects her mother to breathe fire, to flatten this small man where he stands. She is completely unprepared for Maria to say, "He's right."

Carmela wheels on the only grandmother she's ever known, the fiercest fighter. "What are you talking about?"

"Carmela—"

"No, it wasn't even my mother who gave her the poison!"

Father Piero glances toward the windows.

"It was me! They should blame me!"

"Hush, love."

"If you don't go today," Father Piero goes on, ignoring Carmela, as though she hasn't spoken, as though she isn't a burning pillar of fire in the center of the room, ready to incinerate everything and everyone around her, "you will no doubt be executed. What happens to Carmela then?"

Carmela is no longer a pillar of fire. She is a pile of ashes and the slightest breeze will disperse every atom of her being to the farthest corners.

"I'm not inviting you to journey with me. I'm taking a risk simply by being here. But if you're as cunning as you've always shown yourself to be, you'll follow my lead. This very hour."

Without another word, another glance, Father Piero pushes past them through the archway and exits out the back door.

Carmela rushes across the room and grabs Giulia's arm. "Mother, it was me. There's no reason for you to—"

"Hush, love. I need to think."

Helpless, Carmela turns to Maria.

"He's right," Maria says again, this time more gently, to Carmela. "It's Giulia's shop, it's Giulia's recipe. They will execute her, no matter what. If you go claiming responsibility, the most likely outcome is we all hang."

"How can you say that so matter-of-fact?!"

"Because it's true," Giulia says.

"Mother, I can't lose you—"

"I'll try to outrun them. But Maria"—Giulia jolts herself out of whatever reverie she was occupied with and begins to bustle around the room, gathering supplies for travel—"you have to go to the magistrate, tell them I confessed to you, I acted alone, you went to them as soon as I told you and you're bringing them back to arrest me."

"What are you talking about?" Carmela has been dropped into someone else's story. Maria would never do such a thing.

But Maria nods, grim and resigned.

"Why?! Why would we want to convince them Mother is guilty of a hanging crime?"

"I'll be gone before they get here." Giulia pulls remedies from the shelf and tucks them into her sack. "And without me, the shop can go on. If Maria's the one to tell them I'm guilty, it'll throw suspicion off the rest of you."

"There is no shop with you!"

"That's your youth talking," Maria says, pulling Carmela away from Giulia. "There were apothecaries before La Tofana and there will be apothecaries after. And always there will be the women who need us. If the shop closes, think how many will suffer."

"So my mother has to sacrifice herself?"

"I'm in a corner." Giulia moves with an armful of things to the back room. "I'll be sacrificed either way."

Carmela follows her, trying to take things out of her mother's arms.

"If she goes to the convent," Maria says as Giulia fills a skin with water, "we can still correspond. Perhaps even visit."

"Perhaps?!"

Giulia is tying up the traveling sack now, the one she used when she went to Tivoli, but she is not planning to travel for only a few days this time. This is a departure from the shop, from her daughter, never to return again.

Tears course down Carmela's face. Maria, too, is crying. But she holds Carmela tightly as she says, "It's better than visiting a grave. At least at the convent—"

"I'm not going to the convent. You know what the Church did to my mother."

"Giulia." Maria lets go of Carmela, focusing her urgency instead on the daughter of her heart. "Piero was right, the Mother Superior—"

"The Mother Superior would use my sins against me. At least the magistrate would execute me quickly."

"Mother!" Carmela dissolves into sobs.

Then her mother's arms are around her, holding her tighter than she ever has before. "Oh love, I'm so sorry."

She longs to stay there in her mother's strong arms forever. To forget the outside world coming for them, whether to blame them or to need them. Forever they've worried about everyone else, everyone who needs the apothecary. But Carmela needs her mother.

"There's no more time," Giulia says. "Maria, you need to get to them before they come for me on their own."

Maria nods and begins to put on her own cloak.

"No!" Carmela tries to pull the traveling bag from Giulia's arms. "Mother, no!"

"Carmela." Giulia stops her frantic rushing about and grips Carmela by the shoulders. "This is the only way to keep you safe. It's the only way to keep the doors open."

"Can we even do it without you?" Carmela doesn't care if they can. She doesn't care if the shop burns to rubble around them. "It's not Tofana Apothecary without La Tofana!"

Her mother strokes her cheek. "You're La Tofana now. You handle the customers, and Maria makes the remedies."

There's no stopping her. These women are forces swirling around Carmela, stronger than she'll ever be. She cannot change their course. She can only hope not to be swept away and smashed to bits in the maelstrom.

"But no more poison." If she must be La Tofana now, she will do what she has to, but not if it can cause this kind of havoc. "Only love potions and remedies for rheumatism—"

Giulia returns to Carmela. "Those will always be the bulk of what you do. That, and listening to women who have no one else. But there will come a day when a woman needs help only you can give. When all other options have been exhausted. When true evil must be stopped and only your fears stand in the way of giving her the slightest bit of power."

"But . . ." Carmela grasps for an argument. "But I don't have the recipe . . ."

Maria showed her how to make that vial of Acqua Tofana, the one that killed Signora Moretti's husband, that will kill her as well, that could kill Carmela's mother and all of them. But once was not enough for Carmela to learn to carry the weight her mother has handed her. And Maria is old; when she is gone . . .

"Yes, you do." Giulia takes hold of the locket she gave Carmela when she first began in the shop. She opens it and withdraws a tiny scrap of parchment. She hands it to Carmela and turns to embrace Maria a final time.

With shaking hands, Carmela unfolds the parchment. There in a cramped script are the quantities required to make Acqua Tofana. She wants to hurl it into the fire. But then her mother is in front of her, pulling her into her arms.

"I can't do this," Carmela weeps into her hair.

"Of course you can. You're my daughter. You'll make mistakes. I have. But the good will outweigh the bad. Trust me. Trust yourself."

Then Giulia is pulling away from Carmela, who tries desperately to hold on, but Maria is there, restraining her as her mother slips out the back. She hates Maria.

Maria is all she has in the world.

The Women, Part 3

There is a woman
in Campo Marzio
in Regola
in Colonna
in Trevi
in Testaccio
in Sallustiano
in Ludovisi
in Parione

in every rione
of this city
spreading in every direction from the apothecary
throughout the Holy Roman Empire, Europe,
along the Silk Road
across the seas to the colonies
in corners of the world
that don't exist
in the imaginations
of these women

there is a woman
who is completely, utterly alone.
She is surrounded
by children
by siblings
by those who'd call themselves her friends
by church parishioners
by marketgoers

by grasping men
jealous opponents
needy dependents
demanding parents

and still she is alone.

She is the only one
who has ever felt
this unique despair
this singular solitude
this certainty in her own
                    not-enoughness.

If there were another
to bear some of the burden
of course she would go to them
she would ask, she is not proud

it's only that
no one else
could ever possibly
understand.

Carmela barely notices Maria steering her through the Ortaccio and leaving her with a stunned Laura at their apartment. She has no sense of the time it takes Maria to go to the officials and do the unthinkable: turn on Giulia. To lead them back to the shop, and Giulia's apartment, feign dismay at her disappearance—and with her, her traveling essentials. Maria returns to Carmela and Laura with a grim set to her features.

"They'll be watching," she says as she slumps into a chair by the fire. "But for the time being, it seems they're convinced that Giulia has fled."

Carmela wakes in the middle of the night with a desperate certainty that her mother has come to harm. Maria wakes to Carmela's sobs, and then Laura is roused, heating water for tea that Carmela does not want but she will not refuse because it is her mother's blend, her only possible tie to Giulia in this moment.

When she wakes again later, Carmela is alone in the apartment, and the sun is high in the sky. Maria has left to open the shop.

Carmela should dress and head there too. Her mother is relying on her. She is La Tofana now.

Except that's laughable. She's La Tofana like an acorn is an oak tree.

Carmela keeps expecting Laura to return to the apartment, but she's glad when she doesn't. She is still in bed when Maria comes back to check on her several hours later. Maria raises her eyes at the sight of her slumped in the bed but says nothing. She crosses the room and stokes the fire, makes some tea, then kisses Carmela on the forehead, murmuring, "Oh Giulia."

Carmela isn't certain whether Maria is thinking of her mother, or has confused Carmela for another bereft, grieving young woman who ended up on her doorstep all those years ago.

How many times must Maria nurse a girl back into her own strength?

CARMELA DOESN'T COOK, or clean, or make herself useful in any way, like Laura did when it was her turn in Maria's convalescence.

She mopes between the bed and the chair by the fire. She doesn't set foot outside for days. She sips what is set in front of her, nibbles a few bites of food.

Anything more feels insurmountable.

Laura has returned to her work in the shop. Carmela should be grateful, for Maria certainly cannot manage alone, but instead she hates her for it a little. It was too dangerous with La Tofana around, but now that she's sacrificed herself, Laura is at peace?

Maria begins to lose patience. They have all suffered a loss. They have all been through a trauma. But Giulia isn't dead, at least. No one has come to collect Carmela, laying the blame on her instead, which is still a possibility, as long as Patrizia Moretti is alive to say what really happened.

Which won't be much longer. Her execution date has been set, according to the hushed conversations Carmela has heard when she's lying in bed, pretending to be asleep.

One morning, Maria reaches the end of her grace for this lump of girl in the bed. She elbows her upon waking. "Stoke the fire," she says.

Carmela grumbles and slides farther under the blanket.

Maria yanks it off her. "What would your mother say?"

"Maria, that's not fair—" Laura objects, but it is fair. Carmela knows it's fair. She's thought it herself. She simply cannot muster the will to take any action in response.

She does feel guilty when Laura is the one to get out of bed to stoke the fire. That day, she manages to sweep the hearth before she crumples back into the bed.

If Maria notices, she doesn't mention it. She elbows Carmela again the next morning. "Stoke the fire," she says.

Carmela lets out an agonized moan, as though Maria has demanded she undergo the rack, but she gets up, stomps across the room as loudly as possible, and does as she was told. Then she climbs back into the bed and pulls the blanket almost entirely off Maria as she wraps herself away from the world.

After Maria and Laura leave for the shop, Carmela dozes off again. She wakes later from a dream of Giulia on a ship, sailing away to the New World without her. Carmela is propelled from the bed by the image. Carmela is almost certain that if Giulia were going to run that far, she would find a way to take Carmela.

Almost is not nearly enough.

Carmela dresses in a frenzy, bursts out the door into the alley, desperate to find her mother before realizing she has no idea where to begin. If she'd gone to the convent, that would be one thing. But Giulia would sooner die on the side of the road.

Giulia might have died on the road, if she hadn't remembered something in her exhausted delirium.

She had in mind to travel toward Tivoli, the same route she took when she went in search of mandrake. But in trying to stay hidden, she couldn't hire a horse or stop anywhere for lodging, or even to eat and have a moment off her feet.

She purchased the odd bite of something from a roadside vendor, always with her hood drawn tight around her face.

But mostly she walked, and tried to imagine where she might go, what she might do once she reached Tivoli. She couldn't risk going back to the vendor who'd sold her the mandrake, though she'd been a kind woman who felt like a kindred spirit. There was too much danger that Giulia would be remembered.

She probably shouldn't be traveling toward somewhere she had been before at all. For as much as she loved Maria, and Laura, and Carmela, a person could be tortured into admitting nearly anything. She hated to think of the ones she loved suffering like that, and then giving that plague-sore notary useful information on top of it.

The guilt they would live with, when all any of them had ever done was try to serve her and her mission. Putting their faith in her. What a mockery of the human spirit, faith.

She was huddled under a bridge for shelter, somewhere between

Rome and Tivoli, when it came to her, part memory, part vision, part dream. Part women of the cloth, approaching her in their robes and habits, hands outstretched.

"There is refuge at the convent," one of them said.

She turned away. She knew what sort of refuge the Church offered.

"We will feed you," another said.

But then what? Giulia said nothing.

The third one, in a habit distinct from the others, knelt down in front of Giulia. "I am the Mother Superior at Santa Maria of the Angels. You are welcome with us anytime. You have my word: you will be cared for as one of our own."

Still, Giulia said nothing. Later, though, she'd admit she heard something familiar, even then, in the woman's voice. But it wasn't until the woman took her hand and said her parting words that the memory sliced through Giulia like a fresh wound.

"Remember, O most gracious Virgin Mary, never was it known that anyone who fled to thy protection, implored thy help, or sought thine intercession was left unaided."

She'd been twelve or thirteen, a year or so before her father's death—and her mother's—and she'd begun to help her mother in the apothecary after hours. She was never made an official apprentice, but the owner had thrown them a few extra coins when Giulia helped clean up, or restock inventory.

The same sort of tasks she'd started Carmela on.

Carmela.

The apothecary had bid them good night, his eyes lingering a bit too long on her mother. He was a kindly man who saw Costanza's value, and Giulia didn't think he would ever harm her mother, but she was glad to be there as a safeguard.

Now she sees he would have made her mother a much finer husband than her own father had.

He was gone and her mother was tending something over the fire when a face peered in the window.

"Someone's here, Mama," Giulia called.

"Shop's closed," Costanza replied, not looking up.

Giulia couldn't look away. The face was otherworldly, haloed in white. Giulia stepped closer to the window to get a better look. She still believed in angels then.

"Mama!" she screamed when she saw the blood-soaked garments.

Costanza came running and together they brought the young woman in. Not an angel, but a convent novitiate, deathly pale and covered in blood.

"Should I fetch the apothecary?" Giulia asked her mother, but the novitiate grabbed desperately at her arm, willing her to stay.

"All right, love," Costanza said, in the same voice she used when Giulia woke from nightmares. "It's only us here tonight. We'll see you through.

"Hold her hand," Costanza instructed her daughter as she tried to ascertain the problem.

But she gripped a rosary so hard that Giulia could only take her forearm and will the woman to live.

"Remember, O most gracious Virgin Mary," the young woman whispered as Costanza discovered the blood flowed from her womb, "that never was it known that anyone who fled to thy protection, implored thy help, or sought thine intercession was left unaided.

"Inspired by this confidence," she went on as Costanza murmured instructions to Giulia to fetch tinctures of nettle and echinacea and artemisia, "I fly unto thee, O Virgin of virgins, my mother.

"To thee do I come," she said as Costanza asked her what she had stabbed inside her womb in her attempt to end her pregnancy. "Before thee I stand, sinful and sorrowful.

"O Mother of the Word incarnate," she said as Costanza asked if there was someone they could call. "Despise not my petitions but in thy mercy hear and answer me."

She repeated this prayer over and over as Costanza worked and Giulia assisted her, doing what they could to remove the tissue from the womb, to prevent complications, to stop the bleeding.

Giulia had never sat at a patient's side, unless she counted the times she had dressed her own mother's wounds. There had been plenty of those. She much preferred the moments when her mother gave her a clear task to the moments when her only choice was to sit by the woman and bear witness to her horror.

The novitiate never told them her name. Never said a word except the ones of the prayer, begging some unseen spirit to aid her while two women of flesh and blood did the actual work of saving her life.

Saving her life, restoring her womb, and giving her the fresh slate she needed to become the Mother Superior.

Maria and Laura return later than usual, well after the shop should have closed. Their feet are dragging, their movements weary, and their aprons are covered in mysterious substances. A birth, then.

When they find Carmela in bed, the fire gone cold, no food or even hot water ready for them, Laura sighs and begins the necessary tasks.

Not Maria. She marches to Carmela's bed—her own bed—and says, "Tomorrow you will get up early, you will stoke the fire and boil water, and prepare our breakfast. Then you will go to the shop and open it while Laura and I take our time getting there."

Carmela rolls over and faces the wall.

But Maria is not done. "I have indulged you this long because I know what you feel, I feel it too, and don't begin to tell me it's different because she is your mother. She is, in all ways that matter, *my child*. Do you hear me? But I still get up every day and do the work, because that is what your mother would want. That is what she expects. She left you to be La Tofana now, because she trusts you. Look what you've done with that trust."

Carmela did not know she could feel any worse. She waits for Laura to object, to cushion her from Maria's blows. No objections come.

But Maria isn't being fair. Maria cannot claim to know how she feels, because Maria encouraged Giulia to go. She agreed with Father Piero, she convinced Giulia to leave. She has no right.

Carmela rouses herself now. She stands before Maria, and realizes for the first time that she has grown taller than this woman before her, this woman who claims to be a mother to her own.

"If you care so much," she says, "then why did you turn her in to be hanged?"

She doesn't wait for a response, doesn't wait for the inevitable pain in Maria's eyes. She hears Laura calling after her as she runs from the apartment, but they don't follow.

Carmela tries not to look at the apothecary as she approaches the building. She doesn't want to be reminded of that place, which is so inextricable from her mother it's impossible to understand how it didn't crumble to dust the moment La Tofana left town.

Up the stairs, Carmela can pretend it's any other building. She can pretend the scents, the herbs and the oils, don't permeate the walls and ceilings. She bursts into her own apartment, the one she shares with her mother, or did, and throws herself down on Giulia's bed to sob.

The Brokenhearted

There is a young woman
like Carmela
                        but not

sprawled on her bed
in the servants' quarters
of the finest home
in Campo Marzio,
to the northeast of the apothecary
just a few doors down from the notary's

weeping so hard
with any luck
her tears will flood the Tiber
and carry them all away.

She has spent her life in service
and though the work is difficult
she is proud of the money she makes
that supports her grandmother
so the old woman no longer
has to clean up after others.

The day this young woman
became lady's maid
to the daughter of the house
every backbreaking hour
was redeemed.

To think she was paid
to run her fingers through silken hair
to fasten and unfasten buttons on creamy skin
to cherish laughter so delicate
she replayed it over and over in her mind
long after she'd left her lady's side
each night
reluctantly.

She was indispensable.
When her lady traveled to Florence,
this maid accompanied her,
providing for her comfort away from home.
Then to Venice, to Greece, even France.

When her lady shared the news
that she would soon be married,
this maid celebrated.
Her lady would be provided for
and she could share,
for her lady's husband would never
know her the way she did.
Her lady would not need him
like she needed her.

But then it all came apart
like the seam on her lady's finest stockings
when she said,

We'll live in Florence
but you will stay here.

And so the lady's maid sobs
until she finally sleeps
her mind fragmented by dreams
of following her lady
to the ends of the earth.

Carmela is awoken some hours later by a pounding that brings her immediately back to the apothecary, a bloodied Signora Moretti at her side, a man screaming that he will kill her.

Is he back for revenge on Carmela? But no, that man is dead. Dead by Carmela's own hand, in a way.

She gropes for Maria in the bed beside her, but Maria is safe in her own bed, in her own apartment, the one Carmela ran from in a fit of rage.

The pounding continues. Carmela breathes in the scent of her mother's blankets.

"Please!" a voice calls. "Somebody help!" A woman's voice. "Signora Tofana!"

They are calling her mother and her mother cannot answer. This, more than anything else, is what propels Carmela from the bed. She is La Tofana now.

She is already dressed; she only kicked her shoes off after collapsing on the bed. She slips them on without fastening them and hurries down the stairs.

There she finds, slumped in the doorway of the apothecary, a bloodied young woman clutching her shoulder. She is no older than Carmela.

"Please." Her face is white but for the garish spots of rouge on her cheeks and lips.

Carmela looks around for anyone who might have helped this woman here, who might be able to tell her how to begin. The street is silent.

"Come in." Carmela pulls the key from the chain where it clinks against her mother's locket. She has no need of that recipe; tonight is for saving a life, not ending one.

She helps the girl inside, then locks the door behind them.

"What's your name?" Carmela encourages the girl to move her hand so she can see the wound.

"Eleonora," she gasps, relinquishing her hold on the shoulder.

"What happened, Eleonora?"

"A knife," the girl manages before slumping back against the wall where she is propped.

Carmela taps her cheek. "Stay awake, Eleonora, please. I'm going to need your help. You were stabbed?"

Eleonora nods.

Carmela makes some quick decisions. She must boil water, prepare poultices, locate salves. But the girl must have a task, so she does not drift away in Carmela's absence.

Carmela grabs a clean cloth—bless Laura for always keeping the basket replenished—and douses it with yarrow tincture. "Listen to me, Eleonora. You must hold this to the wound as firmly as you can. And you must answer my questions, so I can hear you. Do you understand?"

The girl's eyes are hazy. "I'm dying . . ."

"You are not dying. You are living." The words have flown from Carmela's mouth before she can realize they came straight from Giulia. "You have done so well, getting here. I'm going to help you."

Carmela presses the cloth into her wound, and the hand into the cloth, then rushes to complete the tasks required before properly treating a knife wound.

"How old are you?" she asks. It doesn't matter, but she must keep the girl talking.

"Fifteen," she says, voice barely audible.

"I'm sixteen," Carmela says, as though this makes them the same. As though Carmela didn't just come from a warm bed, while this girl clearly came from the docks in her cheap, scanty clothes. "Were you working?"

The girl nods. Carmela keeps her face neutral. Giulia treated the women who traded their bodies for their living with the same care as the noblewomen like Signora Moretti. She told Carmela about a priest who argued that women like Eleonora must be provided with abortions because the need for them was a hazard of their livelihood.

"And the man who did this," Carmela says. "Could he have followed you?"

"No. He only wanted to get away without paying."

Carmela settles in front of Eleonora. "I'm going to take a look, okay?"

The girl's skimpy coverings are a blessing, as there is not much soiled dress to pull away. Carmela wipes carefully around the edges, to see where the wound begins. The girl is stoic, but when Carmela gets too close, she gasps. Carmela remembers the birth of Nina's twins and reminds Eleonora to breathe. Carmela breathes deeply and slowly herself, which helps as she finds the wound and assesses its severity.

"All right, love," Carmela says, the endearment coming out as though she has known and cared for this girl their entire lives. "The wound is deep, but I don't believe it's hit anything important." That sounds ridiculous as soon as she says it; it's hit skin and flesh and probably bone, every one important. "I mean to say, it could have hit the heart or lungs, but didn't." Perhaps there's a reason Maria and Laura prefer not to speak to patients. "We're going to clean it, and stop the bleeding, and try to relieve your pain. All right?"

Without a task to focus her mind, the girl's eyes grow hazy again.

"Eleonora." Carmela presses a cloth soaked with witch hazel into the wound. The girl gasps. "Tell me about your family. Do you have brothers and sisters?"

She nods. While Carmela works, Eleonora tells her of a large family living near the banks of the Tiber, from the littlest Giacomo, who is only four, up to her brother Paolo, who is nineteen. They all live at home, except for Paolo, who has married and moved away.

Carmela is ashamed at her ignorance. For some reason she imagined the women who sold their bodies as solitary creatures with no one else in the world to care for them. Eleanora has a family. They are not worried about her yet, for they know how she spends her nights. They would not eat without the income she brings in.

But if Carmela were not here to help her, she could have bled so much she died on the street. Then her family would have missed her indeed. Not that she would deserve help any less if she had no one in the world to notice her absence. The amount Carmela has never considered about the world, about the hair-thin lines people walk every day, knocks her off-balance with each new person she helps.

Once Carmela is satisfied the wound is clean, she prepares a poultice of fresh yarrow and lavender, and presses it to the wound, wrapping bandages around the girl's shoulder to hold it in place.

"How does that feel?" Carmela asks as she prepares a willow bark tincture for the pain.

"Much better, thank you."

"You'll want to be very careful until the wound heals. I don't think any muscles were damaged, but if you continue to have pain, you should see a surgeon."

Eleonora makes a face.

"You can take this in water or ale, up to three times a day. If the skin around the wound becomes hot to the touch, or you develop a fever, take this." She holds up a tincture of feverfew and lemon balm. "If those don't help, come back to see me again, all right?"

Eleonora nods.

"If I'm not here," she adds, "the other women who work here will help you too."

Eleonora reaches for her tie-on pocket and now Carmela understands why her mother didn't charge Violetta. She motions for the young woman to put away her coins. It feels wrong to charge her for what is literally only a bandage on a life that will keep tearing her open, over and over.

Carmela eyes the girl as she gets to her feet. Her insubstantial dress leaves the bandage on display, open to the elements. Carmela looks around for a shawl Maria or Laura might have left behind, but Laura is too tidy for that.

"Wait here," Carmela says. "I'm going to be right back."

She hurries up the flight of stairs to the apartment and retrieves a shawl from her mother's things. But when she arrives back in the shop, the girl has gone, and left her coins on the counter.

CARMELA HAS CLEANED UP THE MESS, updated the record books, and started a new batch of willow bark tincture when Maria and Laura arrive at the shop to open up.

Neither says a word, as though Carmela never abandoned her duties here, as though she never stormed out of their apartment like a spoiled child.

"The blood is ready to be dried," Maria merely says as she takes her spot at her worktable and resumes wherever she left off the night before.

The Mother

There is a woman
like Eleonora's mother
                                        but not

in her home by the docks
to the northwest of the apothecary

river stench soaked into every stone
awaiting her daughter's return
the way she does in the early hours
of every morning

not worried exactly
but never relaxed either
until she hears her key in the lock.

It's honest work her daughter does,
nothing more honest really
than money for services rendered
what you see is what you get

and those services
will always be required

but always there's the lurking chance
of danger
of the customer who feels exposed
vulnerable, who lashes out to show his power.
Men are so frail that way.

So she waits, uneasy, uncertain
her daughter will return home
her whole self
her body and mind unharmed
which is silly when she examines it
for every one of her children
faces danger each time they step
outside that door, each time
they pull a little harder
on the tether to home
sometimes so hard
she's sure it will snap.

So far
her children have returned
like her daughter does now
key in the lock
and this mother finally
drops her shoulders
closes her eyes
and lets sleep pull her under.

Not back to normal, never normal without Giulia, but the remaining women of the apothecary learn to muddle forward. None of them have Giulia's charm, or her skills, or her drive, but put together, they make a reasonable understudy.

The trouble is, an understudy is only meant to be temporary.

Whenever a courier passes by, delivering news to their small corner of the world, Carmela cannot tamp down the desperate hope that there will be a letter from her mother. It does not need to say when she is coming home, or even that she is. Carmela only wants reassurance that Giulia has survived her journey and arrived somewhere safe.

But the couriers never stop at the apothecary.

CARMELA IS HELPING NINA with a teething remedy when Laura pushes her way in the front doors, overloaded with flats of small plants.

"Oh, excuse me." Carmela rushes to relieve Laura of the flat she's about to drop.

"I'd help if I could," Nina says, but the two babies in her arms are a very good excuse.

"You had luck," Carmela says. "Actual plants. I thought we'd have to grow from seed."

Laura nods and makes space in the back for the flats. "Benicio said it would be easier this way."

"Benicio?"

Color rises in Laura's cheeks at the same time a baby's wail rises from the shop front. Carmela hurries back to Nina, processing the fact that now that they've blamed Giulia for Signor Moretti's death, Benicio has come around to helping the remaining women of Tofana Apothecary.

It's a good thing, but also.

"You can rub this on their gums whenever they're distressed," she says to Nina of the teething remedy.

"Thank you," Nina says. "You've been so helpful."

Carmela smiles as the second baby joins in the wailing chorus. "Any time."

She follows Nina to the door to hold it open for her, but ends up holding it for Violetta Raso to sail on through.

"What do you want?" Carmela snaps.

Violetta blanches. "Good morning. I was wondering if there's anything you can give me for the pain my stepmother has in her joints?"

Carmela marches past to take her spot behind the counter. She feels powerful there. Or at least, more powerful than when the two of them are on even ground. "Oh, is your mother in pain? That's too bad."

Violetta holds her gaze for a beat. "If you can't help me, I can—"

"Don't scare off the customers," Maria mutters as she passes by the archway.

She's right. Carmela hates it, but she's right. Giulia waited on everyone with the same poise and grace. Carmela is La Tofana now. She takes a deep breath.

"Is the pain constant, or only on exertion?"

A flicker of surprise crosses Violetta's face at Carmela's civility. "Um, I think it's worse in the mornings?"

Oh, to know how her mother felt at any given time of day, to be able to hand her a remedy to make up for destroying her life. Carmela retrieves the tincture of turmeric and ginger, and, upon her return, slams it down on the counter in front of Violetta. "You can pay this time, can't you?"

"Of course." Violetta fishes the coins out of her pocket. "Before I couldn't pay because if my father knew—"

"I understand. That would be terrible if something came between you and your parents."

Violetta falters, but is saved by the ring of the shop bell. Perhaps they are both saved. Carmela wants to be better than her worst instincts, but also, Violetta does not deserve her grace.

"Good morning, Signor Stiatessi," she says in an extra-warm voice to the cantankerous old goat. "What can I do for you this morning?"

He purses his lips tight, then looks around her toward the archway. "I don't suppose Signora Tofana is . . . ?"

Carmela waits, unsure if he's hoping the fugitive apothecary is hiding in the back, ready to help the patients who need her most, or if he's a man with reason to fear his wife, out for her blood.

"I'm afraid not. But I'm certain I can help you with whatever you need."

Violetta backs away from the counter, but she lingers by the electuaries.

Signor Stiatessi lets out an exasperated huff. "It's my toothache again." He glares at Carmela, daring her to know the remedy.

She is La Tofana now. She glides as her mother would have, brisk, but not rushed, and retrieves the clove tincture. She beams at the old goat as though he is her favorite customer in all the world as she hands him the remedy and he hands her his coins.

"Keeping steady with the application is very important," she tells him as he heads for the door.

"Yes, yes, I know." He waves her off, irritated. "Bossy," he says to Violetta. "Like her mother."

As he leaves, Violetta returns to the counter. She sets her coins down and takes the remedy for her stepmother, but she doesn't leave.

Carmela ignores her and goes about her business, marking both transactions in the record book.

"Is your . . . is your mother all right?"

Carmela snaps the book shut. "How should I know? And why should you care?" She whirls around and heads for the back room.

"I do care! So much! Carmela, she saved my life."

Carmela shouldn't engage. She should hold her head high and glide through the apothecary as though she can't be bothered with what anyone says about her, her mother, Maria, or Laura. But try as she might, she is not La Tofana. She's a girl who may not ever see her mother again.

She whirls around. "And yet you'll dump garbage on her assistant in the street, shouting about witches?"

There's a moment where Violetta might be able to deny it, where an unrepentant person could feign ignorance, but that is not who stands before Carmela right now. Violetta's face crumples.

"I knew it."

"I'm sorry!" Violetta's voice wobbles. "I'm so sorry."

"Tell that to Laura," Carmela says. "In fact— Laura! Come out here!"

There's a long pause in which Carmela regrets bringing Laura into this. A confrontation will only make things worse for her. Carmela is being selfish. But Laura is still recovering her place in the shop, eager to show Carmela and Maria that she is a committed part of the team.

She appears in the archway. "Yes?"

"This is Laura," Carmela says, though Violetta surely knows who she is, surely has seen Laura at the apothecary and passed her in the street. Laura may have been present at the births of some of her siblings. "She's worked here for years. She grinds the arnica that goes in your mother's remedy there."

"I do that," Maria hollers from the back.

"She tended the pennyroyal and rue in your abortive remedy—"

"Please," Violetta pleads, checking to make sure there's no one else in the shop.

"That was Benicio," says a miserable Laura.

"Hush," Carmela says. Why are they making this so hard for her? Why isn't Maria, at the very least, out here helping her skewer this horrible girl? "And yet you abuse her and scream at her. Would you have done it to my mother, if you'd seen her at the chandler's stall? Or would that have been too dangerous? The witch might curse you on the spot. Or worse, she might tell your mother what we helped you do!"

"I'm sorry!" Tears stream down Violetta's face, but Carmela feels no pity. "My stepmother saw Laura there, and she was saying horrible things about you all."

Carmela blinks at her. "Is that supposed to make her feel better?"

"She noticed when I didn't agree, didn't jump in. You know what she suspects—"

"The truth?"

"It's fine," Laura whispers.

"It's not fine!"

"I had to do something to keep her from accusing me outright, from telling my father."

Carmela shakes her head. "You're pathetic."

"I know."

"Carmela, stop." Laura steps out into the front. "This isn't what your mother would want."

Carmela looks from Laura's pleading face, to Violetta's. Why is it always about what everyone else wants, when she is the one who wants the most of all? "Well, she's not here, is she?"

When nearly a week passes without word from Eleonora, Carmela begins to fret. She replays her parting conversation with the girl. Did Carmela tell her to return so she could change the wound's dressing?

"She'll be fine," Maria says. "Or she won't. But either way, you did what you could do."

Not if she didn't tell her to come back in. Carmela cannot let the possibility go. "Maybe I should go looking for her."

"Did your mother go tracking down every patient for follow-ups?"

Not since Carmela has watched her run the apothecary. But Giulia also didn't go from apprentice to proprietress overnight. Perhaps when she was younger, when she had more time and less confidence, she did second-guess herself and follow up unnecessarily.

CARMELA IS NOT FOOLISH ENOUGH to venture down to the docks alone at night. So she waits until Sunday when the shop is closed. She packs what she needs to change the wound's dressing and makes her way to the docks in the bright morning sunlight.

She doesn't know where Eleonora lives precisely, but it's a distinctive enough name. She can ask around, and surely someone will know where Eleonora lives with her seven siblings. Her oldest brother was Paolo, Carmela remembers, and the youngest was Giacomo. She listened well, even if she forgot to tell the girl to come back in a few days.

As she draws nearer to the docks, the air takes on the distinctive stench of the Tiber river. A large ship has recently come in, and men stream down the gangplank, some of them carting massive boxes. Languages Carmela doesn't recognize dance through the air around her.

A boy runs past Carmela from behind, knocking her off-balance. A woman around her mother's age grabs Carmela's arm to keep her from falling. "Watch where you're going," the woman says, moving on before Carmela can thank her.

An older man leans on a cart at the side of the road, his produce spread out for sale before him. "Fancy an apple, love?"

Carmela digs into her pocket for a coin. She'll take the apple, but hopefully the coin will buy her more than a piece of fruit. "Signor, can I ask, do you know of a young woman named Eleonora? Around my age, with seven siblings?"

He looks at her with filmy eyes.

"Maybe fifteen years old?" she adds. "I believe she lives near here."

"Can't say that I do," he says, coughing on the produce before him.

"Thank you, anyway." Carmela pockets the apple and looks around. How ridiculous was she, thinking she could find Eleonora simply by pointing herself toward the part of town where the working girls congregate. Eleonora had said she lived near the river, but the Tiber stretches all the way through Rome.

A group of young sailors come talking and laughing boisterously down the gangplank, all coiled muscles and unspent energy.

"Ahoy, Signorina!" one of them calls, waving at Carmela. She waves back, hesitant.

He comes directly to her, his friends trailing him. "I've been two months at sea." The pungent scent wafting off him attests to the truth of the statement. "Will you take five baiocchi?"

Carmela does not process what he means until someone pushes her aside: a woman—a girl really—with rouged lips and a tattered dress.

"She's not for sale, boys," the girl says with a sidelong glance at Carmela.

The young men explode in laughter, and Carmela is forgotten and ashamed for some reason she cannot pinpoint as the working girl leads them away, discussing her price.

"Wait!" Carmela calls. The whole group stops and turns back. The sailor's face is bright, hopeful, as though perhaps Carmela will offer up her goods after all. But Carmela speaks to the young woman. "Do you know Eleonora?"

She wrinkles her brow in confusion and shakes her head. "You should go home, sweetie."

But maybe Eleonora doesn't use her real name at the dock. "Please, she's fifteen. A touch shorter than I am. Reddish curls?"

One of the men hoots. "Lead me to her!"

The girl gives Carmela an apologetic shrug, then turns away without another word.

This was foolishness. Yet again, she should have listened to Maria. She turns back in the direction of the city center.

"Hey!" One of the sailors has broken away from the group and lopes toward Carmela. "I know Eleonora."

"You do?"

"Sure. Redhead, about this tall?" He holds up his hand.

"Yes, exactly. Are you Paolo?"

He grins, gap-toothed and friendly. "That's me."

"Oh thank goodness. She was badly hurt while you were at sea. I bandaged her up, but I wanted to check on her."

"I'll take you to her." He motions toward a quieter side street.

"Thank you." Carmela joins him, relief flooding her. Eleonora is almost certainly fine, but Carmela needs to see it with her own eyes.

He doesn't know how his sister was so badly hurt, but perhaps he can guess. When a horse and cart turn down the alley behind them, Paolo puts himself between Carmela and the cart, shielding her from the muck in its wake.

She has never walked like this, side by side, with a young man down a city street. With any man. Another person has never shielded her from harm, except Giulia, in her way. "Thank you."

He nods but does not put distance between them once the cart has passed. Carmela's shoulder brushes the rough wall to one side, and Paolo crowds her on her other side. He smells of the sea, in all its unfathomable darkness. Earthier things too—sweat and grime and men confined to close quarters.

"Did you get a good catch?" Carmela squeaks, crouching to adjust a boot that has not come unfastened. "Of fish, I mean? You're a fisherman?" A miscalculation, for he only steps closer, his filthy pants at her eye level, enormous hand outstretched to envelop hers and help her up.

"Oh yes, the fish are so eager they nearly jump into our ship."

This is Eleonora's brother; he's leading her to her patient. Sailors are used to close quarters; his months at sea have made him forget social strictures.

"I imagine you're looking forward to seeing your wife after all this time."

"My wife?" He laughs.

Carmela's stomach twists. She looks back over her shoulder in the desperate hope of a witness, someone lurking in the shadows, but the street is quiet.

"Eleonora said you've married and moved out of the family home . . ."

His gait stutters for the briefest moment. "Ah, yes. Eleonora."

The name has never passed his lips before today.

"I—I should return to my apothecary." Carmela stops. "If Eleonora needs to see me, she can come by." She turns back the way they came, but the young sailor grabs her arm.

"What, that's it?"

"Yes. I—I made a mistake. I—"

"What mistake? I'm helping you."

"Yes, well, I've changed my mind. I didn't realize we'd have to walk so far—"

"We don't have to walk." He boxes her in against the wall, muscled arms caging her, making her the wild animal. His breath is hot and sour on her face.

"Signor, I—"

No clever quip will save her here. No fellowship of women, loving support, useless. All the times she wondered how the force that is Maria could ever have been cowed by her lout of a husband rain down upon her in a torrent of shame. For Carmela is frozen between the desire to flee and the knowledge that one wrong move could mean a dagger to her throat.

"If you want money, I—"

"I don't want money."

He presses the length of his body against hers, and Carmela twists her head as far as it will go to the side, to avoid his leering eyes, his jagged teeth, to avoid her unforgivable carelessness a second longer, to pretend she is not trapped in this awful moment but safe where her mother tried to keep her, Giulia had known the world is a cruel, filthy sailor who will rip what he wants from your unwilling hands and leave you shattered on the stones without a backward glance.

He's grabbing at her skirts now, pawing and tugging, fabric rips, and with it something inside Carmela rips open too, a scream from the deepest part of her, the sound an animal makes just before the slaughter.

He laughs at her as one hand finds her thigh. "You think anyone cares down here when a girl screams?" His other hand seizes her face and forces it toward his.

It's instinct, nothing more, that leads Carmela to twist her head and clamp her teeth down on his foul hand. She holds fast, digs in, tastes blood until his other hand is off her thigh and striking her across the face before he leaps back, clutching his bloodied hand to his chest.

"Bitch!" he howls, and in that moment, Carmela knows it was a mistake; she cannot trust her instincts. Now he is feral, lunging forward, uninjured hand gripping her throat, knocking her head back against the stones of this place so inured to violence no one will notice when she suffocates.

A scream in the distance, Carmela barely registers it, it cannot be for her, no one is coming to her aid and they shouldn't, she deserves what she's getting for her foolishness, her arrogance, her—

Glass shatters, shards explode past Carmela's face as the sailor grunts and releases her, crumples to the cobblestones clutching his head, revealing Violetta Raso, the neck of a broken bottle in one hand, the other darting out to grab Carmela.

"Come on!" she shouts, and none of this makes sense, that Violetta Raso should be here, should come to her defense, that they should overpower a man like this, who sees what he wants and takes it.

He's not overpowered, though, only distracted, and now staggering to his feet.

"Now, Carmela, we have to run!" Violetta keeps a firm hold on the broken glass in her hand as she jerks Carmela out of her stupor and they run. They run together.

"You cunts!" the man shouts behind them.

They run and they keep running, melting into the bustling waterfront, still running, cursing heavy skirts that slow them down, but also—Carmela realizes almost hysterically—those despised skirts were a barrier, those skirts delayed the sailor's hands just long enough for her avenging angel to appear and smite him.

The Sailor

There is a man
like this sailor
                                        but not

on the dock near Porto di Ripetta
west of the apothecary

finding his land legs
after weeks aboard the fishing vessel
that carried him along the curves of the Tiber
before bursting into the Tyrrhenian Sea,
Mediterranean blue and endless

not that he spent much time
enjoying the view

what with the backbreaking work
eighteen hours every day
shoulder to shoulder
with his fellows
everyone reeking to high heaven
the fresh fish guts an improvement
over the sailors

but now he's early man
emerging from the sea
trying on these strange appendages;
stirrings, desires long dormant
are suddenly insatiable

as his legs gain surety beneath him
and propel him in search of
something to slake his thirst.

When he finds it
he will deserve it, devour it
demolish it.

He has earned it.

Carmela only makes it back to the shop because Violetta guides her. The blocks between the alley and safety are a haze of pounding heart and pounding feet, hand held fast by the most unlikely of champions.

On the doorstep of the apothecary, Violetta drops her hand, and Carmela is lost.

"Carmela?" Violetta asks when Carmela doesn't move to go inside. "You live upstairs, don't you?"

She does, she lives upstairs, at least when her mother is here, but now she sleeps at Maria's. Does she live there? And if Giulia never returns, what then? Where does Carmela belong?

"There's blood." Violetta brushes a hand against the shoulder of Carmela's dress. "Is it yours?"

The blood on her shoulder focuses Carmela's mind. "What about Eleonora?" she asks.

Violetta frowns. "You can tell me about Eleonora inside. Let's clean you up."

Violetta leads Carmela up the stairs. It's freezing and stale inside the apartment, and Violetta finds no coals to coax into flame. "When was the last time you built a fire?"

Carmela shrugs. "I'm staying with Maria."

"Oh, I'm sorry! Shall I take you there?"

But no, even if it is freezing and stale, Carmela would rather be surrounded by her mother's possessions, the life they built together before Carmela ruined everything. She strips off her bodice and skirts, down to her shift, as Violetta starts a fire. She would burn those things the sailor put his hands on, if she had the luxury. She will settle for scrubbing them until they are fit for a Medici. Her jaw is sore where he struck her, but the bloodstains are his.

When Carmela is newly dressed in Giulia's clothes, Violetta has a fire blazing, tea made, and windows opened to air out the musty room.

Carmela eyes her, suddenly shy. "Why are you helping me?"

Violetta laughs quietly. "You are my wife."

"What?"

"I do remember our wedding."

Carmela takes that in, sits at the table, and accepts the tea.

"Anyway," Violetta says, "I could ask you the same thing. Why did you help me?"

"Because my mother made me."

At that, Violetta laughs full out, a joyous sound Carmela isn't sure she's ever heard, despite knowing this girl for so many years. Violetta joins Carmela at the table. "Are you all right?"

Carmela nods, but winces at the pain in her jaw. "I will be."

Violetta is quiet, but Carmela feels her pulsing with unasked questions.

"What were you doing down at the docks?" Carmela asks.

Violetta's eyes fly open wide. "What was *I*?" When Carmela simply waits for a response, she relents. "My stepmother sends me down on Sunday mornings when the fishing boats are due in. The fish is fresher and cheaper than when it's gotten to the vendors' stalls. What were you doing?"

Carmela stops and starts several times, trying to explain about Eleonora, her wound, her brother Paolo, her need for a change of dressing, but it never sounds reasonable. "It was stupid," she finally mumbles into her teacup.

"It wasn't," Violetta says quickly. "It was kind. You were trying to help her."

Violetta is kind—perhaps the most startling discovery in a day full of uncomfortable new knowledge. Carmela still feels exceedingly foolish. She didn't help Eleonora, and what was more, she'd walked herself straight into danger. Who was she to think Eleonora needed her help at all? That young woman survives on those docks every day, but one morning there and Carmela is still shaking.

"I was stupid," she says.

"Stop saying that." Violetta sets her hand on Carmela's. "Your mother wouldn't—"

Carmela snatches her hand away. "Don't act like you know what my mother would do or say about any of this."

Violetta sits back, stung. "Fine. I only know she never made me feel foolish about everything with Antonio."

"Why would you feel foolish?"

"I thought he loved me. I gave him my purity"—she holds up her hands as Carmela opens her mouth—"and I know I'm not a spoiled piece of fruit, but some of us live in a world that believes I am, and now he's marrying another girl. So yes. I feel foolish."

Carmela sets her hand back on the table. "Do you think he feels foolish?" When Violetta looks up in confusion, Carmela clarifies: "Antonio."

"Are you serious?"

"Deadly," Carmela says. "He certainly should. I once saw him put an entire toad inside his mouth."

This startles a laugh out of Violetta. "What?!"

"We were only six or seven. But still, I bet you've never put a toad in your mouth."

Violetta giggles and stirs her tea.

Carmela sits back, satisfied with the laughter she's gotten out of Violetta. Carmela has laughed nearly every day of her life, mostly thanks to Maria. But she suspects Violetta has not used the same muscles as often.

If only there were more to laugh about.

The Laughing Girl

There is a girl
like Carmela
                    but not

in the alley behind San Giacomo of the Incurables
to the east of the apothecary

emptying bedpans and reminding herself
there are worse things than waste

for example
she could be
one of the poor souls inside
afflicted by the pox,
beset with livid red pustules
then foul-smelling abscesses
that eat into the bone
moaning through the night
of the pain, the humiliation

the inevitability of
            (depending who you ask)
the French disease
the Gallic disease
the Spanish disease
the British disease
the Portuguese disease
the Polish disease
the German disease

the Chinese pox
the Persian fire
the Hindu disease
the Christian disease

everyone pointing pustuled fingers
at someone else
someone
        other
someone to be feared
meanwhile
all of them die in agony

and through it all somehow
this girl in the alley
finds reason each day
to return to the paupers' hospital
and carry out her thankless tasks
for it could be worse

and sometimes
more often than you would think
she finds a reason to laugh.

It should, perhaps, not come as such a shock when Carmela walks into the apothecary a few days later to find Violetta in the back room, helping Maria record inventory.

"What are you doing?" Carmela gasps, unclear whether she's talking to Maria or Violetta or the very bones of the apothecary, to have let such a travesty occur.

"I'm helping," Violetta says. "I came for some lavender pastilles, and Maria asked if I could—"

"Maria!" Carmela wheels on Maria, who stands with her arms folded, jaw set, as though she has been expecting this from tiresome, hysterical Carmela. "What were you thinking?"

"I don't see the problem." Maria hands Violetta a jar to open. Carmela snatches it from her before Violetta can reach for it.

"We can't let just anyone go through our inventory!"

Violetta may have helped her at the docks, but she is the same girl who threw refuse on Laura's head, who screamed at her about being a witch. Her uncle is a notary who loathes the apothecary.

"We're sorting fungicides." Maria's tone implies Carmela is the one who has lost her senses. But Carmela is the only one thinking straight. Her own mother didn't let her back here until she had proven herself. Violetta has proven nothing.

She turns on Violetta instead. "Why are you here? Why are you always here?"

"I don't know!" Violetta grabs the jar out of Carmela's hand. "Maybe I like it here!"

Carmela fumes, at a loss for words.

Violetta carefully notes the name on the jar's label and marks it on her inventory list before speaking. "You're so lucky," she says quietly.

"Lucky? I may never see my mother again."

"And my mother is dead."

Carmela freezes. For all her years of fury with Violetta Raso always getting her way, she has failed to consider the one way Violetta is far more impoverished than she is.

Violetta sets down the inventory book. "It doesn't really heal anything, to compare wounds. But this shop, this life? Coming here every day instead of chasing little siblings and wiping snotty noses and never being destined for anything more? Can't you see what that might mean to me? Can't you see how lucky you are?"

Carmela's breath comes faster, her throat tightens. She is furious at this entitled girl before her, furious that Violetta saw her weak and shaken, that Violetta rescued her in that alley. Furious that Violetta has her own wounds. She does not want to owe this girl anything.

"I'm the luckiest girl in the world!" Carmela cries out, flinging arms wide and knocking a crock off Laura's worktable.

Violetta lunges to clean up the spilled almond oil.

"Leave it," Carmela snaps. "I don't need your help."

"Yes, you do," Maria says.

"Not from her!" Facing Maria, Carmela lets the tears fall down her cheeks. She already owes Maria everything. She has no dignity to lose.

"Don't be absurd. All your mother's taught you about never turning away those in need? It goes both ways."

"We could have done without Father Piero's help," Carmela says, voice low as Violetta carries the dustpan to the fireplace.

"No, we couldn't. Without Father Piero, your mother wouldn't have been able to help the women who needed her most."

"But we don't know if we can trust her—"

"There are always risks. That doesn't mean we stop doing the work."

"I think I got everything," Violetta says. "I'm sorry to have bothered you."

"Are you good with numbers?" Maria asks as Violetta heads for the door.

"What, me?"

"What are you doing?" Carmela grabs Maria's arm, but Maria pats her hand like she meant it as an act of affection.

"Now that Laura's busy keeping up an entire garden, we could use some help with the books."

"Not her!" Carmela's cheeks blaze in indignation.

"She's here all the time anyway. She wants to be here and she already knows our secrets."

"Not all of them," Carmela mutters.

Maria turns back to Violetta. "We can't pay you, you understand. But if you'd like to learn, we'll teach you what we know."

"Maria!" Maria turns slowly to meet Carmela's gaze, fire in her eyes. "My mother wouldn't—"

But Maria cuts her off. "Finish that sentence, young lady. What wouldn't your mother do, exactly? Very few things, which is how she saved my life and this young woman's too."

Another tear falls. Maria is right, but she is also so, so wrong. They don't let just anyone in. They can't trust blindly. That's how Carmela doomed them all with Signora Moretti and Acqua Tofana.

"I'm . . . I'm quite good with numbers," Violetta says.

Maria turns to Carmela, expectant, waiting. She is La Tofana now. It is ultimately up to her, even if it feels like she has absolutely zero control over anything.

They do need the help, because her mother is gone, which is Carmela's fault. How is she to stand in the way of a clear solution? If Maria thinks this is such a good idea, then Carmela will show her the results.

"Fine," she grits out. "Be here at eight tomorrow morning."

When Carmela comes downstairs the next morning, Violetta stands in the doorway, bright-eyed and eager. Carmela is tempted to turn back around and hide under the covers for the rest of the day. But if she does that, Maria will likely be teaching Violetta how to make Acqua Tofana the next time Carmela comes downstairs.

"Good morning," Violetta chirps.

Carmela scowls at her and unlocks the door.

"Shall I build up the fire?" Violetta asks. "Or get straight to the books?"

"Laura will show you the books when she gets here."

Violetta pauses, but when no more instructions are forthcoming, she makes a decision to go forward with building up the fire.

Carmela marches to where Laura keeps the record books and opens them at the counter, poring over nothing, staring at numbers in Laura's precise handwriting, in order to look like she's doing something, like she's important. She turns a page, and her eyes land on her mother's elegant but hurried script, which brings infuriating tears to her eyes. She turns away from Violetta to dash them from her face without an audience.

Violetta isn't even watching her. Or at least, she isn't being obvious about it. She's absorbed with the fire, and Carmela hates her a little when she coaxes a flame to life as easily as she coaxed all the children to play whatever she wanted.

Violetta's life isn't perfect. Or even easy. Carmela wouldn't trade the life she's had or the life before her for Violetta's lot. But she resists a shift away from seeing Violetta as the girl who's always gotten what she wanted.

She's here, isn't she? For no other reason than she happened to be on hand and Maria had a whim. Then again, Violetta wouldn't have given Patrizia Moretti the vial of Acqua Tofana. She wouldn't have sent Eleonora away without all the necessary instructions. Perhaps Carmela should run away like her mother and leave Violetta to be the new face of the shop.

When Violetta has the fire crackling nicely, she hauls water in and sets it to boiling. Then she locates the broom and begins to sweep the shop front, without being asked.

Carmela rains down a curse on her cheery, helpful servitude. Or at least she would if she knew any curses.

"When you said my mother was a witch," she says on impulse, and Violetta's cheer falters, "what did you mean? Did you truly believe she could turn you into a toad?"

Violetta continues sweeping, but more slowly. Finally she says, "I've apologized. To you and to her. I'll keep apologizing, but honestly I don't know how I can—"

"I'm not asking for an apology. I'm truly curious. What did you believe?"

It's a long time before Violetta speaks again. Carmela isn't sure if she's ignoring her or calculating which answer will infuriate Carmela the least.

"Honestly, Carmela? I don't know. I'm not trying to avoid answering. I'm trying to remember and all I recall is that adults said so, and I believed them. Or at least I parroted them."

"So you had no original thought?"

"How much did you have at that age?"

Carmela remembers all the sheep-children doing whatever Violetta declared, while Carmela's suggestions got ignored. "More than you did."

Violetta sighs. "That's probably true."

While Violetta continues to sweep the shop front, Carmela moves to the back and sits at Maria's worktable. A basket of lemon balm waits to be garbled and ground. With nothing else to do until customers arrive, Carmela plucks the leaves from the stems and drops them into her mortar.

"Can I help with that?"

She startles at Violetta's appearance in the back room. She worked for years to be worthy of this space. She respected her mother's wishes, she learned from afar, she waited patiently.

"You can't be back here."

"Oh." Violetta's brow wrinkles. She was back here with Maria the day before, sorting fungicides.

"Come on." Carmela hustles her out to the front. "You finished sweeping?"

"Even my stepmother would approve of those floors."

Carmela cocks her head and considers Violetta. "What did you tell her?"

"My stepmother?"

"About where you were going to be all day. If she hates us so much, surely she wouldn't approve."

"Oh, she'd immediately succumb to the vapors."

Carmela giggles, then berates herself for rewarding Violetta's attempt at humor. Still, she can't help but respond, "That seems unlikely. Vapors arise from a melancholy uterus. But your stepmother is constantly pregnant."

Violetta wrinkles her nose. "A melancholy uterus?"

"Well," Carmela says. "Physicians say an awful lot of things about women's bodies without any basis whatsoever."

Violetta reaches out for Carmela's hand and breathes in her fingers, aromatic with lemon balm. "That's lovely."

Carmela is too shocked to pull her hand back. "*Melissa officinalis.* Calms nerves and relaxes muscles."

"Pregnant or not, my stepmother could probably use some of that."

Carmela retrieves the basket of lemon balm and the mortar and pestle. She holds it out for Violetta to smell the herbs she's already ground.

"It's so much stronger!"

"The leaves are dotted with tiny pockets of aromatic oils. The grinding helps release them." Carmela pushes the mortar across the counter to Violetta. "Here, you try." She strips the leaves from several more sprigs of lemon balm, placing them in the mortar.

Violetta picks up the pestle like it's a highly complex instrument and not meant only for blunt force.

"Go on, grind them."

Doubtful, Violetta pushes the leaves around in the mortar.

"Not like that." Carmela pulls the mortar in front of herself and demonstrates. "Like this."

"I'm sorry." Violetta shrinks. "You said grind. I'm not sure how else—"

"Put your shoulder into it!" Carmela pushes it back in front of Violetta. "It's for a remedy, not a meringue!"

Violetta takes the pestle again and mashes the leaves in the mortar with more force, perhaps imagining they are Carmela's face. "I thought I was supposed to be doing the books," she grumbles.

"I'm starting you off simply," Carmela says. "At least I thought I was." But then she nods in approval. "That's better."

The Friends

There are two women
like Carmela and Violetta
                                        but not

bringing in the laundry
that hangs between their windows
over the north end of the Ortaccio
so close to the apothecary
Carmela could hear their bickering
if she stepped outside

who have been at each other's throats
and in each other's hearts
for more than fifty years

and though they squabbled as children
and nursed petty grievances as teens
and coveted each other's husbands

and judged each other's cooking
and griped at each other's faults
and prodded at each other's insecurities

they are starting to see the end of the road
as all around them more people they've known
have died than not.

The older one
        by sixteen months

    and the younger one
    never lets her forget it
has lost her parents,
her siblings, two of four children
and most recently her husband

who she loved from girlhood
trusted him, relied on him
mourned him deeply.

The younger never had children
but her husband is dying now
and she's ready

though she'd never say it aloud
to anyone but this friend
who even now is tugging too hard
in the opposite direction on the clothesline.

There will be relief
in the end to his suffering
but no matter how quiet the house
in his absence, in the lack of children
in the unlucky fate of outliving most
people she's known

she will not be lonely.

She will haul her laundry
to the fountain every day,
meeting her friend there.

They will scrub side by side
and tell each other everything
that's happened since they last
scrubbed stains from cloth
the day before

and trudge back with heavier baskets
water-laden clothes and rags
which they'll hang from the line
between their windows
griping at each other
over who takes up more space
and who jostles the line out of reach

and it occurs to her to worry
that living alone she may not need
to do laundry every day
but her older friend's husband
died nearly a year ago
and she has continued
the daily ritual

so it seems
there will always
be stains to scrub.

By the time Maria arrives, they've ground the entire basket of lemon balm that had been sitting at her worktable.

"Good morning, girls," she says.

Carmela ignores her look of told-you-so at the sight of them getting along. "Where's Laura? She should be the one to explain the books to Violetta."

"Stopping by Benicio's," Maria says mildly. "It looks like you've found ways to keep busy. How early did you get here?"

The shop bell rings, and Carmela peeks out to see little Serafina, with her mother this time. "Good morning, welcome to Tofana Apothecary." She glides out to make her best effort as the face of the shop.

"Good morning." Serafina's mother nods and then browses the shelves.

But Serafina runs straight up to Carmela at the counter. She stands on her tiptoes and motions for Carmela to lean close. "I have a secret," she says.

Carmela widens her eyes. "Well. Secrets are powerful."

The little girl nods, pleased that Carmela understands. "It's about you."

Carmela keeps her voice even. "Is that so?"

"Lucrecia told me."

Carmela has no idea who Lucrecia is, but it doesn't matter. She steels herself for this child's worst. But then her mother calls her to her side. Serafina goes, with a longing look at Carmela.

As they continue to browse, Carmela retrieves the water Violetta put on to boil. If this little girl thinks Carmela is a witch, she may as well give her a story to tell her little friends. She places a handful of butterfly pea flowers into a glass jug, and then pours the hot water on top. The moment the water touches the petals, it turns a brilliant blue.

Carmela doesn't look up, but she cannot miss the slight intake of breath from across the shop.

Next Carmela retrieves a jar of citric acid from the back, ignoring Maria's inquisitive look. At the counter, she makes sure Serafina is watching, and then pours a spoonful of the powder into the bright blue tea. Instantly it turns from lapis blue to a lush magenta purple.

Serafina gasps. Her mother frowns and draws the girl closer to her side.

Carmela carries on, decanting the vivid liquid into empty vials, as though it is a mysterious potion and not an ordinary tea, as common in some parts of the world as ginger or chamomile.

Serafina's mother pays for a facial serum and a menstrual tonic, and then hurries from the shop with her daughter in tow. But no sooner has the door shut behind them than the bell sounds again. Serafina runs back in, alone this time.

"My friends say," she whispers urgently across the counter to Carmela, "that you're magic."

Little Serafina could knock Carmela over with a breath. She stands there, eyes wide, uncertain whether Carmela is going to laugh at her or scold her or shoo her from the shop.

Instead, Carmela leans across the counter, conspiratorial. "I am," she says, and pushes one of the vials of butterfly pea flower tea across the counter at Serafina. "Take this. It makes you magic too."

THE NEXT TIME THE SHOP BELL RINGS, it's not a customer.

"I've got mandrake!" Laura beams as she holds out a basket full of the pale tubers.

Maria hoots in celebration and abandons Violetta to examine Laura's treasure.

Laura's cheeks are flushed, likely from excitement and the cool morning air, but Carmela cannot help but tease.

"And what did you do to get that mandrake, Laura?"

She goes from rose water to vermilion in an instant. "Nothing!"

"What's mandrake for?" Violetta asks from the archway.

Laura nearly drops her basket at the sight, but Maria is happy to swoop it away to the back, where she will no doubt take the final steps necessary to finish the large order of rheumatism cream.

"We use it in a cream for the joints," Carmela says. "Your stepmother might find it helpful. Our supply has been low for a while, but now Laura did wicked things to procure some—"

"I did not!"

Carmela grins and hugs Laura as she bustles past her to the safety of her worktable.

Violetta laughs, uncertain. She doesn't understand what this mandrake means to them and all they've gone through to get it. But she's still happy for them.

It doesn't heal the gaping wounds, but it's a start.

The convent's herbal workshop is vastly larger than Tofana Apothecary's. Great vats of bubbling potions are overseen by a humorless sister who looks up when Giulia enters the room but does not say a word.

The Mother Superior told Giulia when she arrived that she would be welcome and her gifts were in fact needed. But the sister in charge of the apothecary does not seem at all interested in Giulia's help.

For the thousandth time since pulling herself up the hill to the convent's gates, Giulia feels the urge to flee. For all her mistakes, surely trusting a convent to be her place of refuge is the biggest. Giulia stays out of the humorless sister's way, or at least she tries to. It shouldn't be difficult in such a large workshop, and yet everywhere Giulia moves, it seems she is underfoot.

Giulia peruses the stores of dried herbs, and there the sister is, reaching past her for a jar of mugwort.

She peeks in the boiling pots and there the sister is, waiting to stir whichever one Giulia is blocking.

She looks over the array of herbs growing in pots along the windowsill and there the sister is, impatient to pluck some thyme.

"I hope I'm not disturbing you too much," Giulia says.

"I am used to working alone." The sister does not introduce

herself, but Giulia is almost certain the Mother Superior referred to the head herbalist as Sister Francesca.

"Sister Francesca, is it?"

The nun looks up sharply from where she stands, chopping thin branches of wood into small pieces, but says nothing.

"It's a lot of work for one person."

"I have many helpers. They know how to stay out of my way."

Giulia ducks aside as Sister Francesca bustles importantly toward the back of the room to retrieve another armful of the wood she is preparing. Guaiac wood, Giulia is almost certain.

Giulia does not need to befriend the prickly nun, and she knows better than to mistake her abrasiveness for a kinship with Maria. But Giulia is not used to working alone. She is used to sharing space with women she relies on; she is used to being needed. And if she cannot have that, she at least wants to do something that resembles her normal days. If she cannot have Carmela, at least she can have the plants, the minerals, the knowledge that might help someone.

"I wonder," she says, peering out the window onto the large garden, "do you grow rue here, or pennyroyal?"

Sister Francesca answers deliberately, which is to say she doesn't truly answer at all. "We have no use for rue or pennyroyal."

Giulia remembers this dance. She hasn't set foot in a church since that awful night all those years ago, and she hasn't dealt with church people, aside from Father Piero, who hardly counts, but in an instant she remembers every step of this careful waltz around what one means to say while saying nothing of the sort, but always making one's meaning clear.

"No?" She's almost certain she spots a patch of pennyroyal through the window. It takes all her self-control not to point it out. "Pennyroyal is excellent for muscle spasms—"

"And rue is excellent for joint pain, but that's not why you want them."

A week ago, Giulia scarcely believed the Mother Superior when she told Giulia she ought to make herself useful in the herbalists' workshop.

"Are there any particular needs I might fulfill?" Giulia had asked the Mother Superior. They were a community of women of all ages. Surely the need for menstrual remedies, nerve tonics, and joint balms was no different inside these walls than outside.

But the Mother Superior waved her off. "Oh no, child, we have our own herbalists for that."

Giulia was confused, but that wouldn't stop her from poking at this irritable Sister Francesca.

"The Mother Superior told me I was to continue making the same things I've always made."

The sister places a handful of small wood pieces into a mortar and begins to grind them, carrying on as though she hasn't heard Giulia. Giulia is unaccustomed to being ignored.

"And I suspect," she goes on, "that's because the convent's had need of my particular expertise in the past."

Sister Francesca's eyes dart to the exit, as though she would very much prefer to be anywhere else in this moment.

"I'm happy to make sure the guaiac doesn't boil over if there's somewhere else you need to be," Giulia says sweetly.

Sister Francesca narrows her eyes. "You know the holy wood cure?"

"Of course." Giulia peeks into the vat where guaiac bark shavings boil endlessly. "It's not something I make, though, since I'm not able to monitor patients throughout the treatment."

The sister skims the foam off one of the boiling vats and spreads it thin on a slab of stone to dry.

“For the pox sores?” Giulia asks.

Sister Francesca nods brusquely.

“Are there many sisters with the pox, then?”

Sister Francesca drops her spatula with a clatter. “Of course not!”

Giulia smiles, the picture of innocence. The picture of Carmela.

“We have a ward of pox patients we care for, those whose cases even San Giacomo of the Incurables will not take.”

“Ah. So you do sometimes meet the needs of your community.”

“Sometimes? Always.”

Giulia nods. She doesn’t push her point. Sister Francesca is clearly an intelligent woman, and they’ll need to coexist. Perhaps indefinitely.

“I think I’ll go wander the gardens,” Giulia says. “See for myself what’s in bloom.”

Carmela will never admit it, but Violetta is a natural. She's not only good with numbers, but with plants and customers alike.

She's also infuriatingly helpful.

Laura spends more and more time at Benicio's and the one time Carmela expressed irritation about it, Maria jumped down her throat so fast she'll never bring it up again. Laura deserves her happiness, of course. Though it's hard to see how anyone could be happy in a world without Carmela's mother.

Which sounds like Giulia's dead. She's not, at least as far as they know. But she could be. There's been no word, and Carmela drifts between sleeping in her own apartment and waking with a jolt every night, certain something terrible has befallen her mother, and sleeping at Maria's until the inevitable blowup when Maria proves herself not to be Giulia and Carmela goes huffing back to her apartment.

No wonder Laura keeps disappearing to Benicio's farm on the outskirts of town. She always returns with new plants, new knowledge, a bushel of mandrake, but none of them kid themselves that she's there for the tubers.

While Violetta can never replace Laura, and certainly not Giulia, she does learn how to slide into the wanting places and make herself useful. A lifetime of caring for younger siblings has prepared her well.

Carmela guards the recipe for love potion longer than she should, considering Violetta has been nothing but trustworthy for weeks. But it is one of their best sellers, and no apothecary in Rome sells one that is reputed to be anywhere near as effective. Each day Violetta earns a touch more trust, but Carmela still wouldn't be surprised if she ran and blabbed all their secrets to a competitor.

"We'll start with distilling the rose petals," Carmela says on the day she finally relents.

"I know how to distill rose petals," Violetta says, as though she's known her whole life, and didn't only learn the week before when Maria showed her how to make a skin-calming tonic.

"There are some extra considerations when distilling them for the love potion. How quickly they're brought to boil is important, because too fast and you won't get all the lovely blush color from them."

Chastened, Violetta watches and listens.

When the shop bell rings, they're both peering into the pot, awaiting the impending boil.

"Customer," Maria calls to them.

Carmela must decide: Send Violetta out to see to the customer, or leave her responsible for the rose distillate. "Remember," she says as she brushes off her apron, "the second it boils, remove it from the heat."

If Violetta does it wrong, the distillate will be ruined for love potions, but could still be used for skin products.

"Nina, hello. What can I help you with?" For once, Nina doesn't have her twins in tow. "Are the babies all right?"

Nina bursts into tears.

"Oh dear." Carmela reaches for the carafe. Before, she rolled her eyes at how often her mother turned to that calming tonic. It couldn't be the answer to everything. And it wasn't, but there was something to it.

It might be the confidence with which the apothecary reaches for it and serves it to the distressed customer, or the fact that they must pause to take a drink and a breath before working themselves up further. But there's no question it helps, in its way, most of the time.

As expected, Nina takes a drink and a stuttery breath. "The babies are fine," she says. "Well, no, Giada has a rash, but that's because my mother forgets to use your ointment whenever she changes her."

Carmela shakes her head. The number of people who seem to think simply possessing a remedy will solve the problem is much higher than she would have believed before. "Then what is it?"

Nina begins to cry again. "I'm sorry. I'm so sorry. I swore I wouldn't do this. I stood out there, getting a grip on myself so I wouldn't fall apart—"

"It's all right. Here, sit down."

Carmela guides Nina to the bench and Violetta appears in the archway. She's holding the pot of rose distillate with a smile in her eyes. She removed it from the heat at exactly the right time.

Carmela nods to her. "Leave it to cool now," she instructs over Nina's head.

Nina looks up. "Violetta?"

It would perhaps have been less surprising for Nina to look up and see wanted poison mistress Giulia Tofana herself than to see Violetta Raso in the archway, looking like she belongs there.

"Nina!" Violetta sets the pot down on Laura's worktable, where it will no doubt leave a scorch mark, and rushes to the teary girl. "Whatever's the matter? Is it the twins? Where are they?"

Carmela places a firm hand on Violetta's forearm, hoping to forestall her before she whips Nina back up into more of a frenzy than she was in when she arrived. "Nina was about to tell me." She glances at Violetta. "Though if you'd rather Violetta return to the back—"

"No," Nina says with a sniffle. "She can stay."

"Would you refill Nina's tonic?" Carmela hands Violetta the glass. Violetta can stay, but Carmela has learned from experience that Nina will find it easier to tell them the problem if they are not both hovering.

"It's Sandro."

"Is he unwell, or injured?"

Nina looks confused for a moment, then lets out a shaky laugh. "No, neither. He's healthy as a horse. He thinks nothing has changed and life should go on as it always has, even though we were married for about a fortnight before the twins arrived, so there is no normal to go back to."

Violetta hands Nina her calming tonic. But now Nina's tongue has loosened far too much for tonic.

"He thinks that after I've been caring for the twins all day, and had them hanging off my breasts for most of it, and still managed to make him supper and keep his clothes and his house clean, he thinks I should still be enthusiastic about his roaming hands!"

Carmela freezes. All confidence that she could help Nina with this problem evaporates like a syrup reduction over heat that's much too high. She knows nothing of the marriage bed.

She glances at Violetta, who has at least had sex. But Violetta is wide-eyed.

"That sounds very difficult," Carmela finally says, which is all the prompting Nina needs to tell them how Sandro cajoles and complains and plays the wounded puppy when she does not have anything left to give him at the end of the day.

"Or at the beginning of the day! He'll wake me before dawn when I've been up with the twins most of the night, wanting what he wants since I didn't give it to him the night before.

"Do you have something like a love potion . . . but not?"

"Like to . . . make him fall out of love with you?"

"No," Nina says, though Carmela isn't certain she means it. "I don't want that exactly. I only want him to . . . express it differently."

"Is it really so bad?" Violetta asks, drinking the calming tonic herself.

"I suppose not. He never forces me. But even so, sometimes his touch makes my skin crawl, because he knows I don't want to, but he keeps pushing anyway."

"That's part of marriage, isn't it?" Violetta says. "Maybe one of the tinctures for nervous energy—"

"Nina is not the problem!" Both girls look to Carmela in surprise. "Nina doesn't need a remedy. Or rather there may be some things that would help her cope, but this problem lies with Sandro, who's being an absolute toad!"

From the back room, Maria huffs a laugh.

"Carmela, there are some things you might not understand, since—"

"Since I've never been with a boy?"

The look of alarm on Violetta's face is palpable. Carmela would never give away her secret to Nina, but Violetta still doesn't trust her enough to know that.

"Not that," Nina says. "But more that . . . you've been raised here. By these women. You haven't grown up watching how marriage works."

But Carmela has grown up watching women come through these doors over and over, seeking remedies for themselves, their children, their parents, their husbands, their siblings. She has only ever seen men come seeking remedies for themselves.

The Husband

There is a man
like Sandro
                    but not

roaming the streets
of Campo Marzio
late into the night
never far from the apothecary,
wondering where things went wrong.

One day he had a giggling girl
who snuck out her window
to meet him at the abandoned shed
behind the church, risking everything
for the passion she felt

and next he had
a bedraggled old woman
with time for everyone else
but never noticing him
except to nag and snap and yell
and take for granted

that he would be there
providing for their family
working hard all day
and still wanting, at night,
to curl up with someone
who appreciates him.

Violetta's courses begin.

During her time in the apothecary, Carmela has grown accustomed to knowing more than she'd like about her neighbors' bodily functions, but she could do without an intimate knowledge of Violetta's monthly cycle.

When Laura asks Violetta to water the seedlings on the windowsill, Violetta is stricken. Laura leaves for the farm before Violetta can refuse. Once she's able to form words, she turns to Carmela.

"I can't."

"Can't what?" Carmela has yet another remedy at a crucial stage over the fire.

"Touch the plants."

Carmela never realized how much her mother juggled and with such grace, until she is trying and failing spectacularly to do the same. "Are you too good for such menial tasks?" she says irritably, wondering how she should know when something is about to boil. If it hasn't happened, there is no way to know when it is on the precipice.

"No, it's not that. I . . ." Violetta draws closer, like Serafina wanting to tell Carmela a secret. "My courses have begun."

Carmela removes the cauldron from the fire. She is not going to ruin this entire batch because of Violetta's nonsense. "What on earth do your courses have to do with the lavender seedlings?"

"You know."

As much as Carmela enjoys lording knowledge over Violetta, she is at a loss here. "I don't."

"One can't touch plants while"—she looks around the empty shop and lowers her voice dramatically—"bleeding."

"Whyever not?"

"They'll die! After all Laura's put into raising those little seedlings, I can't do that!"

"What on earth are you talking about?"

Carmela looks to Violetta, incredulous, and Violetta returns the same look. "Everyone knows that!"

"Maria!" Violetta buries her face in her hands as Carmela calls for Maria to join them. "Oh relax," Carmela says. "It's only Maria."

"What do you mean, 'only Maria'?" She stands in the archway, glaring at them both.

"Violetta thinks—"

But Violetta stops her. "No, don't. You'll make me sound foolish."

"I'm sorry if I quote exactly what you said."

Violetta scowls. "Donna Maria, what are the activities one mustn't do during one's bleeding time?"

Maria's eyebrows shoot up, but she considers the question. "You shouldn't push yourself too hard, if you can avoid it, I suppose. Energy stores can be low during the heavy days."

Carmela grins at Violetta's frustration. "Yes, thank you, but is there anything more specific? For example, is there anything to do with plants?"

Understanding flashes across Maria's face. "Such as seeds going infertile and crops going barren at the touch of a bleeding woman?"

Violetta beams and turns to Carmela with crossed arms. "Exactly!"

"Yes," Maria says. "That all depends on what you think of Pliny the Elder. Total donkey brain." She turns around and heads back to her work.

Carmela laughs but tries to stifle it at the look on Violetta's face. "I'm sorry," she says. "Someone taught you that. How should you have known otherwise?"

Violetta busies herself straightening bottles.

"On the bright side, you're not going to cause any fields to go barren by walking by them."

Violetta snorts, then looks at Carmela with a tiny smile. "I'll go get water for the plants."

When Carmela hears the bell a few minutes later, she assumes it's Violetta, so she doesn't hurry to the front. But when it rings a second time, she sees Violetta entering with the water, looking in surprise at Nicolò Tassi. The notary walks stiffly about the shop.

Violetta smooths her surprise over quickly. "Good morning, Don Tassi," she says brightly, loud enough for Carmela and Maria to hear in the back. "Is there something I can help you with?"

Carmela hurries out, but the notary doesn't acknowledge her. Instead he narrows his eyes at Violetta. "Signorina."

"Nicolò." Maria lounges in the archway, denying him the respect he believes his showy clothes afford him. She likely wiped the blood from his slimy body at birth.

"Signora," he says with a mocking bow. He turns back to Violetta, who has been standing very still. "I'd heard rumors, Violetta. But I have to confess, I didn't believe you would sully yourself associating with this shop."

Something flares inside Carmela, a protective instinct. How dare he walk in here and imply their apothecary is anything but a place that helps this community? How dare he remind Violetta that for years she ridiculed and vilified this place?

"Her stepmother sent her," Carmela says. "She swears by our joint cream."

"My sister doesn't swear"—the notary curls his lip—"as she is a good Christian woman. And she most certainly doesn't patronize a shop like this."

"No, she sends Violetta, who she treats like her personal slave."

Violetta squeezes Carmela's arm to shush her. "The truth is, Don Nicolò, this establishment sells the most miraculous remedy for the terrible pains I get during my monthly courses."

The notary chokes on the air. "Well, I— That's certainly none of my—"

"In fact," Violetta goes on, "you should get some for your wife. I know she suffers terribly."

"She does not!" His face now matches his scarlet vest. "Honestly, Signorina—"

"Of course she does. Carla does too. Haven't you noticed how they both get more irritable and lethargic around the same time every month? I think your wife is actually due around our next Sunday dinner." She smiles sweetly.

"Well," he sputters, "but—"

Carmela hands the very remedy to Violetta, who places it on the counter before her stepmother's brother. "A hefty spoonful, morning and evening. That'll be fifty baiocchi."

Nicolò Tassi recoils, bouncing his gaze off every possible object in the room besides the offending bottle. The women present are also apparently beyond his ability to engage with. Finally, he digs the coins out of his pocket, sets them on the counter, then whisks the bottle away and very nearly runs from the shop.

Violetta slumps in relief.

"That was amazing!" Carmela laughs as she throws her arms around Violetta. "How did you do that?!"

Violetta lets out an unbelieving laugh of her own and hugs Carmela back, her arms tentative.

"I think the better question is," Maria says, looking at the happy girls with equal parts fondness and gravity, "why did he come in here?"

"It wasn't to buy a menstrual remedy," Carmela says as Maria's meaning breaks through the mirth.

"When his head clears, he'll be back. We need to make some changes."

Violetta does not arrive before the shop opens the next day, and Carmela is surprised to discover she has dropped the tally of Violetta's wrongs.

When she first started coming into the shop, and then even more so when she first started helping out, Carmela kept a running tally of every questionable action, wrong look, tone slightly out of place. They all went into the column of Reasons Why Carmela Was Right About Violetta All Along.

If she'd been late in her first couple weeks, it would have definitely been a sign of her laziness, entitlement, lack of commitment, and general low quality of character.

But now Carmela is rather shocked by her growing concern. Perhaps Violetta is unwell, or one of her siblings requires her care. Carmela's concern extends to wondering if Violetta will show up at all today, if she will stop coming altogether, if Carmela has lost another person right when she was beginning to trust her. Like her, even.

"Where is that girl?" Maria grumbles, as though they are paying Violetta, as though they have any right to expect her to be anywhere at all.

She is useful. She is nearly as keen as Laura with the numbers and records. But also, perhaps more than any of them would like to admit, she restores the shop to balance. It is meant to have four women moving among each other, sharing the work and conversation. Carmela isn't sure how they managed with three before she came along, for now here they are three again and everything feels deeply, desperately wrong.

When Violetta finally arrives, the wall of irritation that hits her from all three women is not because they are owed her presence, but because they caught a glimpse of what it would mean to lose another of their own.

"I'm sorry," she says, breathless. "Some sort of stomach ailment is passing through my family. I was up all night, emptying chamber pots and applying poultices."

Wordlessly, Maria retrieves a ginger tonic and places it in front of Violetta, then returns to her work.

"Are you feeling well?" Laura asks her.

Violetta nods through a yawn. "Only tired."

"You didn't have to come in, you know," Carmela says, some of the old spikiness returning to her tone. "You could go home." She doesn't want Violetta to go home.

Violetta says nothing, only puts another log onto the fire, then opens the records book.

When the shop bell rings, Carmela puts on her service face for a new customer. "Welcome to Tofana Apothecary. Can I—"

But Violetta interrupts. "Carla, what are you—"

"I knew it!" The woman's face is red, her voice cruel, self-righteous, livid. "Your father defended you when Nico told us, but my brother is a man of honor."

"Violetta?"

"My stepmother," she murmurs as she steps out from behind the counter.

"Signora," Carmela says, wishing all over again that her mother were here. "Violetta isn't—"

"You shut your whore mouth," she snaps. "And I'll thank you to stay away from my family!"

Violetta's face is as white as the rags Carmela helped her scrub clean so this vicious woman wouldn't spread her secret. And now this woman is here, in the place where Violetta finally felt valued. It's a violation of this haven they've built as she looks wildly about the shop, ready to tear it apart for each and every secret she can find.

"What seems to be the problem?"

Carmela sinks back, relieved to let Maria deal with her. She might be the face of the shop now, but Maria is the guts.

"Get away from me, you vile, wicked woman!"

Maria isn't anywhere near Violetta's raging stepmother, nor does she move. "I would gladly have distance placed between us," Maria says, "but as this is my place of business, I believe you're the one who needs to remove yourself."

"Your place of business, is it?" she shrieks. "Since her mother has fled? I suppose it's all the same. You're all witches—"

"Carla—" Violetta places a hand on the woman's arm to placate her, and Carla whirls around and smacks her hard across the face.

Maria is moving now, lunging to place herself between Violetta and this woman she is forced to call family. Carmela surges forward right as the woman shoves Maria away from her and she's so close to reaching her in time, so close, but not close enough as Maria stumbles, smacking her head on the counter and crumpling to the floor.

"No!" Violetta shouts, and the sound that emerges from Carmela is feral as she lunges to Maria's side and Laura is there, as Carla drags Violetta behind her out of the shop.

MARIA'S TEMPLE GUSHES BLOOD.

"It's normal," Laura murmurs, gathering a poultice. "Head wounds bleed excessively."

"Maria, can you hear me?"

"Yes," she mumbles. "Stop shouting."

Carmela's heart surges at the familiar cranky voice. "I'll shout if I want to shout," she snaps with love. "Here, rest your head."

"No, keep her upright." Laura hurries over with the materials she's gathered. "She needs to stay alert."

Carmela kneels behind Maria, resting her body against her own as Laura ministers to the wound. "It looks worse than it is," Laura says, dabbing away the blood.

"Easy for you to say," Maria mutters.

"That horrible woman! We should call for . . . someone? For help?"

"No," Laura says at the same time that Maria shakes her head. "Be still," Laura admonishes.

"Why not?" Carmela demands. "Maria could have been killed!"

"I'm not so frail as all that."

But her voice is weak, and the look on Laura's face tells Carmela this was closer than she's comfortable with.

"Why shouldn't we call someone? That woman attacked Maria! We're all witnesses, and Violetta too!"

"You do realize why Violetta's stepmother showed up today, don't you?" Laura asks.

Carla is the notary's sister. He would have told her all about finding Violetta in the shop. Carla will not be held responsible for her actions.

"And if we start hurling accusations about a crime that happened here in the shop?" Laura goes on. "We're inviting them to open every drawer and bottle, to add to the case against your mother and build cases against us too."

The shop bell rings.

"Oh my goodness!" Signora Abate stands in the doorway with her hand clutched to her heart. "Shall I call for a physician?"

Maria rolls her eyes. "I'm fine."

Carmela helps prop Maria against the counter, then gets to her own feet, shakily. "She's fine," Carmela repeats, trying to believe it. "Can I help you?"

"Oh no, I . . ." Signora Abate backs up, as though Maria 's condition is contagious. "No—I—I'll be fine." She hurries out the door, the bell ringing for longer than it took her to flee.

"What is wrong with people?" Carmela takes the basin full of bloody rags from Laura's side. "Do you need anything else?"

"No." Laura stays on the floor, peering into Maria's face. "We're going to be fine."

The Witness

There is a woman
like Signora Abate
                                        but not

one street over
from the apothecary
hurrying away
from something

she shouldn't have seen
it's none of her business
there's certainly nothing
she can do to help.

So that man smacked his wife
so that boy stole that purse
so that beggar has nothing to eat

if she meddles in every trouble
she'd have no time, no coin,
nothing left for all that's wrong
in her own life and besides

if she meddles with others
that's only inviting them
to stick their noses
where they don't belong

                                        in her life
                                        in her wreckage
                                        in her shame.

Maria is fine, mostly. If she's forgetful or confused sometimes, it's hard to tell if it's new or how she's always been, at least as long as Carmela has known her.

The shop is quieter than usual. Without Giulia, without Violetta, and without the Maria of before, for Carmela is convinced Maria is less talkative, if otherwise the same.

Even the bell above the door breaks, somehow, so Father Piero's arrival a couple of days later is met with complete silence. Maria garbles herbs, Laura peers at the books, and Carmela spreads a paste on the slab where it will dry.

"Ladies?" he finally says from where he stands in the center of the shop, arms full.

"Father Piero!" Carmela abandons her task and rushes to relieve him of baskets overflowing with the herbs Laura has not been successful in growing—among them pennyroyal, rue, and fenugreek. "Where did these come from?"

"I thought you were planning to lead a cloistered life," Maria says from where she sits.

Father Piero smiles, subdued. "We are all suited to different forms of service. Things around the Moretti case seem to have calmed enough that I could venture out."

Carmela wants to be happy for him, but her mother is still on the run and—

"Your mother is well."

Carmela fumbles the basket in her arms. "What? You've heard from her? How—"

Maria gets to her feet but stumbles, knocking a bowl of lavender to the floor with a clatter.

"I'll get that." Laura puts a hand on Maria's arm to guide her out to the front. Maria shakes her off and goes to sit on the bench next to Father Piero.

"Tell us everything."

So he does, mostly, minimizing the suffering Giulia endured before finally ending up at the convent, where the Mother Superior and most of the sisters have welcomed her with open arms. Where she works in their herbalist's workshop and helps to tend the abundant gardens and writes letters to them constantly.

But until Father Piero emerged from his brief foray into quiet contemplation, she wasn't sure how to get the letters to the apothecary safely.

"Where are these letters?" Carmela demands at the same time that Laura asks, "Can we visit her?"

Carmela waits to hear the answer to Laura's far-more-important question.

Father Piero shakes his head. "I don't think that's a good idea. My understanding is there's renewed interest in the shop. You all have perhaps not been keeping as low a profile as we'd hoped."

"We've done nothing wrong!" Carmela's voice pitches high and she doesn't care if she sounds like a whining child. This is so unfair and she wants to lie down and pound the floor with her fists. "Carla Raso attacked Maria and—"

"Hush, child," Maria says. "Father Piero is right."

"In the basket with the pennyroyal," Father Piero says to Carmela.

It takes her a moment to process what he means, and then she is digging the letters out from beneath the fragrant herbs.

Darling Carmela,

My dear, sweet girl. I cannot stop reliving the final moments before we were parted. I hated to leave you like that, in such distress. It was too much like when I was parted from my mother. Except I left you in the company of women who love you nearly as much as I do. I know they are caring for you, as I hope you are caring for them.

How can I begin to put into words how much I miss you? Words have never been how I express my feelings or show my love. I do that through actions, I think. Making you tea, adding another blanket to your bed, teaching you everything I know.

Without being able to do any of those things, I am a pot boiling over. I hope one day this letter finds you. I hope even more that one day we are face-to-face and I can make you all the tea and you can teach me all you've learned. But until then, while this letter must suffice, know that I have everything I need, except for you, and Maria, and Laura.

With all my love,
Mother

Carmela reads the next letter and the next, searching for a change of sentiment. Something that betrays the possibility that her mother might find a way to come home or send for her, might offer her some sort of lifeline.

She thought she only needed to know her mother was safe, but now that she has that assurance, she's dying of thirst with only a drop of water for relief.

She doesn't understand how Maria and Laura can move about their days, knowing now where Giulia is, without abandoning everything and rushing to her side.

But Maria is not rushing anywhere. She walks gingerly since her fall, as though at any moment she might fall again. Carmela replays her mother's advice to customers who've fallen.

The obvious signs, the cuts and bruises, only show us a very small part of the trauma the body underwent. Every muscle and bone reacts to a fall, and they all must be restored.

Carmela and Laura both deposit teas and tinctures in front of Maria until her already-cluttered workspace is unusable.

"Stop treating me like an old woman, Giulia," Maria says to Carmela.

Laura glances up.

When Father Piero comes in next, Carmela could swear Maria doesn't know who he is, at least for a moment.

"What's the best remedy for mouth sores?" Carmela asks when she's got a tricky customer.

"Peppermint oil," Maria says.

But when Carmela goes to retrieve it, Laura meets her there with a shake of her head and directs her to the correct remedy.

When Maria uses the blood basin as a chamber pot, Carmela is through pretending things are as they've always been.

"She's not well," Carmela insists.

Laura stalks away from her, busying herself with an unimportant task.

"Ignoring it isn't helping her," Carmela says.

When Laura turns around, her eyes are full of tears. "I know."

"Should we call for a physician?"

It had seemed an absurd idea when Signora Abate suggested it. Maria would never agree, for one. And Giulia taught Carmela that most physicians treat symptoms without looking for the root cause of a problem. What was more, they consider female bodies nothing but inferior derivatives of male bodies.

Laura shakes her head. "I wish your mother were here."

"HOW LONG DOES IT TAKE to reach the convent?" Carmela asks Father Piero the next time he arrives with letters.

"It's not a good idea, child," he says.

"I didn't ask your opinion. I asked how long to reach the convent."

He pauses and exchanges a glance with Laura. "On your own, you could walk it in two hours. But I suspect you don't mean to go on your own."

"Maria isn't well enough to travel," Laura whispers, joining them at the counter. "I know this is awful, but—"

They all turn at a crash from the back. Maria has—once

again—knocked something over. Recently distilled rose water, from the fragrance that fills the air.

Laura hurries to make sure she doesn't slip in the mess or cut herself on the glass.

"There's a hill," Father Piero says. "An insurmountable one for Maria, even before . . ."

"Can you bring my mother here, then?" Even if there are risks, there must be some way to bring Giulia to Maria, if they cannot bring Maria to Giulia. Giulia will know what is wrong, and what to do. Giulia would be furious with them all if something happened to Maria and she had never been allowed to help.

But Father Piero is firm. "No, child. I'm sorry. We have all sacrificed too much for Giulia's safety to jeopardize it now."

CARMELA AND LAURA close the shop early and help Maria home. Laura is meant to see Benicio that night, but she hesitates.

"Don't worry," Carmela insists. "We'll be fine."

She no longer drifts between the apartments. She will stay with Maria and Laura, at least until Maria is well.

"It's only supper," Laura finally says.

It's not only supper. It's supper with Benicio's parents, who have returned from time abroad and will be meeting Laura for the first time.

"Go. Don't worry."

Carmela has enough worries for both of them. Laura does not look convinced, but she manages to leave, pressing a kiss to Maria's forehead before she goes. If Maria were well, she'd have something to say about that. As it is, though, she smiles and says, "All right, Bettina."

"Who's Bettina?" Carmela asks Laura at the door.

She frowns. "Her little sister. She died of the plague when Maria was ten."

Carmela closes the door behind Laura and leans her head against the wood for a moment.

"Giulia?"

She turns to find Maria standing too near the fire, her skirt almost in the flames.

"Maria, no!" Carmela lunges to push Maria back.

Maria cowers in the chair she is pushed into. "I'm sorry, I won't do it again."

"No, Maria, no." Carmela kneels before her, hands on her knees. "No, you did nothing wrong. I'm the one who's sorry."

If Carmela hadn't given Signora Moretti that Acqua Tofana, Giulia would be here to help them through this, whatever it was. It all comes back to Carmela's failure. Always.

"You're a good girl, Giulia," Maria says, stroking her cheek.

A sound of frantic knocking on the apothecary doors below accelerates Carmela's heart.

That awful man. Would she do it differently, if she had the chance? Would she have handed Signora Moretti back over to the man who was certain to kill her? But that man is dead, and whoever is convinced they'll die without La Tofana's immediate assistance will simply have to find help elsewhere.

Except they're not in Carmela's apartment above the shop. She is at Maria's, and now the pounding is on the apartment door.

"Carmela? Are you there?"

Violetta. Anger flares. Her stepmother did this. Carmela would surely do things differently with Violetta if she could.

"Please!" Violetta calls. "You're in danger!"

When Carmela yanks open the door, Violetta is wild-eyed. "Oh thank God you're here," she says. "They're heading to the shop."

"Who?"

"The magistrate, with my father, and Nicolò and some other officials. They're going to raid it for evidence."

"Of what?"

"Whatever they can find."

Carmela glances at Maria, who is pulling the petals off some bedraggled flowers Benicio sent home with Laura. She pulls Violetta inside.

"Why? What did you tell them?"

"Me? No, I—I overheard them talking. The magistrate came for dinner, with Nicolò, and they were talking about your mother, and the shop. The magistrate thought that as long as Giulia stays gone, the shop is harmless. Carla interrupted to say your mother helped me—"

Violetta glances at Maria, who is now dropping the flower petals into the ash bin.

"Helped you what?"

Violetta fidgets with the hem of her sleeve. "You know. And the magistrate said that's not against the law, but my father interrupted to say that wasn't true, I would never, and La Tofana was guilty of much worse things, so I told them, I—"

Carmela grabs Violetta's hand and squeezes hard. "You told them what?"

"I told them it was true. I'd been with child and your mother helped me. It's not against the law, the magistrate had just said that, and I thought if I confirmed it, maybe the magistrate would think that was the worst of it, that was the only reason people were badmouthing her."

Carmela drops Violetta's hand. Somehow it feels too intimate, standing there, hands joined, as Violetta recounts how she risked her most precious secret to try to help Giulia. To help Carmela. Carmela takes a long slow breath. "What then?"

Violetta's face crumples. "My father lost his mind. He was screaming at me that I was a whore, at Carla for not controlling me, at the magistrate for letting 'those women' bewitch the town, and Nicolò convinced the magistrate to at least search the shop."

"So they're there now?"

Violetta dashes her tears from her cheeks and nods. "I got there first, trying to warn you. But they were right behind me. When you weren't there, I came here. It doesn't matter what they find. They're going to create a reason to arrest you—"

Carmela whirls around at a clatter behind her. Maria has slumped forward and knocked the ash bin from the table.

"Maria!" Violetta cries, and pushes past Carmela.

"Don't touch her." Carmela hovers over Maria and checks for her pulse. Still there.

"What's wrong with her?"

Carmela kneels on spilled ash and flower petals, taking Maria's face into her hands. "Maria, I'm here."

"What can I do?"

Carmela waves Violetta away. She doesn't know what Violetta can do, what she can do, what anyone can do. No one can help Maria, except Giulia.

"If Carla hadn't—"

"Stop."

"Please. Let me help."

Carmela squeezes Maria's hand and considers. Finally, she turns to Violetta. "Can you get a horse and cart?"

There are no other options. That's what Carmela tells herself as she helps Maria into her cloak. She decides against leaving a note for Laura, because if there's a raid on the shop, who's to say there won't be a raid on their homes next. Better to leave Laura ignorant of their whereabouts.

If there were any other options, Carmela certainly wouldn't risk leading Maria out to the street while men converge on the shop right around the corner. But things being what they are, Carmela leads Maria down the stairs and peers out into the alley.

No sign of Violetta. In admitting her pregnancy to her father for the shop's sake, she has proven herself trustworthy, but whether Violetta can somehow procure a horse and cart is another question. Carmela certainly wouldn't know where to begin with such a task.

Maria makes no objections and doesn't ask any questions as they huddle in the alley, which only confirms for Carmela that she is doing the right thing. Maria is not well, and she must be taken to Giulia. Giulia will know what to do.

If Violetta cannot find a cart, Carmela must take Maria somewhere on foot. Not to the shop, and not back to the apartment. She considers the shop's most loyal customers, searching her mind for anyone who would welcome them, hide them, and comes up infuriatingly empty. Not the church, obviously, but perhaps the shed where she hid the arsenic. Only temporarily, but maybe long enough to figure out another way to reach the convent.

Carmela has nearly given up hope when she hears hooves approaching. She peeks down the alley, and there she is: Violetta Raso, childhood ringleader, girl of action, sitting on a cart and directing a horse toward Carmela.

Only when Carmela is helping Maria up into the cart does she notice the seal of the magistrate on the side.

"You stole the magistrate's cart?!"

Violetta hushes her and tucks a blanket around Maria's shoulders. "It was parked outside the apothecary, ready to carry away the shop's inventory." When Carmela does not look convinced, Violetta adds, "Hurry up, unless you want us all to hang!"

"All right." Carmela climbs up next to Maria. "Father Piero said it was two hours walking, so—"

"There are faster ways, but we'll take side streets to avoid notice. My guess is it'll take around an hour."

"What do you mean *we*?"

Violetta gapes back at Carmela in equal astonishment. "I'm helping you."

"Yes, by getting this cart. Thank you."

"Do you know the way to the convent?" Carmela considers lying, but before she can, Violetta continues. "If you get lost, it'll be more time and opportunity for you to be caught with the magistrate's cart. I've been there, and I know how to drive a cart, so stop being so stubborn and get in."

Every minute they argue is a minute wasted. Carmela situates herself close to Maria and takes her hand. "We're going to see Mother, Maria."

Violetta stays on side streets, and Carmela keeps her head down. Beside her, Maria sits quiet and docile. Carmela doesn't take a full breath until they've left the city behind. Even then, she looks over her shoulder immediately after the breath.

"We're all right," Violetta says. "No one's going to bother the magistrate's vehicle. How's Maria?"

Maria's hand is pale and limp in Carmela's.

"Maria?"

She says nothing, only continues looking at the road outside.

"Your mother will know what to do," Violetta says. And then, a few minutes later: "She saved my life. She'll save Maria's."

CARMELA HAS NEVER BEEN SO GLAD to see a church as she is when the bell tower of Santa Maria of the Angels comes into view.

"We're here, Maria," she says. "Mother's here."

"Almost," Violetta corrects. "The convent is up the hill."

The horse slows, plodding his way to the top. Father Piero was right; there is no way Maria could have walked this hill. Finally, Violetta climbs down from the cart and rings a bell at the gate. Carmela squeezes Maria's hand tighter. If someone tries to deny them entrance, she will break down those gates herself.

But the sister who comes out smiles at Violetta. "Signorina Raso, what a blessing to see you again." She glances in confusion at the magistrate's cart. "Have you changed your mind about joining us?"

"No, I've brought two women who need to see Giulia Tofana."

The sister hesitates. "Signora Tofana is not receiving visitors."

Carmela stumbles her way out of the cart. "She'll want to see us. You must tell her."

The woman's face softens. "You're her daughter."

"Please," Violetta says. "And the woman in the cart, she's like a mother to Signora Tofana. She's unwell, and—"

The sister is already moving to open the gates.

"What did she mean?" Carmela asks Violetta as they climb back into the cart to direct it through the gates and up to the front entrance. "About you changing your mind?"

Violetta waves her question off. "It doesn't matter."

The nun from the gate and another are there to help Maria climb down, and they whisk her inside.

"Can you see to stabling the horse?" Carmela asks.

Violetta's expression is unreadable. "No, I—I need to get back."

Carmela frowns, torn between Maria's form disappearing inside the convent and a strange sense that she may never see Violetta Raso again. "They'll already have missed you. It won't make any difference if you take a minute to breathe—"

But Violetta is turning back toward the cart. "I'm sure the convent can arrange a return ride for you, when you're ready," she says. Though who's to say when Carmela and Maria will return to town, to their apartment, to their shop, currently being torn apart by authorities hell-bent on finding exactly what they're looking for.

To Laura.

Carmela grabs Violetta's hand before she can climb up, out of reach. "Can you get word to Laura that we're safe? Warn her before she goes back to the shop."

Violetta nods. "I'll do my best." She throws her arms around Carmela. "I wish I could do more."

Carmela shakes her head, taking in the rosewater scent of Violetta's hair. "You've done so much. I think we might be even."

Not that it matters. Not that it wouldn't be better to continue the push and pull of *I owe you* and *you owe me*, back and forth over years.

"Send word about Maria," Violetta says before releasing Carmela and climbing into the cart.

Carmela hurries inside, following the voices, knowing that one of them will be her mother's.

GIULIA FINDS CARMELA FIRST, darting into a hallway, locking eyes, and then she is upon her, arms fastened tight as Carmela begins to cry, and then sob, and then very nearly wail.

Giulia strokes her hair. "You're here now. It's all right, you're here now."

"Maria too," Carmela says. "You have to see her. She's unwell."

Even though Carmela never wants her mother to let go, they must find Maria.

Giulia leads Carmela to the room where the nuns receive visitors. Maria is seated before the fire, and the same two nuns who received her at the door are fussing over her.

"Maria!" Giulia rushes over, and Carmela is relieved to see Maria's eyes light up in recognition. But then she says, "Costanza, my friend."

Giulia's face shutters only briefly, but she moves forward as though nothing is wrong, sitting at Maria's feet and gathering her hands up in her own. "How was the trip?"

Maria doesn't answer that. Giulia's eyes flicker to Carmela's.

"She fell," Carmela explains quietly.

"And hit her head?"

Carmela nods. "On the shop counter."

"How long ago?"

"Six days." Carmela waits for Giulia to say something reassuring. "The wound is healing well," she adds.

Giulia nods. "Yes, you did a good job of that. It's not the external wound I'm concerned about." She motions to the nun who brought Maria a blanket. "Could you fetch Sister Francesca for me, please? Ask her to bring a water hyssop tincture."

The nun hurries from the room. "Where's Laura?" Giulia asks.

Laura is probably returning home to the apartment after her supper with Benicio's parents to find Maria and Carmela gone, perhaps to find it's been ransacked by Nicolò Tassi's thugs. Laura, who lives with so much fear, may find her beloveds gone and her world upended. Carmela's throat tightens.

"I'm sorry," she whispers. "She wasn't there and I had to get Maria to you, so I—"

"You did well," Giulia says.

A severe-looking nun arrives with the supplies Giulia requested. She takes in the sight of the vacant Maria and teary Carmela. Then she turns to Giulia. "How can I help?"

"This is Maria. Sixty-eight years old, head trauma sustained six days ago. She's not at all herself."

Carmela has never seen Giulia speak to another medical practitioner with such respect.

"She was fine at first," Carmela adds. "But she's gotten increasingly forgetful, confused, clumsy."

The severe nun purses her lips. "Let's move her to my room."

"Sister—" Giulia interjects, but the nun waves her away.

"The infirmary is filled with pox patients. You'll have some privacy this way."

The other nuns hurry out of the room to make whatever preparations are required.

"Mother—"

Giulia squeezes Carmela's hand. "You were right to bring her here."

THE ROOM IS BRIGHT, IF SPARE. Maria is settled on a bed with a crucifix on the wall above the headboard. Otherwise, the walls are bare, and a window looks out onto a garden full of familiar herbs.

Giulia gives Maria a serving of the water hyssop tincture directly, and then presses the bottle into Carmela's hands. "Love, can you please go make a strong hot water infusion with this?"

Carmela is about to object. She doesn't want to leave her mother's side, or Maria's, but the severe nun looks on. Carmela nods and takes the tincture bottle.

She asks the first sister she sees where she might boil water, and the woman wordlessly turns and leads her to a large kitchen where three sisters work together. They move around one another the way Giulia, Maria, and Laura used to move around the apothecary, anticipating each other's movements, passing things before they're requested, stepping aside and making way.

"Excuse me?" Carmela has perhaps never felt more like a foreigner. "I need to boil water, please?"

They all look to her, intruder in their peaceful kitchen. The nun who led her to the kitchen has gone. These three likely have no idea who she is or where she came from. It's as though someone had turned up in the middle of the apothecary workshop asking to use their mortar and pestle.

Except it's not, because Carmela would have chased such an apothecary interloper out of the workshop. But the nuns alter their choreography, leading Carmela to a seat next to a fire where a cauldron full of water is already heating.

"Be at home," one of the sisters says.

Carmela would never be at home in a convent. Not knowing how her grandmother died, how her mother was betrayed. But she finds she is not uncomfortable as a guest for a time.

WHEN THE WATER HYSSOP INFUSION IS READY, she takes it, together with some bread and cheese and olives, back to Maria's room.

"You know, Costanza"—Carmela stops short at the sound of Maria's voice, stronger than it's been in days—"your daughter is a wonder."

Carmela moves slowly toward the doorway, not wanting to

interrupt the moment, but desperate after all these months to be close to her mother.

Giulia sits at Maria's bedside, all traces of the in-control apothecary gone from her face. She is exhausted, brokenhearted. "I agree," Giulia says to Maria. "So are you."

Maria's laughter makes Carmela's heart leap. "I'm a silly old woman."

"No." Giulia grips Maria's hands. "No, you listen to me, Maria. You are a survivor, the toughest person I've ever known, and you've raised my daughter the way I never could."

It doesn't even matter if Giulia is talking about herself as Costanza, or about Carmela. Either way, tears stream down her cheeks.

"Maria, I need you to understand that my daughter and I wouldn't have survived without you. The apothecary wouldn't exist without you. You are the heart of everything. I don't know how we'll go on without you."

That idea, of a world without Maria, sends Carmela lurching through the doorway.

"What are you talking about? She's here. I got her to you in time. Maria's not going anywhere."

Giulia's face is wrecked when she looks up at Carmela, but she tries to arrange it into something resembling calm when she sees her. "Good girl, you brought the infusion?"

Carmela hands her the mug and sits at the foot of Maria's bed. "Why are you talking like that? You can help her, can't you?"

Giulia says nothing while she helps Maria drink.

"She already looks better," Carmela insists, hating the silence.

Giulia nods slowly. "The tincture helped, for the moment. And the infusion will help some too. I suspect that her brain is bleeding, from when she hit her head."

Carmela mentally flips through all the things that can stop

bleeding—yarrow, witch hazel, plantain—but how to apply them to the brain?

Giulia shakes her head. "There's nothing we can do to stop it."

"But . . ." A bleeding brain does not sound like something a person can recover from.

"There's a chance it will stop on its own," Giulia says. "But I think we should be prepared—"

"No! I brought her to you so you could fix her!"

"I know."

"So fix her!" The world is more complicated than that. Carmela knows this. But logic won't stop the fury igniting inside her, the self-righteous insistence that she did everything right and now the world should bend to her will.

"Hush, Giulia." It's Maria who speaks, admonishing Carmela. "Your mother is doing the best she can."

Carmela's heart breaks open. Her mother's best has always been enough. But somehow here they are, needing her the most, and she's falling short. Now more than ever, Carmela wants Maria to look at her and see her and say something gruff but true and set things right.

"I'm Carmela." She takes one of Maria's hands.

Maria frowns a little and her eyes go unfocused.

"It's less confusing to go along with her," Giulia says quietly.

"I don't care," Carmela snaps at her mother, who still thinks she knows best, that Carmela is a child. "If there's a chance, then Maria will take it. She'll heal." Carmela stretches out on the bed next to Maria. This time there is no struggle over the blankets, no elbows to the ribs.

WHEN CARMELA WAKES, no light shines through the window and she's alone in the bed. There is no moment of confusion about where she is. She knows instantly, and the empty bed sends a jolt straight to her heart.

She lurches up and out the door, nearly colliding with a sister delivering a stack of cloths to their room.

"Your mother is down that way," she says softly, pointing.

But when Carmela skids into the room, Maria is there too, propped up on the most comfortable chair.

"She wanted to hear the music," Giulia whispers from Maria's side.

There is music. Carmela hadn't heard it over the blood rushing in her ears, but now she does. Nuns singing, harmonizing, voices blending beautifully.

"The chapel is right through there. They sing at this time every evening."

Carmela studies Maria's face. "She's looking better."

Giulia doesn't respond, only leans her head down to rest on Maria's shoulder.

IN THE MORNING, Laura is there and no one cares about Carmela's apologies for handling everything wrong and leaving without Laura, leaving her to find the ransacked apartment and piece together what had happened.

All that matters now is Maria, who dozes in and out of consciousness as Giulia, Laura, and Carmela rotate around her.

Laura is very pale, saying almost nothing. She grips a rosary and quietly mouths words Carmela has never heard her speak before. They grate on Carmela, the uselessness of them filling this sacred space.

"Why is she praying?" Carmela asks when Laura steps out for a moment.

Giulia looks up at the crucifix. "Because she believes it will help."

"It won't!"

If she thought an act of faith would somehow save Maria, Carmela would take vows that very moment. But that is not what her mother has taught her, what Maria and Laura have taught her. Laura may attend Mass, but like Maria and Giulia, she helps through actions and knowledge and generosity. She doesn't murmur Latin words to an unseen god.

"I don't think it will help Maria," Giulia says. "But it may well help Laura. The repetition, something to fix her mind upon. It may help her feel like she's not spinning out into the universe."

That is exactly how Carmela feels at this moment. Like Maria was the one who kept them all tethered to the earth, and as she fades, the strands of the rope are snapping and any second now the last one will break and Carmela will be untethered from everything she's ever known.

"Carmela."

Carmela jumps to attention at the sound of her name in Maria's voice. Carmela, not Giulia or Costanza.

"Yes, Maria? I'm here."

"You're a good girl."

"I love you, Maria."

"Yes, yes. I need something."

"What is it? Are you cold? Thirsty? What can I—"

"The apothecary."

On Maria's other side, Giulia stills. Laura returns but pauses in the doorway.

Carmela's heart sinks. According to Laura, much of the apothecary's contents were destroyed or carted away. If Maria wants something from the apothecary—

Maria's papery hand tightens around Carmela's. "You must keep it open."

Giulia draws a ragged breath, and Laura moves to her side in one smooth motion.

"Don't worry about that now," Carmela says, struggling to keep her own voice in check.

"Promise me. You will keep doing the work. You will keep listening and helping."

"Of course I will," Carmela says. After all, her mother had said it was better to go along with Maria. "And you'll be there to boss me around."

Maria says nothing to this. Her eyes cloud over again and fix on the wall behind Carmela. Carmela's protestations are as useful as Laura's prayers, said only to comfort herself.

"Carmela." Giulia stands and motions to the door. "Let's give Laura some time alone with Maria."

Carmela follows her mother as if moving through another world. It *is* another world, this place of bare walls, save for broken men nailed to crosses, women clothed in perpetual mourning, constant prayers to a god the whole thing is centered upon but who cannot be bothered to show up for Maria.

They leave the too-close walls and step into the garden, the bright sunshine jarring against their unshakable gloom.

"There's a labyrinth of lavender on the other side of the building," Giulia says. "It's lovely."

"Nice that you're so happy here," Carmela says.

Giulia flinches. "I miss you every second. You have to know that."

Carmela does know, mostly. But she also knows her mother isn't fighting with every breath to get back to her. Just like she isn't fighting to save Maria. When did Giulia Tofana lose all her fight?

"I've learned to make the holy wood cure for the pox," Giulia says. "I could teach you."

"You believe in holy wood now?"

"That's only its name."

Carmela doesn't want to learn a cure for the pox. She wants a cure for Maria.

"I know you're angry with me—"

Carmela breaks away from her mother and plunges farther into the garden, to where the plants are shaggy and overgrown. All this time desperately wanting to be with her mother and now she can't stand another second at her side.

Giulia catches up and sits down next to Carmela. "If there were anything I could do for Maria, I would. Anything."

Carmela nods.

"Maria took me in when my mother died. She raised me, and you. She taught me to fight."

"Then why won't you? Why won't she?"

"Because fighting isn't always the answer. Because sometimes there is no answer, besides accepting what's next."

"I won't."

"I know. But I'm not a miracle worker. Despite my time here, I don't actually believe in miracles. If Maria could survive on her spirit alone, you know she'd stay with us forever. But her body is broken in a way that cannot be fixed."

If an arrow were shot through Maria's heart, Carmela would not expect her mother to be able to fix it. This was a fatal blow, and Maria's fate was sealed the second Carla Raso shoved her. Before that, really, when Maria lunged forward to shield Violetta.

"But if we can't help the ones we love most, what is the point of any of it?"

Giulia sighs. "That we try, I suppose. That we do our best to help the ones we can."

"Maria was trying to help Violetta," Carmela says to the creeping thyme on the path, tiny leaves so minuscule they wouldn't shelter an ant, but massed together they form a canopy at her feet. "She was always trying to help everyone else."

"Yes," Giulia says. "Maybe it's time she's allowed a rest."

Carmela refuses to be so noble and mature that she will simply let Maria go because it is the right thing to do, when Maria is the one who holds her world together. She thought she wouldn't survive her mother's absence. It never crossed her mind that she might lose Maria.

"I want you to know," Giulia says, "that no matter what you promised Maria, no matter what you think I would want, keeping the apothecary open is your decision."

"Are you saying I should go back on my promise?"

Carmela's not sure there's an apothecary to keep open, anyway.

"I think Maria's hope is that you continue the work we started. She doesn't see another way, but you're young. You will find many ways to help, to listen, to use your power."

"You're never coming back, are you?"

Giulia plucks a stem of rosemary and inhales deeply of its woody scent. "Nicolò Tassi had been watching me for years, waiting for me to trip up. I was lucky. Some women are accused of things they never did and executed before anyone considers whether there was evidence.

"But for all the accusations against me, I've helped enough of them to give them pause. Maria was present at their births. Their wives rely on the apothecary. They needed something truly concrete to bring me down."

"Signora Moretti," Carmela says around the painful lump in her throat.

"Yes. Her confession gave them what they'd wanted for so long, and before you say that was your fault, it wasn't. We taught you how to make it, how to administer it. I would have given her Acqua Tofana eventually. Probably sooner than later. And I would have given the same instructions you did, with the same end result. You did nothing wrong."

"Of course I did!"

"You didn't. You had compassion for someone in a desperate situation and did what was in your power to help her. Sometimes that's all we can do. And sometimes it's not enough."

Carmela thinks of Eleonora, of dressing her wound and listening. But then trying to track her down and getting assaulted in the process. And then there's Maria, right inside, apparently beyond even Giulia's help. Carmela can't fix every single ailment in Rome. If she tries, she won't survive long enough to help anyone.

That's what Giulia understands. They have so much to give, but they cannot take on everything.

"They tore the apothecary apart," Carmela says. Somewhere outside the convent walls a cat meows a plaintive cry.

"You can rebuild it," Giulia replies. "But you don't have to. Truly."

"Could I stay here with you?"

Giulia takes a minute to respond. "I believe you could, but I think you would have to take vows. I'm here as a refugee, but you wouldn't be."

"I might. Depending what they found at the apothecary."

"Would you want to be?"

Carmela wrinkles her nose, and Giulia laughs.

"Having truly devout beliefs isn't really required. There are many women who were brought here by their circumstances. Most of them had no other choices. But I would support you if you decide that's what you want. Of course I would love to have you at my side."

Carmela thinks not only about what her mother and Maria want, or even what she wants, but also what she believes is possible. She could talk herself into joining Giulia at the convent. She would have her mother, and that would be no small thing.

But it wouldn't be everything.

It certainly wouldn't honor what Giulia and Maria have passed down to her. But even they didn't push far enough into what might be possible. Giulia has kept the world of the apothecary tight, contained. She's had her reasons, and most have been good. She probably kept them all alive.

At least until now.

But Carmela hasn't been able to shake the feeling, ever since her mother traveled all the way to Tivoli in search of a crop that grows in their backyard, that there is more. That there are others who do the work of Tofana Apothecary, in their own ways, in their own towns. She thinks of Father Piero showing up with a basket of herbs from the convent, and she looks around at the overabundance of this garden, plants gone to seed that could have been harvested and put to use.

She cannot rebuild and sustain the mission of the apothecary, not without her mother. Not as it was.

But if there were others she could rely on, a network like the creeping thyme at her feet, the apothecary just one tiny leaf in a canopy blanketing Rome, and beyond—that would feel worth staying and fighting for.

A sister steps into the garden and motions for them to come. Carmela's heart tightens. She grips her mother's hand, and they hurry to Maria's bedside.

Laura is there, cradling Maria, tears running down her cheeks. The Mother Superior is there too. "It's nearly time, child," she says to Giulia, squeezing her arm as she slips from the room.

Giulia sits at Maria's other side, and Carmela stands at the foot of the bed, watching this trio of women, her trinity.

They are all she has in the world. She doesn't know what she will do as they each fall away from her. How she will survive the inexorable loss. How she will ever go on when the ones who've loved her and grown her and made her who she is cannot guide her way forever.

Giulia holds out her hand and Carmela takes it, sitting with her mother at Maria's side. Laura weeps softly.

Maria's eyes flutter open for a moment and hope soars in Carmela's chest.

"Where . . ." Her voice is faint, her eyes confused.

"Here," Carmela says, taking Maria's cool, papery hand. "We're here." Carmela releases her mother's hand so she can hold on to Maria's with both of hers. She feels the weight of Maria—so light she might float away, but at the same time so anchored to the goodness of the world that Carmela never stops feeling that weight, that reminder of how Maria opened her doors to Giulia, to Laura, to Carmela. Somehow Carmela almost missed the truth that gruff, jaded Maria was the most tenderhearted of them all, constantly flinging her door wide open and somehow still creating a safe place for these women to shelter.

Now another door has opened. Carmela squeezes Maria's hand in hers and guides her through the archway.

Epilogue

There is a child. Like Carmela, but not.

She slips inside the apothecary behind ancient Signora Santori, so that her mother, ever vigilant when the door chimes, might not notice how late she is returning to the shop.

Perhaps her mother will look up from her work, see Flora Maria, and believe she's been there for ages. Unlikely, but possible.

Everything feels possible inside the shop.

Flora Maria hovers behind the potted palm as Carmela greets Signora Santori, congratulating her on the confirmation of her grandchildren the previous Sunday.

Flora Maria had watched, jealous, as the priest anointed first Matteo and then Giada with holy oil, praying blessings over them. Later, as the Santori twins sat apart from the other children, newly inducted into the mysterious world of adults, Flora Maria led the other younger children in their own sacred ritual.

She had ducked into the shop—that back door never was secured—and grabbed the nearest bottle of oil her fingers found. A bright, happy scent confirmed it to be *Melissa officinalis*. That would do. With it, Flora Maria anointed each small child, while droning the best Latin she knew: "*Rosmarinus officinalis, Calendula officinalis, Lavandula angustifolia, Mentha piperita, Passiflora incarnata, Chamomilla recutita, Angelica archangelica, Artemisia absinthium,* amen."

When questioned about the glistening smudge on his forehead, one child had confessed and then a whole string of parents discovered who had confirmed their children into the Order of the Apothecary. Flora Maria's parents stifled their laughter while mumbling their apologies and hurrying her away from the outrage.

Even now, lurking in the shop front, Flora Maria knows she will not be in trouble for being late. Not truly. But even a flash of disappointment on her mother's face and she will wilt like lobelia in full sun.

"Are we out of joint cream?" Carmela asks, and Violetta appears in the archway.

"No, we sent some with Father Piero to the shop in Naples, but there are some still stocked over here."

Violetta comes around the potted palm and startles at the sight of Flora Maria. But then she smiles. "Hiding, are we?"

Flora Maria grins.

Violetta motions that she won't tell a soul and reaches for a bottle above Flora Maria's head.

She watches Violetta take the bottle to Signora Santori and slip behind the counter to stand next to Carmela.

"Oh, thank heavens," the old woman says, paying for her remedy. The twins' grandmother scowls at Flora Maria when she spots her on the way out. "Blasphemous little beast," she mutters.

Flora Maria stifles a giggle.

"I see you over there," Carmela calls when the door shuts behind the customer. "There's a fresh batch of sugared almonds in the back."

It's magical how La Tofana always knows what each person needs as soon as they set foot in the apothecary. And sugared almonds are worth any amount of scolding for Flora Maria's tardiness.

She emerges and sneaks a quick glance at her mother. No scolding yet.

She hurries through the archway to the back room. Only those who know the apothecary best, who truly belong here, are allowed in the back. Even when she's expecting a scolding, Flora Maria puffs up a bit at her belonging in a place like this.

Where the shop front is open and airy, with lots of light for customers to read labels, the back is cozy and cramped, every surface cluttered with bottles and tools, bundled herbs hanging from each beam.

Flora Maria spots the candied almonds and there are no distractions more enticing, even in this room of wonders. She hurries to the tray.

"I'm glad to see you in one piece."

She whirls at Laura's voice, candied almond between her fingers.

Her mother laughs, putting her at ease. "Did you have fun?"

Flora Maria grins and pops the sweet treat into her mouth. She's about to tell her mother how she convinced the other children to play barley break instead of boring old prisoner's base but that they all abandoned the game when Luca showed up with a box full of kittens and she already picked one out and named it Tofana when the shop bell rings.

"Where are my girls?" a deep voice calls.

"Papa!" Flora Maria goes running out to the front, where she barrels into the arms of the enormous man who always smells like growing things.

He hoists her up, even though she is getting too big for that. She frowns at a cut on his cheek, the blood just barely dried. "What happened to you, Papa?"

"Nicked myself shaving," he says. "It doesn't hurt."

She kisses it anyway, because that will make it better, and then pops a candied almond in his mouth for good measure. His eyes light up. "Something sweet from my sweet!" He leans into the archway. "Ready to head home?"

Laura looks up from her already-immaculate station and her face brightens at the sight of Benicio. "Yes, nearly."

Flora Maria's father sets her down and she runs to say her goodbyes to Violetta, and then Carmela.

Carmela leans down, the locket she always wears right at Flora Maria's eye level. Flora Maria asked once to see what was inside the locket, and Auntie Carmela said she'd show her when she was ready. Since Auntie Carmela has never lied to her, Flora Maria waits patiently. Carmela swipes a thumb across Flora Maria's forehead and whispers, "I bless you in the name of the apothecary." Flora Maria giggles. "May you always help those who have nowhere else to turn."

Violetta slips Flora Maria a little package of candied almonds to take home. Her eyes wide, she puts them into her tie-on pocket. She's the only child who has one; her mother says tie-on pockets are for grown ladies. But Auntie Carmela says a girl must always be able to keep her treasures safe, and though Carmela doesn't sew as well as Laura does, she focused her uneven stitches on a child-size pocket for Flora Maria.

"See you tomorrow," Violetta says.

"Keep your parents on their toes," Carmela says.

Benicio laughs, and Laura sighs as they gather their daughter into their arms. Then Flora Maria hurries ahead to hold the door open for them. Once her parents are through, she takes one last look back at her aunties, and the apothecary, and the lives they've all built together. Someday it will all be hers.

And really, it always has been.

Author's Note

My debut novel, *Blood Water Paint*, was about seventeenth-century Italian artist Artemisia Gentileschi, who grew up just across the river from where the events of this book took place. Since its publication, people often ask me what parts of that book are "true."

It's a complicated question. On the surface, people are asking, "Which events really happened?" But all historical records are someone's biased, unreliable version of events. Which makes "truth" particularly difficult to isolate.

Further muddying things is the fact that I am a storyteller, not an academic or historian. Even when I'm trying to answer which events come from a historical record, sometimes things are mixed up in my mind. I work on books for years, and memory is fallible, and eventually even I can't remember what I invented and what I took from someone's historical account.

With *Everything Is Poison*, my answer to this question is made simpler by the lack of historical record. Giulia Tofana was a real person. She existed, lived in Rome, and developed a poison most likely used by women to kill their husbands. Her mother was executed for killing Giulia's father. Giulia is believed to have had a daughter, and several other women were involved in helping her make and distribute the poison.

Giulia's daughter's real name was Girolama, and her associates (according to one account) were named Maria, Laura, Grazioza, and Giovanna, with the assistance of a shady priest named Girolamo. It would be wildly difficult to keep all those G-names straight, so I kept Maria and Laura, but renamed Girolama to Carmela and Girolamo to Piero. Everyone else is entirely fictional.

There is one account where Giulia took refuge in a convent, and received help and support to continue her work. There is another account where the nuns threw her body over the convent walls to the angry villagers. I think you can understand why I made the choice I did.

Nowhere in the historical record does it suggest Giulia Tofana ran an official business like an apothecary. And in fact, a woman at that time would only have been allowed to run a business if she were a widow whose husband had previously run the business. Creating Tofana Apothecary served the story I wanted to tell about women in community, helping the ones who had nowhere else to turn. I am indebted to *Forgotten Healers: Women and the Pursuit of Health in Late Renaissance Italy* by Sharon T. Strocchia for my research into what that might have looked like.

Poison is referred to as a woman's weapon because it doesn't take physical power to wield, and is so easily administered through the domestic spheres women have historically controlled—cooking, cleaning, nursing. Giulia Tofana is far from the only famous female poisoner in history—Agrippina, Lucrezia Borgia, and Catherine de'Medici are only the most famous examples in a long list of female poisoners.

We don't have reliable crime statistics for the seventeenth century, but according to the US Department of Justice's report *Homicide Trends in the United States (1980 to 2008)*, 89.5 percent of convicted murderers are male, and 10.5 percent are female. From the same report, 60.5 percent of convicted poisoners are male, and 39.5 percent are female. This makes the proportion of women convicted of poisoning higher than the proportion of women convicted of other violent crimes (for example, murder by firearm, of which women make up only 7.9 percent of the convictions). But regardless of method, women still make up a small minority of those who kill.

And the idea that anyone—particularly without any formal education and with the rudimentary technology of the time—could have come up with a completely untraceable poison is difficult to swallow. (Sorry.) It leads one to believe that the very idea that a woman might wield such power, especially in supposedly safe domestic spaces, has historically led to exaggeration and hysteria.

Everything Is Poison is based on a play I wrote, called *La Tofana's Poison Emporium*. When it was produced in Seattle in 2022, the theater offered a cocktail at intermission which they cheekily named "Aqua Tofana." It was telling to watch which men made nervous jokes about whether it was safe to drink. Even all these years later, there are some men who can't shake the idea that if women have access to power, no men will be safe.

If only they could imagine how women have felt all these years.

Acknowledgments

Everything Is Poison began as a play called *La Tofana's Poison Emporium*, produced by Seattle's Macha Theatre Works in 2022. That production, directed by Amy Poisson, and the incredible creative team that brought it to life informed much of my process in writing the book. So I am extremely grateful to the talented cast: Alba Davenport, Lisa Every, Melodie Gorow, Sydney Maltese, Bianca Raso, Ilze Riekstiņš, and Amy Van Mechelen. Director Amy Poisson was assisted by Helen T. Mariam, and the designers included Parmida Ziaei, Dani Norberg, Andi Villegas, Zoé Tziotis Shields, and Robin Macartney. Cass Gill, Bailey Dobbins, and Indira Rampersad stage managed. A million standing ovations to you all!

Writing a book is much less collaborative than writing and producing a play. But there are still many people involved in helping the book reach shelves and readers. The very first person in that process is always my wonderful agent, Jim McCarthy. This is lucky book thirteen together! Thank you for being such a wonderful, steady partner in this wild business.

My editor, Andrew Karre, is the kind of man who never felt the need to make a joke about his safety while working on this book. In fact, I think he just might be willing to help me bury a body. If I ever had need. Which I haven't. At the very least he would have thoughtful ideas and research resources to help me do it effectively.

I am incredibly grateful to Andrew, and art director Anna Booth, for allowing my talented daughter Cordelia Carranza-McCullough to create the beautiful map. I hope it is the first of many future collaborations.

Jesse Mockrin's stunning art graces the cover, and Theresa Evangelista and Anna Booth's design throughout is impeccable, as always. Thanks to Rob Farren, Natalie Vielkind, Madison Penico, Vanessa Robles, Chandra Wohleber, and Jacqueline Hornberger for all your careful work. Thanks to the Penguin sales and school and library teams for getting books into the hands of readers who need them. Thanks to teachers, booksellers, and librarians for continuing that important work.

And finally, most importantly, thanks always to my incredible husband, Mariño, and my children, Cordelia and Joaquín, for your endless support and love.